D1360187

# RANGER MAN

**Center Point
Large Print**

Also by William Colt MacDonald and available from Center Point Large Print:

*The Galloping Ghost*
*Incident at Horcado City*
*The Battle at Three-cross*
*Master of the Mesa*

**This Large Print Book carries the
Seal of Approval of N.A.V.H.**

# RANGER MAN

**William Colt MacDonald**

CENTER POINT PUBLISHING
THORNDIKE, MAINE

This Center Point Large Print edition
is published in the year 2009 by arrangement with
Golden West Literary Agency.

The text of this Large Print edition is unabridged.
In other aspects, this book may vary
from the original edition.
Printed in the United States of America.
Set in 16-point Times New Roman type.

ISBN: 978-1-60285-610-3

Library of Congress Cataloging-in-Publication Data

MacDonald, William Colt, 1891-1968.
  Ranger man / William Colt MacDonald. -- Center Point large print ed.
     p. cm.
  ISBN 978-1-60285-610-3 (library binding : alk. paper)
  1. Large type books. I. Title.

PS3525.A2122R36 2009
813'.52--dc22

2009023396

CHAPTER                               PAGE

# CHAPTER I

## "THE FALCON STRIKES!"

FROM one end to the other of the winding, dusty street, the scene presented was one of stifling somnolence. The air was almost too hot to breathe, and there wasn't a single visible indication in the atmosphere that the citizens of Rawhide City were about to become witnesses to a major tragedy. The town lay sprawled under the torrid heat beating down from the siesta-hour sun. To the south of Rawhide City a wide stretch of alkali flats shimmered with an undulating white-heat glare. Upon the shoulders of the town rested but lightly the prestige of being the seat of Creaking River County, while its people drowsed away the midafternoon passage of time.

Along the crooked main street several half-naked Mexican children teased a mangy cur, which was too indolent to bark or even snarl its resentment. A few hens, escaped from some back yard, picked at insects and fallen bits of grain to be found in the wide wheel ruts of the roadway. In the shadows between sunbaked adobe huts and heat-blistered frame buildings an occasional Mexican of the peon type snored lustily. Now and then a cowpuncher, or one of the town's citizens, passed from one building to another, heels striking loudly along the pitch-exuding plank sidewalks. Taken all in all, though, there wasn't much movement along the dusty roadway, except when a vagrant breeze lifted small dust devils to swirl above the earth.

A few cow ponies, scattered along the almost unbroken line of hitch racks that flanked both sides of the street, occasionally shifted reluctant hoofs from one weary position to another, their bodies slumped under the warmth of the day. A shallow river flowed sluggishly near the outskirts of Rawhide City, the scraggly cottonwoods growing at its banks assuming queer, distorted forms when viewed from a distance through the wavering heat waves.

Abruptly, a gunshot sounded from one of the buildings near the centre of town. For a brief moment silence followed the report. Then movement commenced to flow along the street. Men stepped from doorways. Heads popped from open windows. A Mexican woman dashed to the centre of the road and shrilled staccato commands to the youngsters playing there. The children scurried in panic. In an instant the thoroughfare had been cleared from end to end.

At the entrance of the Blue Gem Saloon a man spoke over his shoulder to the massed men pressing behind. "I'm damned if I can see anything wrong. It sure sounded like that gunshot came from the direction of the bank, though."

His glance flashed down the street a short distance to a one-story brick building with a small plate-glass window in the front wall, placed just to one side of an open double doorway. The window bore in faded letters the words: Rawhide City Commercial Bank.

"I guess we must've been mistook—" the man commenced again.

"Either that," another man volunteered, "or some cowpoke has gone crazy with the heat and decided this is a good time for target practice at tin cans—"

Two more shots in quick succession belied the words, almost before they'd left the speaker's mouth.

"By Gawd!" the first man exclaimed. "It *is* the bank! Look!"

The others crowded out to the saloon porch, eyes wide, mouths agape.

From the open bank doorway backed a tall swarthy individual in a high-crowned sombrero, a blue bandanna tied across his nose below the eyes. In his left hand he gripped a small leather satchel. His right fist spurted a cloud of flame and smoke as he emerged into the street. On the sidewalk he whirled, quickly jammed an empty six-shooter into the holster at his thigh and then reached to a second gun stuck in the waistband of his bibless overalls. His glanced flashed contemptuously along the empty street as he moved swiftly towards the hitch rack and his waiting horse.

A tall, thin-lipped man with drooping yellow moustaches pushed through the crowd choking the Blue Gem doorway and glanced across the street. He started suddenly. "By God! That's the Falcon!"

Men in neighbouring buildings heard the words and the name ran from lip to lip along the roadway:

"The Falcon! The Falcon!"

"The Falcon's stuck up the bank!"

"Where's Sheriff Norton?"

Mexican citizens scurrying for shelter took up the cry, *"El Halcón! El Halcón!"* "The Falcon strikes!"

Rawhide City buzzed with excitement. The Falcon wasn't dawdling, nor was he displaying undue haste, but he was alert for the first sign of opposition. He coolly rounded the end of the hitch rack and prepared to mount his horse.

Cries for Sheriff Norton were renewed: "Call the sheriff!"

"Where's Kirk Norton?"

The thin-lipped man on the Blue Gem porch smiled coldly. "I'm here," he announced, half to himself. "By the living devils of hell, I never figured the Falcon would have enough nerve to come to my town. This could be mighty interesting—"

"Interesting or not, Kirk," a man broke in impatiently—"what you aiming to do about it? A lot of us have got money in that bank. You figurin' to let the Falcon get clean away?"

The sheriff sent a sharp glance towards the

10

speaker. "Don't talk like a goddam fool, Banning," he said harshly. "I'll see that he doesn't get away." One hand swept down to his right thigh, then stopped. Norton swore softly. "Damn! I forgot I slipped off my gun a spell back."

He swung around, pushed back through the crowd, and re-entered the saloon.

The Falcon had mounted his horse by this time. Digging in his spurs, he pivoted the animal on hind hoofs and reined it away from the tie rail. His gun flashed up, sending a random shot whining along the street. As his pony came around, he unleashed a second slug in the opposite direction. Those of the curious who had ventured forth to witness what was taking place now withdrew with unusual alacrity. Windows banged closed; men faded into doorways. Black powder smoke hung lazily in the sultry air.

The Falcon's contemptuous laughter sounded in the sudden silence. Carrying the satchel in front of him, he kicked his horse in the ribs. The animal lifted its hoofs and swept into movement, kicking up clouds of dust at the bandit's rear.

Sheriff Kirk Norton again appeared at the Blue Gem entrance. There was no crowd to push through this time. Norton had the Blue Gem porch all to himself. Carrying a Winchester .38-55 repeating rifle, he stepped quickly out to the centre of the roadway.

By this time the Falcon was the length of a city

block distant, and moving fast. Norton smiled his thin-lipped smile, lifted the Winchester to his right shoulder. His finger curled steadily about the trigger . . . tightened. The rifle cracked suddenly.

For a moment the speed of the Falcon's horse was undiminished. Then, quite suddenly, it stumbled and crashed to earth, its hoofs flailing. But already the Falcon had released his feet from stirrups. He hit the dirt, running, the satchel still gripped in one hand. His other hand came up and he turned for a moment to thumb his nose derisively at Kirk Norton, and once more his contemptuous laugh carried along the street. Then he swerved his steps towards a pony standing at a nearby hitch rack.

Again that cold, thin-lipped smile tightened Norton's features as he levered another cartridge into firing position. The rifle barrel lifted once more. Leaden death screamed along the street.

The violent impact of the shot spun the outlaw completely around. Mingled dismay, fright, and astonishment contorted his face as the concealing bandanna dropped to his chest. He raised one protesting hand, then lowered it to his gun. The next instant he had pitched forward into the dust, the satchel dropping from his nerveless grasp.

Yells rose from either side of the street. Men swarmed out to the roadway. A crowd gathered around Norton.

"Fine shootin', Kirk!"

"You got him, Sheriff!"

Norton waved them back. "Just a moment," he said tersely. A third time he raised the rifle butt to shoulder, sighting carefully along the barrel to the motionless figure huddled in the dust. Men saw the Falcon's head jerk as the rifle sounded.

"Just to make certain." Norton smiled thinly. "I didn't want that bustard playing possum on me until I got close enough for killin'."

He left the group, turned back towards the Blue Gem porch, and carefully rested the rifle against the outer wall of the saloon. Then he swung back to the roadway, his long leisurely strides carrying him in the direction of the outlaw he had killed. A knot of men followed in his footsteps. More men had already gathered about the body of the lifeless bandit. The two groups merged as the sheriff arrived, then parted again to let him through. Excited comments filled the air.

The Falcon was prostrate as he had fallen. A few feet away his hat lay on the earth. The satchel rested still nearer the body. Stooping at the outlaw's side, Kirk Norton seized the man's black hair and twisted the head until he could gaze into the sightless eyes. Crimson seeped from the bullet wound at the back of the Falcon's head. A second bloody blot stained the holdup man's shirt.

"Either shot would have finished him, Kirk," a bystander offered.

Norton didn't make any reply. He released his

13

grasp of the bandit's hair and the head fell limply back to earth. Then he rose to his feet, saying, "It's the Falcon, all right." Again the thin smile as he qualified the statement: "It *was* the Falcon."

One of the men in the crowd offered, "Say, Sheriff, don't you think this hombre sort of looks like that Mex Louie what hung around Rawhide seven-eight years back?"

For a brief moment Sheriff Norton let his cold eyes dwell on the speaker. "Are you trying to tell me this isn't the Falcon?" he demanded.

"We-ell"—the man fumbled for words—"I figure it could be Mex Louie. I used to know Louie—"

"Don't talk like a damned idiot, Jarvis," Norton snapped. His tone and look were those of a man who brooks no interference. "This man I killed was the Falcon. There's no doubt of it. *I know.*"

"Yeah—yeah, I reckon you're correct," the other stammered, backing away.

Norton eyed the man coldly a moment longer. "And I don't remember requesting that verification, either," he said in a chill voice.

Jarvis dropped his eyes. "Sorry I spoke, sheriff."

"You should be," Norton said contemptuously. "Most folks would know better than to doubt my word, but I guess all the fools in the world aren't dead yet."

He turned abruptly away, stooped and retrieved the satchel from the earth. "I reckon I'd best take care of this—" He stopped short upon noticing the approach of an individual, wearing a deputy sheriff's badge, who looked as though his clothing had been hastily thrown together about his skinny frame.

"Heard you been havin' a mite of trouble, Kirk," the newcomer said. "Got here soon's I could—"

"No trouble for me," Norton replied shortly. "Trouble for the Falcon. Where've you been, sleeping off a hangover, Jones?"

Deputy Sheriff Jones shook his head. "Something I ate must have went to my stomach," he protested. "I been feelin' peaked. Just couldn't make to crawl out of my bed this mornin'. Knowed you'd get in touch if anythin' went wrong. Didn't figure you'd mind if I coddled myself a mite—"

Kirk Norton said "Rats!" in a sneering tone, then, "Jones, you'd best pull yourself together and earn your salary, or I'm likely to appoint somebody else in your place. I want a man I can depend on when trouble comes."

"Sure, Kirk, sure," Jones said placatingly. "With anybody but you, I'd not babied myself in such fashion, but you've got things running so smooth that there ain't nothin' could come up you couldn't handle—even was I dead. This town don't realise how lucky it is to have a man like you." Norton's manner softened somewhat under the flattery. The deputy glanced down at the dead outlaw, and went on, "You sure handed this feller his quietus, Kirk.

I'd say you done some sharp shootin'—not to mention fast thinkin'."

"I make out all right," Norton grunted.

"I was talkin' to a feller down near the bank," Jones went on. "He tells me the Falcon had a bandanner over his face when he come backin' out, but even that bandanner didn't fool you. You announced right off that it was the Falcon. How could you recognise him with that bandanner across his nose?"

Norton's features hardened. "Now *you're* talking like an idiot," he snapped. "What a damn fool question! Once I've seen a man or read his description, I can recognise him anywhere, bandanna or no bandanna. You can tell by the way a man moves, the set of his shoulders, and the angle he wears his hat. I shouldn't have to tell you—"

"Cripes A'mighty!" Deputy Jones interrupted. "You never told me you'd seen the Falcon before."

"There's a hell of a lot I don't tell you," Norton said coldly. "I don't want to hear any more on the subject. . . . The Falcon's horse is still kicking in the road down there. Get busy and put a shot in its head and see that somebody drags it off the street."

"I'll take care of it at once, Kirk. Just leave things to me," the deputy replied quickly, as he hurried off in the direction of the stricken horse.

Norton looked angrily at the deputy a moment,

shot a hard look at the bystanders. He cast a final glance at the lifeless outlaw before shifting the loaded satchel to his left hand and starting out towards the bank.

Those still standing about the dead body of the Falcon followed Norton's departure with looks which were respectful if not wholly admiring. One man commented, "Judas Priest! What a cold-blooded cuss Norton is. I ain't never seen his like."

An old-timer nodded. "Sort of reminds me of Bill Hickok, used to be marshal up Hays City way. Same blue eyes—icy-like. That long coat Kirk wears—and his hat sort of helps the idea along too. Thin lips and moustache like Hickok had. Hawk nose like Bill's too. Now if he'd only have let that yaller hair grown down to his shoulders like Hickok did, he'd mighty nigh look like a blood brother to Bill."

"I reckon," another voice broke in, "it must be his gun work that most reminds you of Hickok. Course, I don't know how good Norton is with a six-shooter, but he certain used that Winchester neat—"

"Don't you fret none of his hand-gun skill," the old-timer interrupted. "I figure there's dang few men to match him. Say what you like, mebbe Kirk Norton ain't as friendly as some law officers we've had, but he's shore enough the best sheriff ever elected to Creaking River County, and us folks should be grateful. Some of the wild boys sure mind their p's and q's since Norton took'n office—and more left in a hurry. . . . Well, this Falcon hombre has to be took to the undertaker's. Who's helpin'?"

## CHAPTER II

### KIRK NORTON'S PROBLEM

MEANWHILE, Sheriff Norton had progressed a third of the way to the bank, the satchel swinging freely in one hand. Three or four of the crowd were trailing along at his heels. One of them offered to carry the satchel for the sheriff, but Norton refused with a curt negative. Ahead a short distance, there came the report of a six-shooter where Deputy Jones had put a bullet into the head of the Falcon's injured horse. A knot of men stood clustered around the carcass of the beast when Norton came up.

"All right, Jones," Norton said crisply. "No use holding a post-mortem here. Get that dead animal off the street."

"I'm gettin' to it, Kirk," the deputy replied, "but you ain't expectin' me to carry it off by my own-self, are you? Me, I ain't no blasted Samson. Anybody can see it ain't a one-man job. None of these hombres appear anxious to lend a hand. I've asked 'em and asked 'em—"

"Don't ask 'em," Norton said sharply. "Just tell

'em! Here"—he turned to the man who had offered to carry the satchel—"you've been offering to help. See what you can do about this dead horse—"

"Now look here, Sheriff," the man protested. "I ain't no buzzard to be scavengin' dead hawsses. Carryin' a grip is one thing; totin' off dead hawsses is another—"

"I pick a man to fit the job," the sheriff interrupted tersely. "And in my opinion you *are* a buzzard. So get busy." He swung to the others who had been following. "You hombres help him. And I don't want any back talk. The county will pay for your work. Put in a bill for wages. Now, snap to it."

There were no further protests. Norton continued, to his deputy, "You come along with me, Jones. I might need you for something. Leave this job for day labourers. Burying dead horseflesh is" —a sardonic humour crept into his tones as he cast a side glance at his deputy—"is below the dignity of Creaking River County law officers."

Jones cast a dubious glance at his chief, uncertain whether or not he was being "kidded," then fell in at Norton's side as the sheriff continued along the street. A nervous cackle escaped the deputy after they'd proceeded a few paces. "You sure took them fellers down a peg, Kirk. They wouldn't pay me no attention—"

"That's nobody's fault but your own, Jones," Norton stated coldly. "If you're intending to continue to draw county pay, you've got to make men obey you. Perhaps that's beyond your ability. I shouldn't wonder if somebody else needed taking down a peg or two."

The deputy gulped. "Ye—yessir, Kirk. Maybe I've been too easygoing on folks around town. From now on I figure to take hold with a firm rein. I'll show folks I ain't—"

"From now on," Norton snapped, "you'll go on just as you've been doing. If there's to be any running of things with a high hand I'll do it. You just do as I tell you and keep your mouth shut. You talk too much as it is."

They were nearing the bank now. What more Norton might have said, or what reply, if any, might have been considered by his deputy, was cut short by the appearance of a man bursting excitedly from the bank doorway. He was a fleshy, round-faced individual with apoplectic features and a paunchy middle, dressed in town clothing.

"Yonder's Banker Caldwell," Deputy Jones pointed out, "just comin' out of the bank—"

"I've got eyes," Norton nodded briefly.

The banker came plunging through the group of men clustered before the bank's entrance, and paused to gaze wildly in both directions along the street. Then, catching sight of Norton, he turned his stumbling steps in the sheriff's direction. He came panting up, almost staggering. His necktie was awry, one end of his white collar had become unfastened and stuck up past his right ear. His usually neat suit was covered with dust; one trouser leg was splattered with ink. Caldwell's wide mouth was opening and closing, like that of a fish out of water, but no words were issuing. His bulging eyes fell on the satchel in Norton's hand.

"Th-th-thank God," he stammered fervently at last. "You got the money. I—I—"

"And the Falcon as well," Norton said coldly. "Did that bustard shoot anybody in the bank? You weren't hit, were you?"

Frank Caldwell shook his head. His breath was coming easier now. "Nobody hurt but Matt Melville. He's hit bad though. I don't think he's got much chance to live. We got Doc Duncan over right away."

"How'd it happen, Frank?" Norton asked. He slowed pace a trifle to accommodate his gait to the shorter steps of the portly banker.

"I scarcely know how to tell you," Caldwell said nervously. "It all happened so quick I haven't yet got it clear in my mind. To begin with, I'd just made Matt Melville a loan of ten thousand dollars, with his Lazy-Double-M as security. Melville had signed the note and was just starting out with that satchel of money, when the hold-up man came in—you say he was the Falcon?—and shot Melville. Then he grabbed the satchel—"

"Where was your gun?" Norton interrupted.

"In my desk. I tried to get at it, but—"

"In your desk?" sarcastically. "That's certainly a convenient place to keep it. I wonder you didn't have it in the vault, locked up tight."

"Now see here, Kirk," Caldwell bristled. "There's no call for you getting nasty with me. I'm not expected to wear a gun. That's your job—"

"I took care of my job, didn't I?" Norton's tones were cold, contemptuous. "Anybody but a jackass would know enough to have his gun right handy when he's handling money like that. It doesn't pay to take chances—ever. Well, you can thank me for stopping the Falcon and getting your money. The bank would be in a pretty fix if it lost that much money, for all I know. Your clients will lose faith in you if they get an idea you're that careless all the time. You wouldn't want a run on the bank to start, would you? What? What's that?"

Caldwell had been trying to make himself heard for the past several moments. "I'm trying to tell you, if you'll stop talking long enough to listen," he said peevishly. "It wasn't the bank's money—it was Melville's. He'd signed the note and I delivered the money to him in a satchel. Matt will sure be pleased to learn you recovered it—if he lives."

Deputy Jones said, "It's mighty tough. Matt Melville was one square hombre. But he sure didn't look to me like he had much chance when I stopped at the bank a minute—"

"Keep still, Jones," Norton said. "I want to hear what Frank says."

"Not much more to say," Caldwell stated. "Yes, Kirk, I guess you did handle your end of the job, all right. There's no use of me flying off the handle. I figure my nerves is just a bit shaken up yet. Otherwise, I wouldn't of been so sharp with you—"

Norton cut in, ignoring the apologetic words, "What was your cashier doing all this time?"

"The holdup man had backed him into a closet and locked the door. You see, Melville and I were in my office. We didn't hear a thing until the Falcon entered. The Falcon shot Melville and seized the satchel when Melville dropped it. I tried to get the gun out of my desk drawer, but the Falcon sent two shots flying my way. I dropped behind my desk to avoid being hit, stumbled over the leg of my chair, and went sprawling. Tipped over a bottle of ink and everything," he finished sheepishly.

"Seems like," Norton considered, eyes narrowing, "I heard more shots than what you tell about."

Caldwell nodded. "You did. The holdup man shot some more, on his way out, but I reckon that was just to intimidate me more than anything else. He must have nearly reached the street by that time—"

"Is Melville conscious?" Norton interrupted.

Caldwell replied in the negative. ". . . and for all I know," he concluded, "Matt may be dead by this time."

Norton nodded briefly and shifted the satchel to his other hand. "This grip isn't light, by any means. Is this ten thousand in gold?"

"Mostly gold—and gold weighs heavy. There's some silver and bills too. Here, let me carry it."

Without a word, Norton passed over the satchel. Caldwell puffed and panted as he trudged along, the satchel banging against his right leg at every step. Norton said, "There's one thing I don't get. Why in the devil did Melville want that much money in cash? Toting that much cash money is just inviting trouble. Why didn't he just have the amount put to his credit at your bank?"

Caldwell shrugged his bulky shoulders. "I haven't the least idea. I suggested to Matt that he let me give him a cheque, but he said no. Don't ask me, Kirk. Matt wanted it that way."

"I reckon he got more than he wanted," Norton said moodily.

Nothing more was said before the three men reached the bank. A crowd of solemn-faced citizens were collected about the building. Two or three men commented to Norton that he'd done a good job. Norton said stiffly that's what he drew a sheriff's pay for, and added, "You men had best go about your business now. No need of your hanging around here. If anything else comes up, you'll hear about it."

The crowd commenced to disperse. Norton entered the bank, followed by Caldwell and

Deputy Jones. The bank proper was deserted save for a white-faced cashier; a heftily built man whom Norton addressed as "Doc"; and an unconscious, middle-aged individual with greying hair, who was stretched out on the long oak table generally given over to the use of clients of the bank. Norton told his deputy to remain at the entrance to ward off any of the curious who might try to enter, then pushed on into the bank chamber, with Caldwell, still carrying the satchel, at his heels.

Doc Duncan's lined features were serious as he worked over the silent form on the long table. The big man's shirt sleeves were rolled to the elbow; beads of perspiration dripped from his forehead. Norton took a clean bandanna handkerchief from his pocket and dabbed at Duncan's face. Duncan grunted, "Thanks, Kirk."

Norton said, "How bad is it, Doc?"

"It couldn't be much worse—and have Matt still alive," Duncan grunted after a minute.

"He's still alive, though?"

"Just barely—and I got my doubts how long he will last."

Norton said, "Has he been conscious yet?"

Duncan shook his head. His fingers busied themselves about the ugly black hole in Melville's chest. Blood had already congealed on the shirt, which had been ripped open. Duncan swore softly, dipped into a black bag at his feet, and once more bent over the wounded man. "It's so damnably close to the heart," he muttered. "I'll have to—no, I don't dare move this man until I've—Oh hell! Say, Kirk, will you send somebody down to ask Ernie for my other bag. Just tell Ernie it's my other bag I want. He'll know what's needed."

Norton spoke to the deputy stationed near the doorway. The man disappeared into the street. Norton went to the door and called after him. "And don't let any grass grow under your feet on the way, Jones. Tell Ernie that bag is needed plenty pronto."

Norton returned to the side of the wounded man. Doc Duncan was just taking a flask of whisky from Melville's pallid lips. After a moment Melville stirred and his eyelids fluttered slightly. He commenced to regain consciousness. His eyes opened suddenly and for a moment he gazed vacantly at the heads bent above him. Then his vision cleared and he tried to sit up. A sudden groan parted his lips.

Doc Duncan pressed him back on the table. "Easy does it, Matt," Duncan said soothingly. "You've been hit hard and you've got to be quiet for a spell. I'll be getting you fixed up in a jiffy, though. Then I'll move you over to my place." He adjusted the rolled coat beneath Melville's head, and looked worriedly at the wound in the man's chest from which there came a steady oozing of blood.

"The—the money?" Melville gasped painfully. "That—satchel—stick-up man grabbed it—"

26

Norton said quickly, "Rest easy, Matt. I got your satchel. It's right here. Frank's got it. I got the bandit too."

The wounded man's eyes strained toward Caldwell. "You ain't puttin' me off?" he said weakly. "I know I'm hit bad, but I—want to hear the truth—"

"We're giving it to you straight, Matt," Norton replied. "Now just quit your fretting. Everything's going to be all right."

Melville's eyes still held suspicious lights as he looked from face to face. Frank Caldwell said earnestly, "You know us, Matt. We wouldn't side-track you. Look—" He swung the satchel high, panting with the effort. "Here it is—see?"

"Gripes!" Doc Duncan growled. "Open it up and let him see the money. All this talk isn't doing Matt any good. Let him see that his money is safe, then he'll rest easier."

The satchel wasn't locked. Caldwell set it back on the bank floor and unsnapped the catch at either end, saying as he did so, "I guess you're right, Doc. Seeing will do far more good than hearing about it."

He flung open the bag, reached in one hand, then abruptly paused, his jaw dropping. Slowly an expression of amazement, incredulity, and then dismay flooded his florid features. He started to speak, then fell silent.

Somehow, despite Duncan's protestations, the

27

wounded Melville had managed to prop himself up on one elbow. "What—what's wrong, Frank?" he demanded weakly.

Caldwell was finding it hard to meet Melville's gaze. He gulped nervously, then, "Wrong?" he asked with false cheerfulness. "Why, there's not a thing wrong, Matt," he lied. "The money's all here—as it should be. Not a chance of losing it—"

"You—you're lying—to me, Frank," Melville groaned. "I can tell by—the look on your face. You're not speaking truth."

"Swear to God I am," Caldwell insisted, but there was nothing of candour in his tones. "Ask—ask Kirk—or Doc—if you don't want to take my word for it."

Melville tried to speak further, but strength failed him. His eyes closed and he sank back. Only a faint moan passed his lips.

Doc Duncan swore, glanced concernedly at his patient, then toward Caldwell. "Well, what's up?" Duncan demanded tersely. "Hole in the bottom of that grip let some money slip through, or something? Damn it, Frank! Just the look on your face was enough to finish Matt off. I'm expecting one hell of a time pulling him through as it is. And you haven't helped any. Made things worse, if anything. Blast it, man! Speak up! Have you lost your tongue?"

The cashier and Norton were standing over the satchel now, peering into its interior. A sudden oath left the sheriff's lips, followed by a gasp of stunned surprise from the cashier.

"But—but I can't understand it," Caldwell was stammering. "That's my bag—the one I loaned to Matt. See, my initials are on it. It's the bag the money was put in—"

Duncan swore again, took one quick stride across the floor and glanced into the open satchel. He looked sharply at the other three, then something of grim resignation crossed his features. Without another word he returned to his patient.

Sheriff Norton's eyes were narrowed in thought. He knelt near the bag and thrust one hand within. It emerged a moment later, bearing something wrapped in a piece of newspaper. He unrolled the package, then dipped into the satchel for a second similar parcel. Certain low profanity left his thin lips. Caldwell was on his knees beside the bag now, unwrapping other packages.

"I knew something was wrong the minute I saw that newspaper-wrapped stuff," he was saying over and over.

A harsh laugh from Norton interrupted the remarks. There was nothing of humour in the sound, though. "We've been out-foxed," the sheriff stated. "Now I know why that satchel was so damn heavy. Nothing but broken pieces of rock inside, each one wrapped neat so if the chunks knocked together a man wouldn't get suspicious of the sound—" He broke off. "I wonder who in hell got that money—and how—and when?"

"That, Kirk," Doc Duncan said heavily, without turning his head from his patient, "is your problem."

"Yes," Norton agreed grimly, "it's my problem, and one I aim to solve too. If I don't, by God, I'll be handing in my star of office."

"Matt would sure be grateful—if he lives," Caldwell put in.

"I'm not thinking of Melville," Norton stated flatly. "It's my reputation that's at stake. Nobody's going to come into my territory and get away with anything like this. I'll get to the bottom of this piece of skulduggery if I have to jail every man in this town—"

Deputy Jones's voice interrupted from the doorway. "Here's that other bag you wanted from Ernie, Doc. I fetched it as fast as I could—" He broke off, noting the furious look on Norton's face. "What's up?"

No one answered for a moment, then Doc Duncan said, "Get that bag over here pronto. I need it bad. There's something else needed here, too, but it's nothing I can help the sheriff on—"

"The sheriff," Norton cut in curtly, "isn't asking for any help. I'll work this out my own way. Doc, if Matt regains consciousness long enough to talk, I want to see him. There may be something he can offer to explain what's happened. Let me know as soon as possible."

Without another word, Norton left the bank in long strides and stepped into the street. Duncan hadn't made a reply. While he worked over Melville, he was thinking that beyond a first gasp of surprise when the bag's contents were discovered, Jay Summerton, the cashier, hadn't had a word to say.

## CHAPTER III

### A MATTER OF CLIMATE

TWO riders were pressing their weary, sweat-streaked ponies across the alkali flats which lay south of Rawhide City. The two were approximately the same age—somewhere between twenty-five and thirty years of age, and probably nearer the twenty-five mark. Both wore faded denim overalls, riding boots, and woollen shirts. There the resemblance came to a halt. One of the riders was a Spanish-American, or what is generally called a Mexican.

The other, Johnny Barlow by name, was snub-nosed and freckled-faced, the freckles so prominent they even showed through his dark tan. He had grey eyes, and his bronzed jaw was lean and sinewy. Barlow's shoulders were so wide that he had the appearance of being shorter than he actually was. There was a devil-may-care quirk to his wide mouth, and his roll-brim Stetson was cocked at a jaunty angle atop his unruly mop of auburn locks.

A casual observer would have put Johnny Barlow down as a cowhand; a close observer would have stated definitely that Johnny was a hell of a good cowhand—and something more. The latter observation might have been prompted by the cartridge belt that encircled Johnny's slim hips, and the well-worn appearance of the short-barrelled Colt .44 six-shooter that hung at his thigh in its holster. Smart gun fighters realise that when a fast draw becomes necessary, the short-barrelled gun can be drawn a fraction of a second faster than the weapon with the longer barrel. However, if Johnny Barlow was a gun fighter, he certainly didn't look the part.

In contrast to Barlow's holster, the Mexican's was a handsome affair of hand-tooled leather, as was his cartridge belt, though the six-shooter he carried appeared to be fully as serviceable. The Mexican—Miguel Vallejo was his name though his friends knew him as Mike—was slim, swarthy, black of hair and eye. A handsome cuss, this son of the old Spanish dons, with his even white teeth, small jet moustache above cleanly-cut lips and jaw, and finely chiselled nose. A scarlet neckerchief encircled his throat, and his heavily embroidered steeple-crowned sombrero of fine felt was equipped with a beaded chin strap. More of a dandy, Miguel Vallejo, but in his way fully as efficient as Johnny Barlow, and with every inch of his tough whipcord-like frame in full commission.

Barlow squinted at the terrain that lay ahead, lifted the blue bandanna at his throat, and wiped the salty perspiration from his face and eyes. "I'm blasted if I know," he stated, as the two men pulled their ponies to a slower gait, "how a man can be so parched and sweat so much at the same time." He reached to the saddle horn of his buckskin gelding, lifted the canteen that hung there, and swallowed the last of the lukewarm water the container had held. "I'd give a heap right now, for some real cold water."

Vallejo said, "And that you weel hav' before too long, Johnee. Theese, I promise."

"I'll take your word for it." Barlow smiled, and added emphatically, "I know now why they call this the Creaking River country: she's so dry, she creaks. And I haven't seen that river yet, either. You weren't just running a whizzer on me, were you, when you stated this was a short cut to Rawhide City, across these alkali flats?"

Johnny's grin was infectious. The Mexican's teeth flashed a gleaming white reply. "No, Johnee, I speak the truth. But I know how you feel. Almos', eet ees so dry your tongue feels like thee sandpaper—no?"

"Yes," Barlow said definitely. "Burning sand-paper."

"*Es verdad,* Johnee. But look you, eet will not take a great deal more of the time, theese journey." His right arm swung to the northwest. "Already you may view the Sangre de Santos Range. Directly north, if you look closely, you will see the buildings of Rawhide Cit-ee. Beyond, to the north, is fine grazing country. To the west, and also to the north, runs Creaking River. To the north-east runs the Dominion River."

"Where do those two rivers run to?" Barlow asked.

Vallejo replied, "After watering the range, north of Rawhide Cit-ee, both of theese streams turn to the south and flow to theese alkali flat. After that, *quién sabe?* Who knows? The rivers just sink into the flat and make the disappear."

"Anything wet would disappear in these flats," Johnny said. "They're so damn gleaming white it hurts my eyes. I'm glad we haven't much farther to go."

He glanced ahead in the direction Vallejo had indicated and caught sight of the blocky shapes of buildings, low on the burning white horizon. Through the heat waves that partially obscured his vision the buildings appeared twisted and distorted. Even while he watched, Barlow saw a square adobe shape lengthen to an oblong, then the indistinct lines faded, wavered, and were blotted out by other weirdly changing angles of architecture.

"Is queer, no," Vallejo continued, "that nevair before you have visit Rawhide Cit-ee?"

"It is, at that." Johnny nodded agreement. "Come to think of it, I've covered nearly every other part of this territory, but somehow my business always swung me wide of the Creaking River country."

They rode on in silence for a short time, then Vallejo, too, emptied his canteen. He touched spurs to his chestnut pony and, with Barlow riding at his side, they quickened pace. The sun swung to westward. Now occasional spots of plant growth commenced to appear. The riders passed small clumps of prickly pear, creosote bush, and pickle weed. Stunted mesquite trees began to break the monotony of sand and alkali. The town ahead assumed more definite proportions.

The westering sun was picking out bright highlights on the serrated peaks of the Sangre de Santos mountains and forming purple shadows in the draws and ravines when the men entered Rawhide City's main street at the eastern approach. There were a few scattered huts here and there, before the buildings grew closer together along the winding, dusty thoroughfare, which was hoof-chopped and rutted from the weight of passing wagon wheels.

Barlow commented, "Some drunk must have laid out this street. It makes a sort of staggering design. Even the buildings look as if they'd been thrown down helter skelter. It's hard to find two

35

with their fronts lined up even, on the sidewalk. And I can't decide whether these cross streets we pass are really cross streets or just wide spaces between buildings."

"I'm theenk no one else is sure either." Vallejo smiled. "You take your choice. To the north of theese main street are many houses where people leeve, but neither do they have any appearance of order. Is like as if the *bueno Dios* throws down the handful of houses and says to the people, 'Here you weel leeve,' and here they have stay."

The ponies had been pulled to a walk by this time and were nearing the centre of town. Several pedestrians were seen on the sidewalks. Cow ponies and vehicles stood at hitch racks. Barlow had noticed a couple of general stores, several saloons, a brick bank building, three or four restaurants, and various other places of commercial enterprise. Most of the buildings were of either rock-and-adobe or of frame construction, with high false fronts.

Barlow said, "I keep remembering I'm thirsty."

"*Por Dios,* Johnee! Deed you theenk I can forget eeet? My own throat ees like the channel of burning lava. But there ees one certain place I weesh to stop. Ees not far now."

Eventually they drew rein before a false-fronted building of faded pine-board construction from which the paint had long since been blistered and sand blasted by sun and desert winds. Across the false front a barely discernible sign proclaimed it to be Doc Duncan's Clinic Saloon.

Barlow commented dryly, "Clinic Saloon, eh? Mike, I sure enough feel like I need some medicine."

"In the form of a stimulant—no?" The Mexican's teeth shone whitely through the caked dust on his swarthy features.

"In the form of a stimulant—yes." Barlow laughed.

Vallejo led the way along a passage between two buildings. At the rear of the Clinic Saloon the two men dismounted stiffly. Here they found water for the ponies and washed some of the sweat from faces and arms. Saddles were stripped off and the horses given a light rub. Then the rigs were replaced and loosely cinched. With the ponies taken care of, the two men now remembered their own thirsts. They led their mounts back to the hitch rack and headed for the saloon entrance. The sun was farther to the west by this time.

Barlow and his companion were grateful for the cool dim interior of the bar-room, after the sun glare of outdoors. The saloon was nearly empty. One customer lounged at the far end of the bar behind which presided the bartender, a wizened, slick-haired individual with prominent gold teeth and a genial smile.

"Howdy, gents," the barkeep greeted and immediately set out two glasses of cool water. Barlow and Vallejo brushed more alkali dust from their clothing and moved up to the bar. They acknowledged the greeting, downed the water, and requested second glasses.

Barlow heaved a long sigh of relief. "Now that I've sluiced down my pipes, I'll continue the good work with a bottle of suds."

The bartender nodded, opened a bottle of beer, and set it on the bar with a glass tumbler. He next turned to Vallejo. "Same for you as last time, I suppose," he said, reaching for a bottle of tequila.

Vallejo stared. "Las' time?"

The bartender's smile widened. "Am I mistook? Didn't you take tequila that other time you were here?"

Vallejo gulped and looked somewhat staggered. "Ees likely I did drink the tequila, but—but—*socorro*—!" He broke off and burst into a torrent of Spanish directed at Johnny Barlow. After a moment he calmed down somewhat. "Look you, Johnee, this hombre ees what you call the marvel. Only once have I been in hees place—five or seex year ago—and he remembairs what I dreenk—"

"Five years and seven months, to be more exact," the barkeep stated confidently. "Give me a coupla minutes and I can state how many days,"

Vallejo stared, dumbfounded. "Johnee! You hear? The day of the miracle ees not yet pass."

"You were just passing through," the bartender said proudly. "Me, I ain't never forgot a customer once I've served him. Your pard is a stranger, though."

"I am," Barlow acknowledged, amused. "Name's Barlow, Johnny Barlow."

"Glad to meet you," the barkeep said. "Ernie Braughn's my moniker. Your pard's name is—lemme see—Vallejo. Miguel Vallejo. Is that correct?"

Vallejo made helpless floundering movements with his hands. "*Diantre,* Johnny! Nevair have I witness theese equal. Is unbelievable—no?"

"Ernie's got a right fine memory, if you ask me," Johnny said.

The man at the far end of the bar got into the conversation, considerable disgust in his tones as he approached Johnny and Vallejo. "It's a *terrible* memory. He don't even keep an account book, and he ain't never yet forgot any drinks that was charged. I borrowed a match from Ernie, nigh ten years ago, and he ain't never given me any chance to forget it."

Johnny Barlow chuckled. "Why don't you repay the loan?"

"I'm trying to outlast him in the hope he will forget something," the man said gloomily. "If he'd just forget one thing—one little thing—I could be happy. But he don't." The man sighed deeply. He was a tall, cadaverous-looking fellow in black clothing and flat-heeled boots, and possessed a long bony horse face and the sad eyes of a St.

Bernard dog. A gun dangled loosely at his right thigh, and Barlow spotted a deputy sheriff's badge pinned to his limp vest. Ernie Braughn introduced him as Meticulous Jones, Deputy Sheriff of Creaking River County, with headquarters in Rawhide City.

"You'd better get in on this, Deputy," Johnny invited as Braughn commenced setting out another glass.

"Thanks, I'll do that," Jones accepted. "Ernie, I'll take about two fingers of bourbon in a tall glass."

Johhny had started to pour his beer. The bartender shoved a bottle of bourbon and tumbler in front of the deputy, then set the tequila before Vallejo, together with a salt shaker and a slice of lemon. "Just like you had it last time," Braughn said proudly to the Mexican.

Vallejo nodded, smiled, and poured a small shot of tequila. Placing a pinch of salt on his tongue, the Mexican dashed down the fiery tequila and pulled the lemon through his teeth. Johnny was appreciatively downing half a glass of beer meanwhile. He had noticed that Meticulous Jones hadn't yet poured his drink. Vallejo tossed a silver dollar on the bar and Braughn turned to place it on his till on the back bar.

The instant Braughn's back was turned, Jones seized the bottle of bourbon and poured his water tumbler nearly full of whisky. At that moment, Braughn turned back to the bar.

"Hey, wait a minute," he protested. "Meticulous, you said you just wanted two fingers of bourbon. You nigh filled that tumbler."

"Well, what you squawkin' about, Ernie?" Jones asked aggrievedly. "Ain't this two fingers?" He raised one hand to measure the contents of the glass. Holding the two middle fingers back against his palm, he spread his little and index fingers from the bottom to the top of the tumbler. "There"—triumphantly—"just like I said. Two fingers! My drink measures a mite under, if anythin'."

Ernie Braughn looked helplessly at Johnny and Mike Vallejo. "Can you beat that? A fat chance I've got to make Meticulous pay me back a borrowed match when he'll run a two-fingered whizzer like that on me. Well, it's just something I'll have to try and forget." He placed some change in silver before Vallejo. "Drink up, gents. The next drink is on the house. Except this time, I aim to pour Meticulous's drink my ownself."

Johnny laughed. "I'd like a chance to buy one. This beer just hits the spot."

"You'll have plenty chance," Ernie promised.

The four men conversed for a few moments. Finally Vallejo asked, "Did theese place not used to be called the Gold Dollar bar?"

Braughn nodded. "Doc Duncan bought it out— leeme see just three or four days after you was in here before."

Vallejo looked helplessly at Johnny. Johnny said gravely, "Ernie, can't you be sure if it was three or four?"

"Nope, I can't," Braughn admitted. "The deal took place and Doc took over plumb on the stroke of midnight—midway of the twelve strokes, so you see you can't blame me for any uncertainty."

Mike's jaw sagged. "Johnee, you cannot beat this man."

"I'm not going to try." Johnny chuckled. He said to Braughn, who stood, eyes twinkling, waiting for the next question, "I take it Doc Duncan isn't a regular medic, then."

"That's where you're wrong, Johnny," Braughn replied. "You bet your bottom dollar he is. Regular college graduate, got a deeploma and everything. He came here to practice, but this country's so danged healthy there wasn't many to practice on, so he bought this saloon. Now he's just like one of the oldest residents—savvys cow language and all. We got another doctor here too now, but he just sort of takes care of kids' 'hoopin' cough and measles and such. Folks with bullet wounds or broken limbs sort of relies on Doc—but neither of these medics gets much business, to tell the truth."

"How come?" Johnny asked.

"Healthy climate, for one thing. That takes care of disease. As to bullet wounds, we got a sheriff here that really keeps the peace—that is, with an occasional exception. But crime's at a minimum in

Rawhide City. Sheriff Norton runs things with an iron fist. Meticulous, here, if the truth has to be told, is just sort of a figurehead and could probably be dispensed with—"

"Aw—aw—aw—" Meticulous Jones sputtered indignant protest.

"Ain't it the truth, Meticulous?"

Jones swallowed hard and finally admitted sadly, "I reckon that's right. But it ain't my fault. You know how Kirk Norton is—refuses to designate authority, runs the whole show. If I do show any initiative, he jumps down my throat. Consequently, I just do as he says and draw down my salary. If he wants it that way, who am I to kick?"

"That's the way of it." Braughn nodded to Johnny. "And with this healthy climate I figure the taxpayers will be providing for Meticulous for a good many years now." A smile twitched at his lips. "Why, you probably might not believe it, but the fact is when it came time to start a Boot Hill in this town, we had to kill a man just to get a corpse."

Meticulous snickered. Vallejo smiled quietly.

Johnny said gravely. "I don't doubt it. Sort of reminds me of my old home town. There was a place that couldn't be beat for climate. The air was invigorating. Just a few days there and a man could peel years off his life. The city fathers put up a big hotel, when a lot of these big eastern millionaires come out for their health. You'd watch them arrive, looking like old, old men, with one foot in the grave and the other on a banana peel. It sure braced them up, though, when they'd had a few whiffs of our climate. Trouble was, it just about put the owner of our general store out of business."

"How was that?" Meticulous wanted to know.

Johnny explained: "This general store proprietor saw a heap of business coming his way, when those millionaires arrived, and he figures he can lay in a stock of frock coats, plug hats, and gold-headed canes—that sort of truck. So he went ahead and laid in a full stock, borrowing from the bank to raise the money. So help me, that poor hombre just about bankrupt himself."

"Is that so?" Ernie looked puzzled. "How do you explain it?"

"All those millionaires," Johnny finished sadly, "just wouldn't have anything to do with the silk hats and canes and so on. No sirree! After they'd been in town just a few days our climate made 'em all so much younger that all they wanted to buy at the store was little red wagons and alphabet blocks and other such kid toys. A heap of them million-aires even went back to three-cornered pants, with safety-pins—"

"Aw, you go to hell." Ernie laughed genially. Meticulous Jones's eyes were bulging from his head.

Vallejo smiled. "Johnee, theese air of the climate you mention must have been of the mos' invigorateeng." He paused. "What is known as hot air, I'm theenking."

Meticulous finally got to the point. His face reddened. "Aw—aw—you two," he sputtered. "All right, I'll admit I been took in. This time the drinks are on me."

# CHAPTER IV

## SUDDEN WITH HIS IRONS

T HE laughter at Deputy Jones's expense died away as his drinks were finished. Johnny Barlow rolled a brown-paper cigarette and tossed the "makin's" to Vallejo. A match was struck and blue smoke spiralled through the bar room. Johnny asked after a few minutes, "Say, Ernie, how do we get to the Lazy-Double-M spread from here?"

The bartender turned suddenly serious. "You figuring to visit there, or are you looking for a job—?"

Meticulous Jones cut in, "If it's a job, you might as well save yourself the ride. The Lazy-Double-M ain't hirin'."

"We just plan to visit a spell," Johnny explained. Braughn and the deputy exchanged glances. Johnny asked, "Something wrong? Is the road barred, or something?"

"No, the road to the Lazy-Double-M is there,

right enough," Ernie Braughn said somewhat heavily. "You and Mike just turn north-west from Main Street when you leave town. You can't miss the trail." He paused a moment. "You got friends out there?"

"Matt Melville and his daughter," Johnny replied. "I haven't seen 'em for years, though. I get a letter from Matt, now and then—not often."

"Melville," Meticulous stated bluntly, "is in town right now. But I don't reckon Doc Duncan will let you visit him."

"Doc," Ernie expanded on the subject, "spends most of his time with Matt. That's why he hasn't been in this afternoon, and why I've been putting in double-duty hours at this bar."

Johhny said quietly, "All this sounds like bad news. Let's have it."

"You haven't heard about it, then?" Ernie asked.

"Nary a word," Johnny answered. He said again, "Let's have it."

"When I boasted about our town not having any crime," Ernie continued slowly, "I should have mentioned a certain exception. The Falcon rode in here and—"

"*El Halcón!* The Falcon—here?" Vallejo exclaimed, following a sharp intake of breath. Johnny Barlow's eyes had narrowed.

"Yeah, the Falcon," Meticulous said. "You act like you'd heard of him. Mex bandit—holdup man. Been operating around these parts."

Johnny nodded. "Yes, we've heard of him. There've been various pieces in newspapers. But I thought he just worked close to the border. Never heard of him operating this far from the line."

"Well, he did," Meticulous growled. "Raised plenty hell too. Damn nigh finished off Matt Melville."

Johnny looked concerned. "Matt? Gripes, I'm sorry to hear that. Is he all right now? Get on with the telling."

"He's got a chance to pull through." Ernie took up the story. "It happened just eight days ago. Matt Melville had just raised a loan of ten thousand dollars from Banker Caldwell. He'd signed a note and had the money in a satchel, preparin' to leave. It was hotter'n hell's hinges in town, and everybody was holed up inside. Meanwhile, the Falcon rides in without being noticed, walks into the bank and throws a gun on Jay Summerton, the cashier. There was nobody else in front of the bank at that moment. The Falcon backed Summerton into a closet, then goes back to Banker Caldwell's office. Matt was just starting to leave when the Falcon pushes in. The Falcon shot him down, threw a couple more shots at Caldwell—which he missed—then grabbed the satchel of money and lined out for his horse, waitin' at the hitch rack—"

"I'd been up all night playin' stud"—Meticulous soothed his guilty conscience—"and was catching

47

up on my shut-eye, at the time. Otherwise, I'd probably stopped that damn bandit."

"Theese Falcon, he escape' with the money—no?" Vallejo inquired.

Ernie Braughn shook his head. "No. Didn't I mention that Rawhide City's got a dang efficient sheriff? Kirk Norton. Norton just can't be beat for handlin' law busters. He owns the Quarter-Circle-N Ranch and the Blue Gem Saloon as well, but he still finds time to handle the sheriff's office in fine fashion. Anyway, the Falcon had everybody bluffed with the promiscuous lead he was slingin' reckless-like both ways along the street, and was makin' a clean getaway when Kirk Norton stepped into the picture. He come walkin' cool-like out of the Blue Gem with his Winchester, like he had all the time in the world, stepped out to the road and drew his bead. Gents, I'm telling you, Norton stopped that stick-up man plumb pronto. Downed the hawss first, then when the Falcon was running to get another pony, Kirk lets him have it. Killed him instanter. The Falcon was dead before the first man reached him. Kirk thrun another slug through the Falcon's head, just to make sure, as he put it, though that extra shot wa'n't really necessary. But that was typical of the sheriff; he just don't take any chances. He likes to make sure."

"Did the Señor Sheriff collect the reward offered for the Falcon's death?" Vallejo wanted to know.

Ernie shrugged. "Ain't never heard anything to that effect."

"I suppose," Johnny put in, "the body of the Falcon would have to be identified by somebody who knew him before the authorities would pay the reward."

"Norton himself identified the Falcon," Ernie said. "Recognised him right off, when he first see the Falcon backing out of the bank doorway—and the Falcon with a bandanner across his face too."

"So?" Johnny started to say something, then changed the subject slightly. "Well, I'm danged glad to hear Matt Melville didn't lose his ten thousand, anyway. How bad was Matt hit, exactly?"

"So damn bad," Ernie said seriously, "that Doc Duncan didn't even dare move him out of the bank for three days. The bank had to stay closed for three days, except for Frank Caldwell having access to his office. Caldwell brought sacks of money down here, some of his books and such, and his cashier, Jay Summerton, ran the banking business from here, for the benefit of folks who couldn't wait to do their bankin'. And every minute this Clinic Saloon was open for bankin' hours Kirk Norton stuck close to make sure no holdups were attempted. Even had his meals brought in—"

"That's correct," Meticulous Jones nodded. "Kirk wouldn't even let me relieve him." His face clouded up. "Kirk wouldn't trust me, I reckon."

"Melville's down to Doc's house now," Ernie went on. "He's still right bad, but Doc thinks he's got a chance to pull through, with careful nursin' and proper medicine."

"And something else"—Meticulous Jones addressed Johnny—"that money wa'n't recovered, like you think. It plumb disappeared."

"Disappeared?" Johnny frowned. "I don't understand—"

"Neither does anybody else," Ernie interrupted. "I'll let you figure it out if you're able. That satchel of gold was in plain sight of folks from the instant the Falcon left the bank, and yet when the satchel was taken back to the bank, and opened, the ten thousand had plumb vanished. There was nothing in that grip but broken chunks of sandstone, wrapped in pieces of newspaper."

"*Diantre!* The devil you say!" Vallejo exclaimed. "Someone make the exchange of the satchels—no?"

Johnny's eyes narrowed in thought. "It sure looks like somebody switched bags all right." He pondered a moment, then frowned. "Damned if I see how, though—if that bag was in full sight all the time. It was mighty slick work."

"Nobody'd believe at first them bags had been switched," Ernie continued. "Caldwell's initials were on the bag the gold was put into; his initials were on the bag the rocks were found in. Caldwell swore the rock bag was his'n, at first, but now he

50

ain't sure. He's sort of up in the air about the whole business. He ain't certain if it's his bag or not."

"The sheriff thinks," Meticulous pointed out, "that a switch was made right after the Falcon was knocked out of his saddle and got hit by the first slug. You see, before Kirk could reach the body, a crowd had collected around. In them few moments anythin' might have happened. The satchel was completely out of Kirk's sight. A fast worker, it might be, could've made the exchange durin' the excitement, with folks millin' around and all, and made a quick getaway."

Johnny shrugged unbelievingly. "It's possible, of course," he conceded. "What's the sheriff doing about it?"

"Getting crabbier every minute," Meticulous complained. "A body would think it was all my fault. Well, I'm admittin' Kirk is a sharper hombre than me, and if he can't figure it out, I can't give him the answer."

"If you can pin him down," Ernie Braughn said, "the sheriff will admit he's up against it. He threw out some vague remarks about having clues, and he arrested several suspects who was known to have been near the Falcon, after the sheriff downed him, but Kirk had to let said suspects go free after givin' 'em one hell of a grillin'. Not a one would confess to anythin', and Norton didn't have any proof agin' 'em. Kirk had their houses searched and everything, but the money has just plumb van-

51

ished. I guess the loss will put Matt Melville into a tight too. Doc Duncan says the shock of the loss dang nigh finished him."

"I can imagine," Johnny said sympathetically. A fresh idea suggested itself. "What about this Summer—what's his name?—the cashier? What does he say?"

"Jay Summerton," Ernie supplied the name. "Hell! He can't—and don't—say nothin'. All he knows is that the Falcon shoved him into a closet at the point of a gun. After that, until Caldwell unlocked the closet door and released him, Jay didn't see nothin' important. He could hear the shots, but he didn't know what was goin' on in Caldwell's office."

Vallejo asked, "Ees eet likely that theese cashier would be in—how do you say eet?—cahoots?—weeth the Falcon, and somehow make the exchange?"

Ernie shook his head. "Not a chance, as I see it. Jay is loyal to Frank Caldwell. You see, Jay came out here three years back, sufferin' from lung trouble. He tried to get work, but nobody would hire him. Finally, Caldwell gave him the job as cashier—Jay knew bankin'—and since then he feels that Caldwell saved his life. Anyway, you don't want to forget that Jay was locked in that closet when the money was grabbed."

"Me, I'm convinced that one of the first to get near the Falcon's dead body is the skunk that stole

Matt's money," Meticulous Jones stated definitely.

"Which same idea," Ernie snorted, "you adopted from Sheriff Norton. Now if the Sheriff only knew every man who was gathered around that body, he could grill 'em proper, but in the excitement he only remembered a few—"

"He should have had you there," Johnny smiled.

Ernie nodded seriously. "If I'd seen 'em, I'd have remembered, but I didn't, so there's no use of speculatin'. Kirk just remembered a few of the fellers, and he couldn't learn nothin' from them."

Johnny asked casually, "What's this Kirk Norton like?" He was looking at Meticulous Jones.

"We-ell—" Meticulous paused and groped for words.

Ernie made answer. "Meticulous don't like to say too much about his boss, but I don't have to keep my mouth shut—not yet, anyway. I can give you Kirk Norton in a few words. He's harder'n ice and just as cold. He's a dead shot with six-shooter or rifle. He ain't friendly enough to be popular, but he's got folks' respect—"

Meticulous put in, somewhat defiant tones, "And if he can't get respect he bullies folks. One way or another he pulls folks to his way of thinkin', or shuts their mouths—but don't let on I said so."

"Meticulous is right." Ernie agreed. "I will say this though: it's Kirk Norton who has kept Rawhide City free of crime. If he'd just unbend a mite, I think folks would like him fine. To sum up,

Kirk is one hell of a fine sheriff, in my opinion, though there have been times when it seemed to me he was a mite sudden with his irons."

"In other words," Johnny said, "if he wasn't a law officer—and a good one—it wouldn't take much of a jump over the corral bars to turn him into a professional gun fighter. And killer."

Ernie squirmed under this direct statement, but conceded reluctantly, "I reckon you called the turn, Johnny."

Barlow asked next: "Who carried the satchel back to the bank?"

"Norton, most of the way," Ernie said promptly. "Caldwell took it when Norton had nearly reached the bank. You see, Caldwell had run out to meet Kirk—"

"Could the exchange of bags have been made then?" Vallejo asked.

"Hell's bells on a tomcat!" Meticulous exploded. "An exchange then? In broad daylight? With the whole town lookin' on, and Norton in plain sight when he handed over the bag to Banker Caldwell?"

Johnny continued, "Who was in the bank when the satchel was carried inside?"

Meticulous answered that too. "I'd come awake at the sound of the shooting and hurried to the bank. I'd helped to lift Matt to a table. Then I left to find Kirk. I followed him back to the bank. I stood in the doorway to keep the crowd out.

54

Caldwell and Kirk were there with the satchel. Jay Summerton was there. Doc Duncan was there, workin' over Matt, who was stretched out on the table. That's all. Doc decides he has to have another bag, so he has Kirk send me over here to get it from Ernie—"

"What bag did you bring?" Johnny cut in quickly.

"A bag of surgery tools and medicines," Meticulous snapped. "Hell, feller! They'd already discovered the money was missing before I git back with Doc's bag—"

"And Doc Duncan is as straight as a die," Ernie chipped in belligerently. "Don't you go suspectin' him of a hand in the robbery."

Johnny laughed softly. "All right, you two, you can climb down off your high horses. I'm not suspecting Doc Duncan. I was just looking for information. I'm sort of curious, but it don't mean a thing, so quit fretting."

Ernie smiled suddenly. "It's all right, cowpoke. Only I think a heap of Doc. He's four-square. And don't get any ideas about Meticulous, here, either. When he says it was Doc's bag of tools he fetched, he speaks truth. I know, 'cause I gave 'em to him."

"That's correct," the deputy verified. He muttered something about being "poor but virtuous," then added in a louder tone, "Cripes A'mighty! I wouldn't know what to do with ten thousand if I had it, so that clears me."

"Meticulous," Johnny said solemnly, "I never even give you a thought. Far's I'm concerned, you're pure as the lily in the dell." Meticulous said thank you, and Johnny continued, "Ernie, you said that Norton identified the bandit as the Falcon."

Braughn nodded. "That's right." He hesitated, then, "There's three or four fellers around town think he might be wrong, though."

"Who?" Johnny asked. "And why?"

"Oh, just fellers around town," Ernie replied evasively. He and the deputy exchanged quick glances.

"If not the Falcon," Vallejo asked, "who did these men theenk eet was?"

Ernie hesitated a moment. Meticulous cleared his throat. "I've never said anything to Kirk, but I'm one of the fellers who is not sure that dead bandit was the Falcon. I saw the body at the undertaker's."

"You got any idea who it was?" Johnny asked.

"We-ell," Meticulous said cautiously, "it might have been a hombre called Mex Louie, who lived here one time—some years back. I won't say for sure, but he certain resembled Mex Louie as I remembered him." Johnny asked a question and Meticulous replied, "Mex Louie's mother was a big blonde woman. His father was a Mexican. The mother is dead now, but I think the old man still lives in town. Louie never amounted to much as a kid and he got worse as he grew up. He left town a long while back. He visited his father about four years ago for a few days. I had a hunch then he might be hidin' out from somebody. I don't know where he holes up. Some place across the border, could be, but that's just a guess."

"What did Sheriff Norton have to say about the bandit being Mex Louie?" Johnny asked.

"Damn little," Ernie replied. "He rode roughshod over anybody that disagreed with him, and insisted, definite, the bandit was the Falcon. Them that thought he was mistook sort of changed their minds after a spell. I've already pointed out that Kirk don't brook no interference."

At that moment Doc Duncan entered the saloon. He nodded to Ernie and Meticulous and glanced questioningly at Johnny and Vallejo. Ernie introduced the two and a smile broke over Duncan's lined face as he shook hands. "Friend of Matt Melville's, eh?" he said to Johnny.

Johnny nodded. "Haven't seen him for a good many years, though. Not since his daughter Irene—we used to call her 'Rene—and I were youngsters. My dad used to be sheriff of Paso County, back in Texas. Matt Melville was his deputy. Then, when 'Rene's mother died, Matt took his daughter and pulled out for this section of the country, so as to help forget his grief, I suppose. Then my parents died, and I sort of drifted around. Mike and I have been knocking about down in *mañana* land for a spell. When we got close to the border, I happened to remember that the Melvilles lived near Rawhide City, so I figured to drop in and say hello to 'em. Never thought to find Matt hurt. Is he able to see visitors?"

Duncan frowned and shook his head. "I'd just as soon you didn't come to see him, right now. The least excitement might set him back. My wife is as capable a nurse as there is in these parts. She's taking good care of him. I *think* I can pull him through, but I don't want to risk anything that might bring on a relapse."

"Sure, I can understand that," Johnny said. "I sort of think we'll stick around a few days anyway. Maybe I can see him later. I want to slope out to the ranch and say hello to 'Rene, anyway."

"It's too dang bad 'Rene didn't know you were in town," Duncan said. "She rode in this afternoon to see how Matt was doing, and just pulled out about twenty minutes ago. I imagine she'll be pleased to see an old friend."

"We'll drift out to the Lazy-Double-M later," Johnny said. "Right now, I could stand some chow. My stomach's beginning to think my throat's been cut. How about you, Mike?"

"*Si,*" Vallejo agreed instantly. "I'm theenk we can do weeth some food, Johnee."

Duncan said, "I can recommend either the Kansas City Chop House or the T-Bone Restaurant. Will you have a drink before you go?"

"Thanks, no." Johnny shook his head. "We'll be seeing you some more, Doc. Ernie and Meticulous have told us about the holdup and so on. I'd like to talk to you about it sometime. That missing money puzzles me."

"It's got us all puzzled." Duncan frowned.

They talked a few minutes more, then Johnny and Vallejo left the saloon. Ernie Braughn's eyes narrowed as they passed through the swinging doors. "Now, I wonder . . ." he mused. "I just can't believe it was ordinary curiosity spurrin' that Barlow hombre's questions."

"What do you mean?" Duncan asked.

Ernie didn't reply for a moment, then, "Doc, I'm not just certain what I mean, but somehow I got a feeling those two know something we don't."

"Concernin' the robbery?" Meticulous asked.

"Damned if I can say." Ernie scowled. "It's not all clear in my mind. But if there isn't more to that Johnny Barlow than you see on the surface, I'm mighty mistaken in my hunches."

And with that not quite satisfactory reply, the other two had to be content.

# CHAPTER V

## WARNING

THE sun had dropped below the peaks of the Sangre de Santos Range when Johnny and Vallejo stepped into the street. Within a short time a brief twilight would ensue, then darkness would settle down. The day had cooled considerably and a slight breeze had commenced to stir across the range. The two men went directly to their horses at the hitch rack, then Johnny said, "Wait a minute, Mike." He appeared lost in thought.

"What's on the mind, Johnee?" Vallejo asked after a few moments.

"Let the ponies stand," Johnny replied. "We can make to find the restaurant on foot. But first, if you can stave off your appetite, I'd like to try something else—"

"You are theenking of theese Sheriff Norton," Vallejo surmised shrewdly.

"Right." Johnny nodded. "I'd like to get a look at that hombre and see how he sizes up. Mike, I've got a hunch there's some underhanded business being pulled hereabouts. I'm going to stay around until I learn what's what, if possible—"

"You theenk Norton is behind the underhanded work you mention?"

"I didn't say that." There was a slight trace of irritation in Johnny's voice. "I just don't know what to think, and it bothers me. But, as I say, I'd like to give Norton the once-over. Let's find the Blue Gem Saloon that Norton owns—along with his ranch and a job as sheriff. Good lord, all that must keep him busy. What I'm getting at is this: we might find Norton in the Blue Gem. Does the idea appeal to you?"

"Whatevair you say, Johnee, is all right weeth

me," Vallejo returned agreeably. "I'm think the Blue Gem is down this way"—pointing toward the east.

The two sauntered leisurely along the plank sidewalk. Now and then a pedestrian passed, or a rider raised dust in the street. A few lights appeared in store windows, though it would be some short time yet before night descended. Less than five minutes' walk brought them abreast of the Blue Gem, a solidly built structure of rock and adobe, with a dust-encrusted window at either side of the swinging-doored entrance. From beyond the batwing doors came the clink of bottles against glasses and men's voices. A yellow glow sprang into being; the Blue Gem was just lighting up.

Followed by Vallejo, Johnny stepped to the plank platform that fronted the entrance. Unbeknown to Johnny, another man was just on the point of taking his departure from the saloon. As his hand touched the swinging doors, Johnny was performing the same action from his side. The swinging doors resisted Johnny's light shove as he started through. Unthinkingly, he pushed harder. Too late, he saw the outline of a man's head and shoulders above the doors, as the batwings swung sharply in under Johnny's emphatic push. One door struck the departing client sharply against a shoulder, partially throwing him off balance.

The man staggered back as Johnny and Vallejo stepped inside. Johnny was instantly apologetic.

"Excuse me, mister," he commenced. "I didn't realise you were leaving. I reckon if you and I had each kept to the right as we started through—as is intended with these doors—we'd not—"

The words were cut short by a torrent of abuse as the other righted himself. ". . . and you'd better look where you're going after this, you lousy sonuvabuzzard," the man concluded, with a couple of additional curses.

Johnny's lips tightened. "Take it easy, hombre," he advised coldly. "I've tried to apologise. Maybe we were both in the wrong, but I'm willing to take the blame. Now just cool down and everything will be hunky-dory—"

The man's face flooded crimson. He called Johnny a name. "I just figure I'll have to teach you a lesson," he snarled.

"I've told you once to cool down," Johnny snapped. "I don't want to have to repeat myself. If you hadn't been drinking, you'd know enough to use your head—"

The man repeated the name.

Johnny didn't hesitate a moment longer. His clenched fist shot out, catching the belligerent one on the side of the jaw. The man stumbled back, legs moving rapidly in the effort to save himself. Then his spur rowels became entangled and he crashed down in a heap. For a moment he sat there, dazed, shaking his head groggily.

Johnny sent a swift glance towards the bar. A

number of men stood there, with glasses before them. Behind the bar the bartender craned his head forward, mouth agape. There was no time to see more.

The man on the floor was clambering up now, a lurid stream of profanity gushing from his lips. Once on his feet, his right hand started to claw at his holster, though Johnny could see he was somewhat dazed still.

At that moment Johnny recognised the man. The jutting jaw, the small eyes placed too closely together, the triangle of black hair hanging across the receding forehead . . . Johnny had made no move as yet to draw his own gun. He stood a few feet inside the entrance, legs wide, thumbs hooked in cartridge belt. At his back, Mike Vallejo waited, alert for the first hostile move on the part of any of the men at the bar.

Then Johnny spoke sharply. "Don't draw that gun, Deever."

Vink Deever paused momentarily, squinting at Johnny from a bleary daze. One hand was still pawing at his holster as he weaved about, uncertain on his legs. He swore again.

The next instant he felt Johnny's gun barrel slammed into his middle with considerable force. Air was expelled violently from Deever's open mouth and he grunted with mingled pain and anger.

Johnny said again, "Don't draw that gun, Deever," in the same whiplike tone.

Deever's hand left his holster. His mouth closed, then sagged open again. For a moment he couldn't find his voice as a light from an overhead kerosene lamp revealed Johnny's once familiar features. Something like a gasp left Deever's lips, and his face turned chalk-white.

"Barlow," he whispered hoarsely, unbelievingly, and again, "Barlow!"

Johnny nodded. "You haven't forgotten me, eh, Vink?"

Deever's eyes had cleared now. "Forgot *you?*" His voice trembled with resentment, anger. "Why, God damn you—" Abruptly his voice changed to a whine. "What you doing here, Barlow? You ain't got a thing on me. I'm living honest. You can't do anything to me."

Johnny laughed softly. "No, Deever, I haven't got a thing on you—yet."

"And you won't get nothin', neither, Barlow. I paid, didn't I?"

"As far as I know, you paid." Johnny nodded. "That part wasn't my problem."

Deever shifted nervously, his eyes darting from side to side. He wanted to leave, yet felt something more might be required. He'd owned a certain prestige in Rawhide City. Now he could see it being swept away by the sudden, unexpected appearance of this damn Barlow. Hot rage flooded through his body, but he lacked the requisite nerve to take the step that might restore his lost reputation.

Seven or eight men, in cowpuncher togs, standing at the bar, looked on in wide-eyed amazement. Sheriff Norton, among them, was taking in the scene, the curiosity in his gaze veiled by narrowed lids. It was plain to Norton that Deever's courage had evaporated into thin air.

Suddenly the sheriff acted. He left the bar and crossed the floor to Deever's side. "You, Vink," he ordered tersely. "Get out! You've been drinking too much. Go get yourself some sleep."

Deever was thoroughly sober by this time. He nodded, speaking in jerky tones. "Just as you say, Kirk. I don't want to make any trouble here." He cast a look of hate at Barlow, then shoved past and plunged hurriedly through the swinging doors. His footsteps pounded across the saloon porch.

Norton swung back to Johnny. Johnny took in the hawklike nose, thin merciless lips below the yellow moustaches, the hard gaze. He faced Norton squarely. "Sheriff Norton, I take it," he said quietly, slipping his six-shooter back into holster.

Norton flicked one hand toward the metal star on his coat lapel. "You take it correct." His voice was hard, flat, emotionless as he continued, "Undoubtedly, Deever was in the wrong. What you gave him he deserved. Apparently, you two have met before. That's your business and his. I'm not concerned in that part. What does concern me is your gun. You can't tote a gun in this town. If you intend to remain, you'll have to give it into my

65

care until you leave." He repeated, "You can't tote a gun in this town."

"No?" Johnny's face assumed a look of surprise. He cast a glance towards the men lining the bar before his gaze returned to the sheriff's. "That must be a new ordinance, isn't it?" Johnny asked cheerfully. "Everyone else seems to be packing his hardware. With a little effort you may remember that Deever even tried to get his gun into action—or didn't you notice that?"

"I noticed it. I said before that he deserved what you gave him. But that doesn't change the situation. Neither does Rawhide City have a new ordinance against gun toting," Norton said coldly. "But in this case *I'm* the law, and I say you can't wear your gun in this town. That settles it. I know these other men. I don't know you nor your pardner. If you remain here, you can't wear an iron. Make up your mind—disarm, or leave!"

Johnny grinned, but the grin had nothing to do with the look in his eyes. "My pard and I were aiming to give the Blue Gem a mite of business," he said easily.

"The Blue Gem," Norton replied, clipping the words short, "will be glad of *your* patronage, so long as you understand the conditions. As for your friend"—his gaze rested but briefly on Vallejo—"he'll have to find his drinks some other place. I do not allow greasers to be served in the Blue Gem."

Vallejo stiffened, his eyes flashing hotly. "Sheriff

66

Norton," he protested with considerable dignity, "I do not care for theese 'greaser' word you employ so carelessly—"

"It's not my habit," Norton snapped, "to consider greasers' feelings in such matters. You *pelados* must be taught your place—and it's not with white men—"

*"Diantre!"* Vallejo flamed, swinging swiftly to one side as Norton's hand went to gun butt. "That you mus' take back—"

"Easy, Mike!" Johnny exclaimed. His left hand fell to Miguel's right, preventing the Mexican from drawing his six-shooter. At the same instant Johnny's own gun flashed again into view, covering the sheriff. "Don't pull it, Norton; don't pull it," Johnny finished.

Norton swore, but relaxed the grip on his own weapon, various ideas coursing swiftly through his mind. Though his face didn't show it, he had been considerably surprised at the speed with which Johnny had covered him. "You're making a mistake, cowpunch," Norton stated severely. "You'd best hand over that gun to me."

"Do you think I'm a fool?" Johnny demanded.

"As a matter of fact, I do," Norton said angrily.

Johnny grinned exasperatingly. "All right, I'm a fool, then. Now don't tell me you expect a fool to act sensibly." His gun tilted a trifle, still bearing on Norton's middle. Vallejo had relaxed and made no further attempt to draw his weapon.

"This is a pack of damn nonsense," Norton swore wrathfully. He turned his head to appeal to the men at the bar. "One of you hombres get busy and—"

"You men keep your hands away from your guns," Johnny spoke warningly. "The sheriff don't mean what he says, or he's another fool. Norton, you'd better reconsider. Even if one of those men succeeded in dropping me, haven't you realised the shock of being hit might explode my gun—and then where would you be? . . . Mike, you keep out of this. I can handle it."

"*Bueno,* Johnee. I do as you say."

Norton's eyes were cold flames of hate, but he realised the sense that lay in Johnny's advice. Grudgingly, he spoke again to the men at the bar. "All right, hombres, no need for you to take a hand in this game. This is my problem."

The men at the bar relaxed, though none of them had shown any great desire to take part in the argument.

Norton spoke to Johnny again. "You can't get away with this—"

"I'm getting away with it, ain't I?" Johnny laughed derisively.

"I demand you surrender to my authority."

"Demand and be damned to you," Johnny grinned. "Look here, Norton, you're just making things worse for yourself. I've heard you were smart. Why don't you try to prove that to me? Use your head, for cripes' sakes, and you'll be able to see you haven't any real complaint to make. I'm regretful this happened, but you've got to admit I saved some bloodshed, probably. You may be fast with a gun, but Mike's no slouch either. Maybe I've saved somebody's life."

Anger struggled with reluctant admiration in Norton's features. He was breathing hard, fighting to hold his temper, knowing all the time that Johnny was right and thinking that only an idiot keeps banging his head against a stone wall. A smart man extricates himself from an untenable position in order to save himself for the next attempt.

Johnny guessed what was taking place in the man's mind, and followed up his advantage: "Look here, Sheriff Norton, I've already stated I'm regretful this happened. What more can I say? We didn't come here looking for trouble. This whole fuss isn't of our making, but apparently we got off on the wrong foot with you. What harm's been done, is done, but there's no use crying over spilt milk. Mike and I realise we're not popular here, so we're sloping. . . . Now, I'll put my gun away if you'll promise not to plug me in the back when we leave."

Norton said stiffly, "I'm not in the habit of shooting men in the back."

"A thing can be done once without becoming a habit," Johnny pointed out, "but that one shot can

69

raise merry hell with a man's carcass. Come to think of it, didn't your first shot hit the Falcon in the back?"

Norton tensed. "What do you know about the Falcon?"

"Why ask me?" Johnny shrugged. "I wasn't here when it happened. But I've heard folks telling about it."

"The shot that struck the Falcon first was a different matter," Norton said coldly. "I was just trying to make it plain to you that I do not make a habit of—"

"Oh hell," Johnny spoke wearily. "We're fed up with all this palaver and this place too. We're leaving. Do you figure to stop us?"

"I'm as sick of this talk as you are," Norton said frigidly. He was cooling down now. "All right, I'll agree that you probably did save some bloodshed. That being the case, I'll agree to forget this trouble, providing you men leave the county *pronto*. I'll give you one hour to get out of town. Sixty minutes from now I'll be taking you in—or shooting you, I don't much care which—if you cut my trail again."

Abruptly, he turned his back on Johnny and Vallejo and returned to the bar. At the bar he spoke over his shoulder: "You've had your warning. Now get out!"

"We'll do that," Johnny said quietly. "Come on, Mike."

Vallejo preceded him through the swing doors. Johnny backed through the exit. Only after he was outside did he holster his gun. Then he gave vent to a long breath of relief.

On the sidewalk Vallejo said, "For one minute eet looked like the bad situation, Johnee."

Johnny nodded, then shrugged his shoulders. "I've been in worse though, Mike. C'mon, let's go find some chow. We've got an hour left."

## CHAPTER VI

### EX-CONVICT

BREATHS of suppressed excitement were exhaled slowly as Barlow and the Mexican disappeared into the night. Norton ran his sharp glance along the bar. No one met his eyes. Finally Norton said in quiet tones to his barkeep, "Set 'em up, Jiggs. Drinks are on the house. And on me, personal. That's the first time in many a moon that anyone got the drop on Kirk Norton. I've got to admit I don't like it a bit, but there you are. That redheaded cowpoke accomplished what nobody else has done in twenty years."

Shaking his head in self-disgust, he rounded the end of the bar and took a seat on a high stool, his back resting against a back bar. Jiggs, a tall thin individual with a sober countenance, poured a drink for his boss, handed it to him, then took orders from the men in front of the bar. For several minutes nothing was heard but the clinking of glasses and the smacking of lips.

A cowboy from the Rafter-G Ranch broke the awkward silence: "I doubt if the waddie would've got the drop on you, Sheriff, if you hadn't been watching that oiler at the time."

Norton replied instantly in flat, definite tones, "Whether or not I was watching that Mex hombre excuses me not a particle. As sheriff, I'm supposed to be on the alert for such moves. I got careless and quit watching the white fellow an instant too long. I've nobody to blame but myself for my own stupidity."

And that, too, was according to tradition. Men said that Kirk Norton was fully as just as he was hard.

"Still," another man put in, "that feller was a heap faster'n usual with his draw. You couldn't have been expected to know about that."

"He was fast all right," Norton conceded. He gazed moodily a moment into his glass, swirled the liquor around the tumbler a moment, and then drained it off.

"You figurin' to arrest them two later, Kirk?" a Circle-Cross hand asked.

Norton's lips tightened. He cast a quick glance at the cowboy and replied coldly, "You should know better than to ask such a fool question, Winston. You heard my warning. If he stays, he'll have to hand over his gun. There's your answer. I don't expect any fuss about it. I could see that white hombre was trying to avoid trouble, and the Mex was followin' his lead. He come here peaceful enough. I got to admit that much. It was that fool Deever caused the trouble. And I don't suppose either of 'em could be expected to know about my rule regarding not serving greasers in the Blue Gem. Evidently the white hombre—What did Deever call him?—Barton? No, Barlow. That's it, Barlow. Evidently Deever and this Barlow had had a run-in some place before. Sounded like there'd been a feud or something between 'em. Deever sure looked scared as hell when he recognised Barlow, and I never looked on Deever as a man who scared easily. That all makes Barlow sound sort of dangerous."

"Yeah," a puncher from the HB-Connected put in, "the way Vink Deever acted, I'd say he lost the pot in whatever game him and this Barlow was playin'."

Oh hell," Norton said irritably, "we're making a lot of *habla* about nothing important. I reckon we'd best forget the whole matter. Barlow and his Mex pard will, like's not, slope out of town *pronto*. If they don't"—and Norton's thin laugh sounded brittle—"it won't take long to forget 'em anyhow."

The others nodded sheeplike agreement. Norton told Jiggs to set up another round of drinks on the house, then slipped from his seat and strode without further words through the swinging doors of the entrance. Seating himself on a beer keg under the wooden awning that graced the Blue Gem porch, he gave himself over to angry meditation. The street was spotted with squares of yellow light now. Overhead, stars were twinkling into being, though there was no sign of the moon as yet. Diagonally across the street stood the T-Bone Restaurant. Norton's sharp glance carried through the window to the lighted interior where he could see Johnny Barlow and Vallejo seated at a long counter. He cursed in a low undertone; unconsciously his right hand stole to the gun in holster at his thigh.

"I give 'em an hour to get out of town," Norton muttered. "They've already wasted fifteen minutes of that time. Well, we'll see. . . ."

Vink Deever emerged from a dark passageway across the street, then came over from the opposite side and stepped to the Blue Gem porch. Norton glanced at him without speaking. Deever took up a position beside Norton, his back braced against the front wall of the saloon.

"They're across the street, in the T-Bone, Kirk," Deever said after a moment.

"I've got eyes of my own," Norton said briefly. He took a long thin cigar from his pocket, savagely bit off one end, lighted it and exhaled a cloud of grey smoke. "I'm waiting for your story," he said finally.

Deever asked, "What happened after I left?"

"Plenty," Norton said tersely. "We had some words." He explained in a few clipped sentences what had happened. "That Barlow hombre got the drop on me while I was watching the greaser."

"He did? My Gawd, Kirk—"

"Shut up! I'm telling this. I was in no position to push trouble then—though I was within an ace of cutting a notch for the Mex. I've give 'em both an hour to leave town. Time's a-burnin'. Then, we'll see." He chewed savagely on the cigar.

"You—gave Barlow—one hour—to leave town?" Astonishment spaced the words in Deever's question.

"One hour. Not an instant more."

Deever's laughter started with a low chuckle, then increased in volume. There was something derisive in the sound that grated on Norton's nerves.

Norton's head jerked around abruptly. "You damned fool, Vink! What are you laughing at?"

"Didn't Barlow—*haw, haw*—tell you—*haw, haw, haw!*—who he was?"

Norton lifted a vicious left hand and gave Deever a backhanded slap across the face. "God damn it! Will you quit that fool laughing, or have I got to stop you?" The cruel tones and the slap restored Deever to sober humility. Norton went on, "No, he didn't tell me who he is. Is he somebody I should know about? Where'd you meet him? Is he a famous gun slinger, or something of the sort? That draw of his—"

"Yeah, something of the sort," Deever said soberly. "To be exact, Barlow is a member of the Border Rangers—"

A nasty oath interrupted the words. Then both men were silent for a time. Norton had to draw hard to bring his cigar back to life. When he spoke again, his voice was hard and steady. "All right, it's a body blow, but I can handle it. Tell me about Barlow. What's he got on you?"

Deever's words shook a trifle. "Not a blasted thing—now. Except maybe—well, unless—"

"Shut it up, you fool." The command came in a terse whisper.

A puncher from the HB-Connected pushed through the swinging doors of the Blue Gem, and, without noticing Deever and Norton on the porch, rocked a trifle unsteadily out to the hitch rack and mounted his pony. The pony was turned and went drumming down the street.

Norton said, "All right, go on."

Deever said, "It happened a long spell back, before I ever come to Rawhide City. Barlow was new with the Border Rangers then. I got mixed up in a rustling mess. I was innocent of stealin' the cattle in question, but—"

"Get on with your story and skip the lying."

Deever swallowed hard. "I thought I'd make a clean getaway, but that damn Barlow picked up my

76

trail. I'd underestimated his abilities and got careless. Tried to shake him off with every dodge I knew, but it was no good. I led him a three weeks' chase and started across the Muerto Desert, but he hung on like a bulldog. Finally I got tired of running and tried to ambush him, but he had all the luck and outsmarted me. We shot it out. I nearly got him too, but he was a mite the faster. I've practised my draw a heap since those days, though, and I figure—"

"You had a chance to try out your figuring when you met him inside a while back," Norton interrupted brutally. "Get to it. How long did you serve?"

"Twenty-eight months in the pen. Got some time off for good behaviour or it would have been longer."

Norton swore at him. "Why didn't you tell me this when I hired you? I'll have a fine reputation if this sort of news gets around—me, Sheriff Norton, hiring an ex-convict."

"Honest to Gawd, Kirk," Deever said in a whining voice, "I would have told you, only I was afraid you wouldn't take me on. I needed a job, money, bad."

"You been riding a straight trail since you got out of the pen, Vink? I want the truth now. None of your damn lying."

"You should know I've worked for your interests ever since you put me on your pay roll, Kirk. You—you ain't goin' to fire me, are you?"

77

"Don't talk like a jackass, Vink. So long as that Ranger man hasn't anything on you, I'll forget what happened before—as long as this news doesn't get around town. If folks should get indignant, I'd just have to let you go, naturally, so watch your step. I don't forget easily—" Norton paused as a new thought struck him. "Well, this means just one thing."

"What's that?"

"If Barlow isn't on your trail, somebody's called him in on Melville's case to find the missing money."

Deever considered that before replying. Except for lights here and there, the gloom along the street had deepened. A few pedestrians passed without noticing Norton and Deever on the porch. A customer entered the Blue Gem, passing a few feet from Norton without being aware of the sheriff's presence.

Deever finally said, "I'm not so sure you're right about that, Kirk. Maybe Barlow's just passing through, headed for someplace else. Course, unless his business was pressin', he might stay here, should he get wind of that missin' satchel of cash—"

"I figure he's heard about it."

Deever sighed. "Along the border east of here, where Barlow used to be stationed, they used to call him Lucky Barlow. He was always stumblin' in where he wa'n't wanted—and winnin' glory. There's a chance he just stumbled in here."

"He'll win no glory here if I can help it," Norton snapped. "This business of the missing money is my job to handle, and folks should realise it. I wonder if somebody has sent word to the Rangers about it. Maybe it's somebody in town who thinks I'm not big enough for my job. I wonder if it could have been Irene Melville—or someone else on the Lazy-Double-M."

Deever disagreed. "I think you're lookin' for trouble where trouble doesn't exist, Kirk. This town seems to have plenty of faith in you. Matter of fact, I heard one of Melville's hands say yesterday that he expected you to turn up the guilty man and restore that money most any day now. No, I got a hunch that Barlow just landed here through chance."

The words helped restore Norton's confidence. He puffed energetically on his cigar. The end of the weed glowed red. Smoke drifted lazily out to the street. "Well, perhaps you're correct, Vink," he said finally. "Just the same, if I learn anybody in Rawhide City notified the Rangers and asked for an investigation, I aim to resign my office plenty *pronto*. There isn't room in this town for more than one law officer while I'm sheriff."

Deever's snicker sounded through the gloom. "How about Meticulous Jones?"

"I said law officer," Norton replied ironically. "Jones is all right to serve court notices and round up men to serve on juries and so on, but no sane

person would call him a law officer—even if, the-
oretically, he acts as my deputy—" He left the sentence unfinished.

Diagonally across the roadway, Johnny Barlow
and Vallejo had finished their supper and were just
emerging from the T-Bone Restaurant. For a
moment the two stood talking at the edge of the
sidewalk. Norton started to rise from his seat, then
dropped back once more. "I suppose," he said
reluctantly, "in view of Barlow being a Border
Ranger, some words are demanded from me. I'll
have to admit that I talked too much—but I'll wait
awhile, I reckon. Maybe I won't see him again."
He looked thoughtful.

Vink Deever cast a quick glance at his chief,
trying to ascertain exactly what Norton had in
mind. "Do y'know," Deever said after a minute, "I
think I could pick that Barlow hombre off from
here."

Norton remained silent. Deever didn't know
whether the sheriff was giving some consideration
to the suggestion, or hadn't heard it. Barlow and
Vallejo were still standing in front of the restaurant, engaged in lighting cigarettes.

"Don't talk like a brainless fool, Vink," Norton
said at last. He took the cigar from his teeth. "You
wouldn't be able to get both Barlow and Vallejo.
You'd have that Mex coming after you like a
wildcat—"

"Maybe I could get them both. I could try.

Anyway, what would you be doing? You could handle the Mex—"

"Don't talk like a brainless fool, Vink," Norton repeated. "You should know I wouldn't have no part in anything like that." He added. "Not right in front of the Blue Gem."

Deever shot a narrow-eyed glance at his employer. "Where, then?" he asked eagerly.

"As sheriff," Norton said coldly, "I should put you under bond to keep the peace after listening to such talk as that. Now shut up. I want to see what those two aim to do—stay or leave town."

## CHAPTER VII

### "I'M NOT THROUGH WITH NORTON"

JOHNNY BARLOW held the lighted match to Vallejo's cigarette, touched it to his own, snapped the match between his fingers, and tossed it into the road. The two drew silently on the tobacco a few moments in the light from the T-Bone Restaurant before Johnny said, "Feel as though you got your strength back, Mike?"

"That suppair," the Mexican said with a smile, "just about put me back on my feet. Where do we go now, Johnee?"

Johnny shoved his sombrero to one side of his head and scratched meditatively at his thick red hair. "You know, I'd like to see Caldwell, the banker, and talk with him a mite—see what he thinks of Norton, get his opinion of where that money went. And I'm not through with Norton yet, either. Not by a long shot! He can wait until *mañana,* though. By that time he may be more amenable to reason, when he finds I have a right to be here, and that I don't aim to let him ride roughshod over me—like he's apparently been doing with everybody else in this town."

"You do not plan to leave, then?" Vallejo asked dryly.

"Mike, you know better than that. Who do you think you're joshing? You're damn right I'm not planning to leave. I sort of smell trouble here-abouts, and I'm mighty intrigued. Do you feel like sticking around for a while and help me smell?"

Vallejo wrinkled his nose and sniffed the air. "I'm theenk you are correc', Johnee. Ees eet a polecat makes that odair?"

Johnny nodded. "A polecat that steals money from honest men. I'd like to scare him into the open before he spoils this whole atmosphere, and hand him his quietus."

"*Bueno!* Good. I'm stay and help you hunt theese skonk."

"It might be dangerous, Mike," Johnny reminded.

Vallejo shrugged. "What the hell! A man can live only once. I'm stay."

"That's fine. I thought you would, but I wanted

82

to be sure. After all, this isn't really your responsibility—"

"Johnee! *Basta!* Stop! Must you talk so much, when already eet ees decide I stay?"

"Right! I'll shut up. . . . Let me see. I reckon it might be a good idea to ride out to the Lazy-Double-M and hear 'Rene Melville's side of the story. First, though, let's find the post office. That restaurant feller said the night stage wasn't due to leave for a spell yet. I'd like to send off a couple of letters. While I'm doing that, you can be looking up some oats for our ponies. Then we'll line out for the Lazy-Double-M."

The two fell into step and proceeded down the street. Opposite the Clinic Saloon, Vallejo crossed to attend the needs of the horses. Johnny continued on a few doors farther and found the post office. Here he wrote two short letters, purchased envelopes and stamps, and handed the letters to the postmaster, who was grumbling about the lateness of the stagecoach making him stay open after hours. At that moment the stage came sweeping in to the accompaniment of jangling harness, pounding hoofs, and clouds of dust, and Johnny escaped from the long-winded postmaster.

That business concluded, Johnny left the post office and headed diagonally across the street in search of Vallejo. The Mexican was just tightening the saddle cinches when Johnny arrived.

"All set, Mike."

"All is in readiness, Johnee,"

Though the moon wasn't yet up, it wasn't any job to locate the well-worn trail that led to the Lazy-Double-M Ranch. Johnny and Vallejo turned toward the north-west, once they were clear of Rawhide City, and followed the wagon-rutted way. The two riders conversed but little as they loped along at a ground-devouring speed that left miles rapidly to their rear. An hour passed. The trail swerved slightly to the west and pursued a course with the cottonwood-bordered Creaking River on the left. Here the riders paused long enough to rein their ponies into the shallow stream. When the horses' thirst was slaked, they turned back to the road and pushed on. By this time the moon was well above the eastern horizon.

It must have been close to nine-thirty when Johnny first caught sight of the Lazy-Double-M buildings—ranch house, bunkhouse, cookhouse-and-chuck building, stables and blacksmith shop, corrals and a windmill that clanked monotonously in the breeze lifting across the grasslands. The ranch buildings were constructed of adobe and timber combined; they looked substantial, comfortable, and rambling. There wasn't much movement from the horses in the corrals.

A light shone from the ranch house. Down in the bunkhouse a cowhand's voice could be heard crooning the words of "Little Joe, the Wrangler," to the accompaniment of a discordant banjo.

Johnny and Vallejo alighted near the back door of the ranch house. Johnny knocked. The door was answered by a Mexican woman. She barred the entrance to the house, one hand on the doorknob.

"Is Miss 'Rene in to visitors?" Johnny asked.

The Mexican woman peered at the two men and paused uncertainly. From the front of the house a throaty voice called, "Who is it, Jovita?"

Before the woman could answer, Johnny called back, "Two gentlemen callers for Miss 'Rene Melville, and is she in the mood to do some entertaining of said gents, or is she enjoying one of her ornery moods?"

Something like a gasp was heard from another room and there was the sound of quick steps. Jovita faded into the background and turned up the wick of the oil lamp suspended in a bracket against one wall. A tall slim girl in a brown dress trimmed with lace at throat and wrists appeared in the kitchen. She was dark-haired; her dark eyes had unusually long lashes, and her lips were very red, making a vivid contrast to the well-tanned, smooth skin of her face. Irene Melville wasn't exactly beautiful, but there was a wealth of character in her features and firm, determined chin. Johnny decided in that moment that she was "plumb ornamental", far more so than he had remembered her.

The girl didn't recognise Johnny at once. She stood hesitant, frowning at the two men. "What—who on earth—?" she commenced.

Johnny grinned. "Don't say you've forgotten me. You'll break my heart if you do, 'Rene. Maybe it was announcing myself as a gentleman that threw you off the trail. I'll admit I don't look it. 'Rene, do you still hold it against me for tearing your party dress on my spur that time? Seems like we had words—or you did—at a dance one time. That's all of ten years back, of course."

"Johnny! Johnny Barlow!" the girl exclaimed. "You come right on into the house. Say, we did have a fight once, didn't we?"

"At least once." Johnny chuckled. "You gave me Hail Columbia, if that's what you mean by fighting. I can't remember, though, that I was even able to get a word in edgewise."

'Rene Melville laughed. "At any rate, you were forgiven years ago, Johnny. I'd forgotten all about it."

Johnny suddenly remembered his companion. " 'Rene, this is my good *amigo,* Miguel Vallejo *y* Cordano. Mike really is a gentleman—one *bueno caballero*—and if you like him one half as well as I do, I'm going to be jealous as the devil."

"I can imagine *you* being jealous," the girl said sceptically. She released her hand from Johnny's grasp and extended it to Vallejo, then went on, "I've yet to see the girl who could make you jealous, Johnny. Whatever brings you to this part of the country? Not Dad's trouble?" She sobered suddenly. "Or is it?"

86

Johnny shook his head. "No, though I've heard about that. I've already written for permission to stay here and look into that business. It's mighty tough for your dad. It's only about two months back I had a letter from him, saying you were getting along fine. . . . No, it was just luck I stumbled into this. I've been enjoying a furlough. Ran across Mike down in Mexico. He was drifting north, so I drifted along with him. Figured I'd stop in for a short visit before I returned to duty. And here we are."

"I'm more than glad to see you. Both of you. Good grief! We don't have to stand here talking in the kitchen. Where are my manners? I'll call Jovita and we'll rustle some food *pronto.*"

"Thanks, don't bother," Johnny refused. "We had supper in Rawhide City."

"How about some Java?" 'Rene asked. "I've yet to see a cowman who didn't like coffee at any and all hours. You could handle a cup, couldn't you, Senor Vallejo?"

"Call him Mike," Johnny cut in.

"I'm theenk," Vallejo replied, his teeth shining whitely, "that Miss 'Rene could call me anything—jus' so long as she remembair to call me. A cup of coffee would be *muy bueno.*"

"All right." The girl laughed. "Mike it is, if you'll leave off the 'Miss.' I'm plain 'Rene to Johnny and his friends. Anyway, that's settled. You boys put up your ponies. While you're down at the corral, Johnny, stop in and see Tex Houston at the bunkhouse. You remember him, don't you?"

"I'll tell a man I do. Your dad's last letter said he'd promoted Tex to foreman. I'll be dang glad to shake that old coot's hand, again. . . . C'mon, Mike."

'Rene called after them as they stepped outside, "Don't stay long, Johnny. I've a million things to talk over with you. As I recollect it, you didn't have much time for girls the last time I saw you."

"Proving," Johnny spoke over one shoulder, "that I wasn't showing good sense. Me, I was still wet behind the ears, those days. Sure, we'll drift back in ten-fifteen minutes."

After the horses had been unsaddled and turned into the corral, Johnny and Miguel stepped through the open door of the bunkhouse. A cowhand was seated on the edge of one bunk, strumming a banjo. Two other punchers were engaged with a third, dour-faced individual in a game of seven-up. A lean, grizzled man with piercing eyes and sweeping white moustaches was frowning over a tally book at a rudely constructed pine desk. He glanced up quickly as Johnny and Vallejo entered. The banjo player ceased strumming.

The man at the desk frowned, then a broad smile crossed his rugged features. "May I be everlastingly hung for a sheep herder if the Rangers ain't dropped down on us!" he exclaimed, rising.

Johnny grinned. "Right you are, Tex. One

Ranger, leastwise." The two men gripped hands.

"Johnny Barlow! You unwhipped, young good-for-nawthin' *orejano!*" Tex Houston continued. "It's good to see your ugly mug again."

"Same to you, Tex, you uncurried maverick, you. Meet my friend, Mike Vallejo."

Houston had already crossed the bunkhouse floor in quick strides and was reaching for Vallejo's hand. "I'm sure glad to see you two hombres. I sort of thought a spell back I heard some noises down to the saddlers' corral, but Slim Pickens, over there, makes so much noise with his caterwaulin' and that banjo contraption that a man can't scarce hear himself think. Slim, get up on your hind hoofs and shake dew claws with these fellers."

Slim Pickens put down his banjo and shook hands. The three men at the card table were introduced. Two of the hands answered to the names of Murphy Swartz and Quinn Taylor. Swartz was round-faced with tow-coloured hair. Quinn Taylor was weatherbeaten, lean and tough as whip-cord, with amazingly frank eyes and a fighting jaw. The dour-faced cardplayer proved to be Soup-Kettle Simpson, cook of the outfit.

"You'll be staying the night," Tex Houston said. It was a statement, not a question.

"Got room for us?" Johnny asked.

"If these lazy good-for-nawthin' cow nurses can't make room," Houston replied, "I'll make 'em give up their bunks and sleep in Soup-Kettle's kitchen."

"Oh no, boss, no!" Swartz exclaimed in pretended horror. "Don't force us to stay in that dirty hole—"

Slim Pickens groaned. "The kitchen? That garbage can? Don't say that, Tex. I'm willin' to sleep on the floor, or under a hawss shelter, but not in that torture chamber of damaged chow—"

"To hell with you hombres," Soup-Kettle Simpson snorted indignantly. "You won't get to sleep in my kitchen. I cleaned out all cockroaches years back, and I don't aim to have another invasion. Barlow, I want you and your pard to know there ain't no cleaner kitchen to be found from here to the border—and north of here. Matter of fact, you and Vallejo would be far better off in my diggin's than tryin' to sleep through the snorin' that goes on here. Mornin's when I come in to rouse 'em out of their blankets, I ain't never sure whether I've stepped into a sawmill or a locomotive-whistle factory."

"Pay no attention to all this talk, Johnny," Quinn Taylor stated genially. "There's bunks and there's blankets. It's good to see a couple of new faces here."

"We'll be able to sleep you all right," Houston promised. He shoved straight-backed chairs in the direction of Johnny and Mike. "What brings you to this neck of the range, Matt's trouble?"

Johnny shook his head. "Didn't hear about that

90

until after we'd hit Rawhide City. Said trouble, however," he added meaningly, "is going to keep me here for a spell."

"I'm danged glad to hear that," Houston nodded.

Quinn Taylor said, "I reckon we all are. Matt's in a mighty difficult position, even if he has passed most of the danger from his wound."

"We'll talk it over later," Johnny said. "I told 'Rene we'd be back in a few minutes and hear her side of the story. Anything she can't set me straight on, I'll ask you hombres."

"We'll give you what we know," Houston said, suddenly moody, "but it ain't much, boy."

Murphy Swartz put in, "Johnny, we'd be glad to have you and your pard sit in on some cards with us. Mebbe we could fix up a little game of draw, and take Cookie's wad away from him. He can't play poker for sour apples."

"No honest man," Soup-Kettle growled, "has got any business playing with a pair of sharks like Murphy and Quinn. Them two would skin a blind man of his eyelashes, give 'em a chance. Don't you and Mike come into no game, Johnny. Take my warnin'. They're pow'ful wicked, them two."

Johnny looked wistful. "I've always wished I could find somebody to teach me to play poker" —this statement was greeted with sceptical snorts—"but I promised 'Rene I'd be back and so did Mike. Howsomever, we'll both be glad to take a lesson some other time."

91

There was some laughter at this. Johnny and Vallejo talked to the men a few minutes longer, then retraced their steps to the ranch house, where 'Rene led the way to the dining room. Steaming coffee was on the table. As the two men and the girl seated themselves, the Mexican woman brought in a dried-apple pie.

'Rene asked innocently, "Do you still like pie, Johnny?"

Johnny cast a quick wary glance at 'Rene, then eyed the pie with some scepticism. "Is this another of your jokes, 'Rene?" he asked cautiously. "I still remember you made a pie for me once before—on All-Fools' Day." He turned to Mike. "It was supposed to be an apple pie, but 'Rene had used cactus pads, cut up, for apples."

"The prickly-pear cactus," Mike said, "is veree good for the eating. You peel the pads and slice into strips, then cook and serve like you do the—how do you say eet?—the streeng bean? Many of my people in Mexico consider the prickly pear a veree good food, veree healthful—"

"But you don't understand," Johnny cut in. " 'Rene's cactus was supposed to be cooked like apples. The pads were cut up, all right, but they weren't peeled and the thorns were still intact. The crust of the pie was salt and flour—mostly salt. What I figured to be cinnamon on top turned out to be red pepper."

Vallejo laughed softly, his eyes dwelling appreciatively on the girl. "Was veree good joke—no?"

"No!" Johnny glowered at 'Rene. "I always promised myself I'd wring your neck for that little caper, girl. But you moved away before I could get around to doing it. But don't think I've forgotten. I'll square that score yet."

'Rene was wiping tears of laughter from her eyes. "Oh, Johnny, what a fool thing that was for me to do. Even eating a little bit of that pie might have resulted in something serious to you. I couldn't blame you if you had wrung my neck. But it *is* good to see you again, even with that threat hanging over me. I promise you this pie is all right. I just made it this afternoon, and I used real dough and apples."

"That being the case," Johnny replied, as Jovita cut the pie and placed it on plates, before leaving the room, "this latest experiment of yours shouldn't do any more than give me a case of acute indigestion." He drew the plate towards him, forked up a chunk and thrust it into his mouth. He chewed silently, smacked his lips and observed sourly, "This tastes pretty terrible. It hasn't been cooked long enough, and the crust is tough as an old boot sole." He immediately belied the words with a second attack on the pastry.

"I hope," 'Rene observed sweetly, "that it sticks in your gullet and chokes you."

"Probably it will," Johnny agreed. "I'm only eating this to show my good manners while I'm visiting. Likely I'll go down in posterity as a martyr to etiquette and bad cooking. . . . Mike, you don't have to be polite. You don't know this girl like I do—even though I haven't seen her in years. Stand up for your rights and lay down that fork. Don't eat the pie if you don't like it. There's not a bit of doubt it will give you ptomaine poisoning."

"Theese potato-mine poisoning I weel risk, Johnee, and gladly. Your plot does not work. You want I should quit eateeng so as to leave more of pie for you, I'm theenk. I am not so stupid, to believe in your talk. Or perhaps you are just crazee." He turned to the girl. "*Es verdad,* no?"

"That's the truth, Mike." 'Rene smiled. "Don't pay any attention to Johnny. Fighting is the only means he and I have ever had of getting along on friendly terms. Besides, I think his head is swelled because of the record he's made with the Border Rangers. It has probably affected what he calls his mind."

"You flatter me," Johnny said, grinning, "regarding what you say about my record with the Rangers—"

"But not about the mind, eh?" 'Rene laughed.

Johnny didn't reply at once. He gazed meditatively at the oil lamp suspended on one wall across the room. Then he sighed deeply. " 'Rene, I sometimes wonder if there isn't a mite of scorpion in you. Just about the time a feller tries to be nice and polite, you whip your stinger into him."

"Anybody knows you like I do," 'Rene protested, "knows better than to trust you when you go polite—unless you've changed." She turned to Vallejo to explain. "I used to sit just in front of him in school. He was always telling me I had pretty hair, and I didn't mind him handling my pigtails—until the day I discovered he was dipping them into his bottle of ink—"

"Aw-w-w," Johnny sputtered, his face reddening. "C'mon, let's cut out this bickering and cut me another piece of pie, 'Rene. I'll let bygones be bygones if you will. And I can use another cup of Java too."

Coffee and pie were finally finished. 'Rene picked Johnny's papers and sack of Durham from the table and rolled a cigarette for him, and another for Vallejo. Johnny laughed as they lighted the cigarettes. "Haven't forgotten how, I see," he said. "Y'know, 'Rene, I think it was when I first knew you could roll a cigarette like a man that I decided there might be some good in you after all. The more I think of it, the more I regret that you moved away when you did. You and me were just beginning to get really acquainted."

"That's probably why I moved away." 'Rene smiled.

"All right, I give in," Johnny said grouchily. "I doubt there ever was a man lived who could really win an argument from a woman. Maybe we'd better declare a truce right now."

"Anybody who asks for a truce admits he's licked," 'Rene stated.

"All right, I'm licked, then," Johnny said sadly. "Sometimes I think, where you're concerned, I've always been. That's why I'm asking for a cease-fire order from your forces."

Vallejo excused himself after a few minutes and headed for the bunkhouse. Jovita could be heard moving about in another room, softly humming to herself.

"Mike has an eye on that game down in the bunkhouse," Johnny explained after the Mexican's departure. "When we were down there, a couple of the boys were talking about dealing a few hands of draw. They claimed they were after Soup-Kettle's money."

"I'm not worried about Soup-Kettle," 'Rene said. "As I get it, he's been holding most of the high hands for the past few months. You're sure you don't want to leave and get into the game too?"

"What? When I can stay here and talk to you. You know I'd rather do that than—"

"No flattery now, Johnny. If we talk, it's got to be serious."

"That's one of the things I came out here to do," Johnny returned. "I was never more serious in my life."

# CHAPTER VIII

## A SHOT IN THE NIGHT!

JOVITA cleared away the dishes, and after extinguishing the light on the side wall disappeared in the direction of the kitchen. 'Rene pushed aside a second kerosene lamp on the table and asked, "Do you want to go in the main room, or shall we stay here?"

"I'm comfortable here. I want to hear what happened when Matt was shot. I'd like to get a line on certain people in Rawhide City. To be brief, I want to get your side of the story on what's happened and exactly how you feel about men who are connected with Matt. He was always inclined to be too trustful with folks, and I'm wondering if somebody he thought was a friend has double-crossed him."

'Rene rested her elbows on the scarred surface of the old oak table, her chin in her hands. She looked steadily at Johnny for a few moments, then said, a trifle wistfully, "More than once, Johnny, I've wished you were here. We're in a terrible mess. It could have been worse, of course, if Dad had been killed. Even so, things are plenty bad. Somehow, just the past few days I've been thinking about how you used to lick the boys who teased me at school." Here dark eyes glistened.

"Cripes," Johnny said awkwardly, "nobody's going to get away with teasing you now, either. Me, I'm just realising what a fool I've been for not coming to see you—you and Matt—long ago. Now you quit your fretting. I've talked to Doc Duncan and he tells me Matt is going to make it all right. As for all the rest, while there's life there's hope, and things will work out. Just meet each day's problems as they show up, and don't try to look too far ahead. Things will finish up just fine. You see."

'Rene blew her nose, smiling through tears that were very near the surface. "Darn it," she said, "I've been just ripe to sob my grief on somebody's shoulders, and then you had to show up. I don't need to tell you how glad I am."

"That goes double, 'Rene. And my shoulders aren't going to mind a mite of soaking. So go ahead and sob, if it will make you feel any better—though I don't think it will. Just keep your chin up, and tell the whole adverse world where it can go."

"You're right. And that shoulder is safe. I'm not going to do any weeping. . . . Yes, I guess Dad is beyond danger now. But it's going to break his heart to lose the outfit."

"What makes you think he'll lose it?"

"I can't see any hope for anything else now. You aren't acquainted with the circumstances, Johnny."

"I came here to get 'em. I know what happened, more or less, from the time of the holdup on, but what led up to it? Why was your dad borrowing that money?"

The girl explained: "You see, we've had two bad years. Drought. Cattle prices were low before that. This whole range has had a long run of bad luck. Two years back, Creaking River practically dried up. And the Dominion River too. All the outfits have been hit hard—especially Kirk Norton's Quarter-Circle-N. Norton is the only sizable rancher around here who has to depend on water holes. The Creaking River—most of it—runs on Lazy-Double-M holdings."

Gradually the story was pieced together. "It's always been a struggle for Dad to get the ranch paid for and make both ends meet. Then the drought came. The first year the drought hit us Dad had to borrow some money—ten thousand dollars. If things had gone right, we'd have been able to pay that off this year, though it would have practically taken every cent. But that was the way Dad had planned. His note for that money still has nine months to run—"

"Does the Rawhide City banker—Caldwell?— hold that note?"

"Not the original note. Caldwell wasn't in a position to lend that much money when Dad first needed the loan. Everybody else around here was borrowing from the bank too—and Banker Caldwell just had to call a halt somewhere if he wanted to remain solvent. But he did suggest that

Dad try a bank in Capitol City. Dad went up there and got the loan. Ten thousand dollars at ten per cent—"

Johnny's soft indignant whistle interrupted the words. "That's mighty steep interest these days. Matt must have fallen into the hands of a gang of loan sharks."

'Rene smiled slightly. "They claimed to be just hard-headed businessmen. Ten per cent. is steep, all right. But what could Dad do? When you have to have money, you pay the price, and that's all there is to it. Dad had his choice of paying that price, or losing the outfit. What would you do in his shoes?"

"I reckon I'd pay the price," Johnny conceded. "But I'd feel I'd fallen among thieves."

"Undoubtedly. But remember, money was scarce—to borrowers. Dad took the money. Then, a little over a month ago, Frank Caldwell's bank was in a position to lend. Conditions had improved slightly and Mr. Caldwell wanted to help Dad out. They've always been close friends. Mr. Caldwell suggested that he lend Dad the ten thousand to pay off the Capitol City bank loan—"

"I'm hanged if I get that idea," Johnny frowned.

"It's simply this. Mr. Caldwell let Dad have the money at six per cent. interest—"

"Ah, a saving of four per cent." Johnny's face cleared.

"Right. And while four per cent. doesn't seem much at first glance, it adds up like the deuce, and every cent. counted with us. Dad figured it was well worth while. Besides, he preferred to let the Caldwell Bank have the profit on the loan. And so matters were arranged. Dad went to the bank, signed the note, and started out of Mr. Caldwell's office. At that moment the Falcon appeared, shot him, and seized the satchel of money—"

"And now the money has disappeared," Johnny said.

"Now the money has just vanished," 'Rene said hopelessly, "and we owe twenty thousand dollars, instead of ten. You see, Dad had planned to catch the stage for Capitol City, after he got the money, and pay off the first note."

Johnny scowled. "I'm danged if I can understand why your dad took cash money. Why didn't he get a cheque from Caldwell?"

'Rene shook her head. "You know Dad. Once he gets an idea in his head, it's hard to shake him loose from it. He's a hard-money man—has been for a good many years now—ever since he got a cheque from some man who went bankrupt before the cheque could be honoured. Dad always said, from then on, he just didn't have any faith in paper, and he refused to accept it. He always figured he was strong enough to take care of any money in his possession. Well, as things have turned out, I guess he wasn't. But that can't be helped now."

Johnny pondered the subject. "If the money isn't paid to the Capitol City bank, I suppose that outfit will take possession of the Lazy-Double-M. Is that the idea? And then Caldwell's bank puts in a second claim?"

'Rene shook her head. "The Rawhide City bank has the sole claim now. Mr. Caldwell has been awfully kind. He insisted on loaning us a second ten thousand dollars. I signed the papers. Mr. Caldwell said that wasn't quite legal, but under the circumstances the bank would take a chance. And of course Dad would back up anything I signed for. Mr. Caldwell went up to Capitol City himself and paid off the bank there, then gave me back Dad's cancelled note. Do you want to see it?"

Johnny shook his head. "You say you have the cancelled note. That's good enough for me. As it stands now, then, the Lazy-Double-M owes Caldwell's bank twenty thousand dollars, at six per cent. interest. When does that come due?"

"On the same date the Capitol City bank was due to be paid off—a trifle less than nine months now. But Mr. Caldwell says for us not to worry about it. He says he'll renew when payment comes due, and all we have to do is keep up the interest payments. He means well, but it isn't as though it was his own money. It's the bank's money he loaned, and it must be paid on time. The bank has its stock-holders to answer to. Golly, Johnny, we could probably have paid off ten thousand dollars, but I'm darned if I know where we'll ever get twenty thousand. All this sure does put us in a hole."

Johnny grinned encouragingly. "Mebbe not, 'Rene. Perhaps we'll locate that missing satchel of money. You know, it's just didn't turn into chunks of rock of its own account. There's some buzzard back of that slippery little move, and I aim to uncover him, if possible."

He reached for his "makin's", but 'Rene had anticipated his need and was rolling a cigarette for him. He absentmindedly touched flame to the cylinder of tobacco, and inhaled deeply. For several moments he pondered the situation, smoking in silence, then, "You mentioned something about drought having hit this range hard. Who exactly was hit? Give me a line on the biggest outfits, hereabouts."

"Well, so far as water for the stock is concerned, the Lazy-Double-M has the Creaking River to draw on. Directly east of us lies Norton's Quarter-Circle-N. Next to Norton's outfit comes Guy Gerard's Rafter-G. Southeast of Gerard lies the HB-Connected, owned by Homer Boggs, and south of Bogg's holdings is Jim Cross's Circle-Cross outfit. You see, the five outfits are spread fanwise from northwest of Rawhide City to directly east of the town."

"Yeah." Johnny scowled thoughtfully. "Now where do all these spreads water their herds?"

"As I said, we have the Creaking River to draw on. Norton has several rather undependable water holes. The other three ranches are strung along the

Dominion River. That takes care of them, unless a drought and unusually hot weather comes in summer."

Johnny nodded. "With Norton having to count on water holes, I'd say that leaves him most susceptible to a droughty season. To be brief, he needs water the worst of the five spreads."

"That's correct." 'Rene nodded. "Of course, this spring Creaking River was bankfull, as was the Dominion. Norton approached Dad then, asking to buy water from us. That is, he tried to get permission to water his cows at the Creaking, so as to conserve his water holes. Dad refused. If the summer did turn hot and dry, we might not have enough water for our own cows."

"What did Norton say? Was he sore?"

"I imagine he was, but he didn't let on. He's never very friendly with anyone, of course, but he did say he didn't blame Dad a particle. If the weather does turn dry, however, we may have to sell water to him now. Lordy, we could use the money. . . . But why are you asking all this, Johnny? Surely you're not suspecting Norton of having a hand in our trouble."

"Me," Johnny said grimly, "I'm suspecting nigh everybody until he's proved innocent. Norton needs more water. Should Matt lose the Lazy-Double-M to Caldwell's bank, there's nothing to prevent Norton from buying your outfit and getting the water he needs. No, I don't insist that's what would happen. But it's a probability we can't afford to overlook. I'm just trying to pin the stealing of that money on somebody, and I have to start someplace with my suspicions."

'Rene shook her head. "Suspicion doesn't give you any proof against Kirk Norton. After all, it was Kirk who shot the Falcon and got that satchel, even if the money did disappear. Kirk did his best. Just because he wants our water is nothing against him. Guy Gerard, of the Rafter-G offered to buy us out once too. Does that make you suspect him?"

Johnny said, "I've told you I'm suspecting everybody. What do you know about Frank Caldwell?"

"He's been might friendly to us. Dad likes him a lot. Since this trouble hit us, Mr. Caldwell has continually gone out of his way to help in any way he could."

"Except to cancel your loan," Johnny said.

"Don't be cynical, Johnny. You couldn't expect even a friend to do that."

"Some friends might. Forget I mentioned it. How about this Summerton hombre, the cashier?"

"Jay Summerton? I can't say I know much about him. We have a speaking acquaintance, that's about all. He came out West for his health. Mr. Caldwell says he lives a very quiet life—he doesn't smoke or drink."

"I'm suspicious of saints too," Johnny grunted. "If his health is bad, he could probably use a nice chunk of money so he wouldn't have to work. Do you know his health is bad?"

"Not for a fact—no, but his appearance tells me he is. He's rather frail and there's very little colour in his face."

"I've seen ex-convicts with a prison pallor too," Johnny observed.

"Johnny, I told you once not to be cynical."

"In my business, lady, it pays to be cynical. I reckon I'll have to have a talk with Jay Summerton. . . . Say, where does Vink Deever fit in around here? What does he do?"

"He works for Kirk Norton. Acts as a sort of all-around man for Norton. He's the foreman of the Quarter-Circle-N, for one thing, though he's in town as much as he's at the ranch, I've heard. He rides errands for the sheriff. I think Kirk keeps him at the Blue Gem much of the time to sort of guard the cash."

"I can't say much for Norton's choice."

"More of your cynicism, Johnny? Do you know anything about Deever?"

"Nothing that reflects any credit on him. I was forced to arrest him one time. He stood trial and went to the penitentiary for rustling. You don't need to repeat that. Maybe Deever's going straight these days, I won't interfere with him if he is."

'Rene frowned. "I wonder if Kirk Norton knows about that. I don't think the sheriff would hire a man with that sort of reputation."

106

Jovita passed through the dining room on her way to bed, said good night, and vanished through an open doorway.

Johnny said somewhat irritably, "You sure seem sold on Norton's integrity, 'Rene. If he does know about Deever, I can't say I'd put much faith in him. Deever may be going straight, but what I saw of him didn't convince me."

"I think Kirk Norton is straight," 'Rene said. "He's a mighty cold-acting individual, but everyone says he's just. He's made a good sheriff for Creaking River County. There's been very little crime while Kirk Norton has held office. Besides"—and she flushed—"I can't actually dislike a man who has proposed to me."

"Huh? What!" Johnny's jaw dropped and his eyes widened. Then he slowly shook his head, saying dryly, "Jeepers! Some men will do anything to get water for their herds. The drought must have been really bad in these parts—"

"Johnny!" 'Rene's face flamed. "I don't think you're very flattering."

Johnny chuckled. "I just couldn't resist that one, 'Rene. But, look, did Norton actually ask you to marry him?"

"I don't like the way you say that. Why shouldn't he?"

"'Rene, that Norton hombre has got his nerve. He should know that he's reaching for the stars—and him with his feet stuck in the mud—"

"Now you are flattering me."

"I'm speaking only truth. That Norton hombre is just too damn aspiring to suit me—" He broke off. "What did you tell him."

"We-ell," 'Rene said primly, "you must admit he did things the old-fashioned honourable way. He asked Dad, first, if he had any objections. Dad said it was strictly up to me. I said 'no', of course."

"Sensible girl." Johnny looked more easy in his mind. "Well, probably that accounts for Norton ordering me out of Rawhide City."

"Johnny! He didn't!"

"I'm throwing a straight loop. Mike and I had started into his Blue Gem place. . . ." From that point, Johnny went on with the story of what had happened.

When he had concluded, 'Rene's eyes were wide. "Johnny, I don't like it. . . . But—but what does that have to do with me? I can't see what my saying 'no' has to do with Kirk Norton ordering you out of town—and threatening you besides."

"It's all plain as the nose on your face—and a right pretty nose it is, too, 'Rene," Johnny said offhandedly. "When you refused him, you likely added that your refusal was due to the fact that you were intending to marry the handsomest man in the Border Rangers. I imagine he recognised me immediately, and started to ride roughshod over me—"

"Johnny Barlow," the girl said severely, rising to her feet, "you certainly don't lack conceit. I think it's time you left. Besides, as you told it, Kirk Norton didn't even know you were a Border Ranger. So you're just handing me a line of palaver. Go on, you'd better head for the bunkhouse. It's getting late and I've got to get to bed. I can't afford to miss my beauty sleep, you know."

Johnny grinned his open admiration as he rose and reached for his stetson. "Beauty sleep? Gosh, 'Rene, I didn't figure you ever needed that."

"Thanks, mister. I see your tongue is just as smooth as ever."

Johnny shook his head. "You're wrong. I'm all out of practice. It's years since I've had a chance to talk to a good-looking girl—"

"Get going, Johnny. You know I don't believe that. And I don't intend to have you practise on me."

Johnny turned serious momentarily. "All right, I'm leaving. But don't forget what I told you: keep a stiff upper lip and don't fret. This business is going to come out all right."

The girl accompanied him through the kitchen to the rear door. The two stood a moment on the back porch. Johnny glanced at the sky. Apropos of nothing in particular, he commented, "It's commencing to cloud up a mite."

"Those are not rain clouds, that's sure," 'Rene answered.

"They're just passing over."

"That's a darn nice moon, though," Johnny said innocently.

"I've heard that once before, too," 'Rene said promptly. "Now, get along with you. You're neglecting your friend Mike."

Johnny turned suddenly, looking directly into 'Rene's dark eyes. "Are you still my girl, 'Rene? You used to say—"

"Johnny Barlow! After all this time? Certainly not. That was all foolish boy-and-girl stuff."

"Boy-and-girl stuff, sure. And foolish about each other, eh? But answer me. Are you?"

"I've already answered you. Certainly not." Her words just reached him.

Johnny laughed softly. "You're rather a lovable little liar," he said tenderly. He reached for the girl's hand, but she eluded him, slipping quickly to one side and stepping back to the kitchen. An instant later she had slammed the door.

He heard the key turn in the lock, then her voice through the wood, "If I'm a liar, I scarcely know how to answer." She laughed. "Good night."

*"Adiôs,"* Johnny replied. "I'll see you *mañana.*"

He stepped down from the porch and started towards the lights gleaming from the bunkhouse. He was nearly halfway there when something struck him a tremendous blow in the middle. At the same instant there came the sharp crack of a Winchester rifle.

Johnny caught 'Rene's scream from within the house, even as he spun half round and crashed down to the earth.

# CHAPTER IX

## TWO CLUES

JOHNNY was still down when the men came sprinting from the bunkhouse. The rear door of the ranch house banged open as 'Rene came running out. Some distance off sounded the fast-diminishing drumming of horse's hoofs.

"What's wrong up there?" Tex Houston yelled as he plunged from the bunkhouse, followed by the other hands.

Johnny was braced on hands and knees now, struggling to regain his feet. 'Rene reached his side first and started to help him up, then changed her mind. "No, Johnny, you'd better lie quiet until we see how hard you're hit."

Johnny shook his head but could only make painful gasping sounds as he insisted on rising. Vallejo was at his side by this time too, and was lifting him by one shoulder. The others gathered around, anxious-faced in the moonlight. Again Johnny tried to speak, but words wouldn't come. He raised one hand in a meaning gesture toward the swiftly departing hoofbeats. He staggered a bit uncertainly on his feet and groped for his six-shooter. Both Vallejo and 'Rene were urging him to take it easy.

Tex Houston shouted swift orders. Slim Pickens

and Quinn Taylor departed at a run for the corral. 'Rene dashed into the house and returned with a glass of water, which she held to Johnny's lips. Soup-Kettle Simpson produced a small flask of whisky. Meanwhile, Vallejo's swift hands and eyes were surveying Johnny's body for the wound. Suddenly he straightened up. Johnny's fingers were fumbling at his belt.

Then surprisingly, something like a feeble laugh left Johnny's lips. It was a gaspy sort of laugh, but it was, nevertheless, a laugh. He struggled for breath to speak.

*"Poder de Dios!"* Vallejo exclaimed. "Strength of God, Johnny! It is the buckle that is shot from your belt!"

Johnny finally found his voice. "Yeah . . . bullet struck the . . . belt buckle. . . . Knocked the wind . . . out of me. . . . That's all. Nothing to . . . worry 'bout."

'Rene gave a low relieved cry. Johnny brushed off the sustaining hands. There came a swift pounding of hoofs as Slim Pickens and Quinn Taylor swept past on their ponies and headed toward the roadway.

"Johnny's all right," Tex Houston yelled after them. "But catch that bush-whackin' skunk if you can."

If the two riders replied, their voices were lost in the rush of wind that drove past them. Sounds of the would-be assassin's pony had long since receded in the distance.

"Those boys will be just wasting their time, I'm afraid," Johnny said, his voice more certain now. "That skunk had too much start to be caught now. I'd better get my pony and go after them—"

"Let 'em ride," Houston said. "They might have some luck. If that coyote's hawss should stumble and break a laig, they'd sure get him—" He broke off. "You feeling all right now, Johnny?"

"Right as can be," Johnny said, "though my pants feel sort of loose. I'm glad that slug didn't hit my cartridge belt. I wouldn't want that ruined. A pants belt don't amount to much—except in this instance. It sure saved me from being hit, though I certain lacked wind for a spell."

"Eet was a close escape, Johnee," Vallejo commented.

"Too dang close to be comfortable," Johnny agreed. "I reckon that slug just sort of caromed off the belt buckle, but took the buckle along with it. Tore it plumb loose from the leather. It sure walloped when it struck. I felt as though a mule had cut loose with both hind hoofs at my middle."

'Rene, who had gone into the house, returned carrying a belt. "Here's a belt of Dad's, Johnny. I think it will fit you." Johnny thanked her and commenced threading the belt through his belt loops. The girl's voice had been calm, but in the moonlight Johnny could see the considerable concern in her dark eyes. "You haven't any idea who it was, have you, Johnny?"

"Sure I have," Johnny laughed. "Some buzzard who figured I'd been cheatin' the undertaker long enough. Or maybe the president of some coffin factory—"

"Johnny Barlow! I do believe you'll make jokes on your death-bed."

"I hope I'm able to."

'Rene shook her head. "You're hopeless. You haven't sense enough to know when you're in danger. Well, I must go in and pacify Jovita. That shot scared her senseless. I'm beginning to think the same thing happened to you. . . . Good night."

Johnny and the others said good night. Soup-Kettle announced that he was going to turn in to his blankets. At Johnny's request, Tex Houston sent Murphy Swartz for a lantern.

"How'd your game go?" Johnny asked Vallejo.

"The cards brought only the *malo* luck to me," Vallejo admitted. "Howevair, for Soup-Kettle eet was good luck. I am out the sum of nearly ten *pesos*."

"That cookie," Houston said, "plays a shrewd game."

Within a few mintues Swartz returned with the lighted lantern. He, Johnny, Houston and Vallejo proceeded to scan the earth in the hope of finding "sign". Johnny's badly battered belt buckle was found on the ground several yards off. Johnny glanced at it, laughed softly, and tossed it away.

"I don't reckon there's any use looking for the

slug that spoiled that buckle," Tex growled. "I'd sort of like to see what calibre it is though."

"It'd be like looking for a needle in a haystack," Johnny pointed out. "No use to bother with it." He gazed about the landscape, then pointed towards the south-east. "As near as I can locate it, that rifle shot was fired from over there, near the road."

Tex Houston took up the lantern. "We'll go give a look-see for prints."

"Wait a minute," Johnny suggested. "It might be a good idea to look close to the house first. That shot wasn't intended for just anybody—it was definitely meant for me. Whoever fired it would want to make sure I was here, so he could throw down on me when I left. It was light enough to make out my form, when I started down towards the bunkhouse, but the moon wasn't throwing enough light to show up my features from a distance."

They carried the lantern to one side of the house. Beneath the window of the room in which Johnny and 'Rene had been seated, they found dim traces of a footprint, though the earth was baked too hard to leave much of an impression.

"Hmmm," Johnny grunted as he bent closer to inspect the faintly outlined depression in the earth. "Someone stood here, all right, and looked in on 'Rene and me."

"Big foot or little foot?" Tex asked.

Johnny shook his head. "Right hard to determine, Tex. Too faint and not enough of it. Just a sort of toelike impression, where that hombre may have raised up to peek in the window. The other foot doesn't show, and this mark is too scant for me to even make sure it's a cowman's boot."

He raised up and mentally reconstructed the scene, then relayed his thoughts to the others. "That bustard, whoever he is, came out here, tied his horse near the road someplace, then sneaked on foot to the house—"

"Maybe we can find some other footprints," Swartz interrupted.

"Maybe we can. We'll look later, though I haven't much hope of locating 'em on this earth. It's like rock . . . When the feller got to the house, he peeked in the window, made sure I was here, then sloped back to the road to wait until I left. The front of the house is parallel with the road, so he'd have to move down a short distance to shoot from an angle that would reach the rear of the house."

"Smart thinkin', Johnny." Houston nodded. "Let's look some more."

They scanned the earth in wide arcs about one side of the house, but found no further footprints. Then the four men walked out to the road and followed a short distance along the wagon-rutted and hoof-chopped way, until they'd reached a clump of chaparral. Here they quickly found evidence that a horse had been tethered among the trees and brush. The men spread out to the extent allowed by the lantern's rays and scrutinised the earth.

Murphy Swartz finally grunted with disgust. "Too chopped up around here to read much sign," he growled. "I was sort of in hopes we might find an empty ca'tridge shell."

"I doubt that hombre took time to eject his shell," Johnny guessed. "He was in too much of a rush to make his getaway. Likely when he saw me drop, he figured I was done for—" He broke off abruptly, reaching down one hand and retrieved from among the blades of tangled grass a shining bit of metal. There was a quick intake of breath before he said, "Now here's something important, men."

"I, also, have found sometheeng," Vallejo announced at almost the same instant.

The four men gathered in the rays of the lantern. Johnny's find proved to be a tarnished silver badge in the form of a five-pointed star. Across the face of the badge was the single word: Sheriff.

"Geez!" Murphy Swartz exclaimed. "Kirk Norton!"

"The so veree just an' upright Sheriff Norton," Vallejo said ironically.

"I'll bet the pin wore through the cloth of his vest and fell off," Tex speculated. "I'll be damned. It was just his bad luck it dropped here."

Johnny laughed softly. "Well, I guess we'll just have to talk to Mr. Norton about being so careless with his badge. Anyway, we've found one clue to—well, to something. Mike what did you find?"

Vallejo produced a partly consumed plug of chewing tobacco. There was no tin tag on it to denote the brand. Johnny examined it carefully by the light of the lantern. "Some folks are sure careless dropping their belongings," he mused softly. Then to the others: "Does Kirk Norton use eating tobacco?"

Murphy Swartz and Houston nodded simultaneously. "I've seen him take a chaw often," Tex added.

"What kind of teeth has he got?" Johnny asked next.

Houston frowned. "What kind of teeth? Why, I reckon the same as all other humans."

"I mean," Johnny explained, "are they good teeth or bad? Loose or solid? Are they worn down to snags? Or maybe he has a set of China clippers. Do you happen to know?"

Houston's frown deepened. "Hell! I don't know. Ain't never took any notice. They must be all right though, or I think I would have noticed 'em. Mebbe if he'd smile once in a while I'd know for sure, but between them tight lips of his'n and his yellow moustaches, I don't remember that I ever saw his teeth even. Off-hand I'd say they was all right though. He looks a pretty solid specimen."

"Maybe this isn't his plug, then," Johnny said. "Whoever lost this chunk of tobacco has bad teeth, I think."

"Is that so?" Houston said. He looked blank.

Johnny explained: "Mostly hombres who chew tobacco bite off their chew, providing their teeth are solid. This plug has been sliced with a knife."

"By cripes, it has!" Houston exclaimed. "Now all you have to do is find a hombre with bad teeth."

"That'll be simple." Johnny laughed dryly. "All I have to do is examine half the teeth in Rawhide City—maybe more—of young men and old men. Still, it won't hurt to keep my eyes open."

"I'd like to know," Swartz growled, "how you ever expect to get a look at Norton's teeth. Even when he talks he sort of clips his words fast."

"I'll just ask him to open up, like I would a horse," Johnny said with a grin, "and tell him I want to know his age."

"That'll be a hawss on the sheriff, if you can work it," Tex chuckled.

Johnny changed the subject slightly, "Well, anyway, let's not say anything to folks about what we've found—not for a spell. Of course, it's all right to let Slim and Quinn know, when they come back, but I don't want the information spread promiscuous."

They looked over the ground for a few minutes more, but failed to locate any further evidence. Within a short time they returned to the bunkhouse. Soup-Kettle was just leaving for his own quarters in the combination chuck house and kitchen.

"Cripes, Cookie," Houston commented, "I thought you'd be in the hay by this time."

"I come back to pick up my poker winnin's," Simpson grunted. "Then I thought I'd wait around a spell to see if you hombres uncovered anything."

They told him what they had found, cautioning him to silence.

"Sheriff Norton, huh?" the cook exploded. "Well, may I be everlastin'ly damned for a hawss thief. And I've always figured him as on the square, even if he wa'n't congenial." Simpson considered a moment. "You say that shot come from a rifle, Johnny?"

Johnny nodded. "Near as I can tell from the sound—and from that distance—"

"Kirk Norton is a bearcat with a rifle," the cook cut in. "I ain't forgot how he downed the Falcon, though I wa'n't in town that day to witness the shootin'. From all I hear tell, though, it was one whale of a good shot."

"By the way," Johnny asked, "it was Norton who identified the bandit as the Falcon, wasn't it?"

Tex Houston nodded. "That's it. Though there's some around town what think the holdup man looked a heap like a hombre who was known as Mex Louie around Rawhide City, a few years back."

"I've heard something to that effect," Johnny said. "How come Norton was so certain in his identifying?"

"The sheriff said he'd seen the Falcon's picture on a reward bill—one that carried the description and all. Kirk claimed he'd heard the Falcon was working over this way, and consequent was on the look out for the bustard."

"What an alert law officer," Johnny commented with a touch of sarcasm.

The talk drifted to the disappearance of the money. Johnny had Tex and the others tell him what they knew of the affair, what they'd heard, but, so far as Johnny could determine nothing of import came to light. It all tallied with the story the barkeep of the Clinic Saloon had related.

"What sort of crew does Norton hire on his outfit?" Johnny asked next.

"Just the ordinary run-of-the-mill cowhands," Houston replied. "With the exception of Vink Deever, they seem like pretty good hombres. I never did cater to Deever, but I've got to admit I know nothing against him. For that matter, I don't know of any cowhand in these parts that doesn't shape up pretty well. I've scanned a long list of names in my memory, and I can't find suspicion pointin' to any single one of 'em."

"And so," Johnny said, smiling thinly, "we've got just two facts we're sure of. One, the money has disappeared; two, Border Rangers aren't welcome hereabouts. That proves somebody hereabouts is guilty—but who is he?"

The conversation swerved to other subjects. Soup-Kettle went off and returned after a time with beef sandwiches and a pot of coffee. Around two-thirty in the morning, Quinn Taylor and Slim Pickens returned on tired ponies. Johnny and the rest went to the corral to meet them.

"What luck?" Johnny asked.

Quinn swore, adding, "Not any."

"I was afraid you wouldn't catch the bustard. He had too great a start on you, and his horse was travelling fast."

Slim said, "We went clear to Rawhide City. That cuss that shot at you—Hey! Johnny! You're all right. What happened, anyway? We figured you wa'n't hurt bad by what Tex yelled at us, but we didn't get it all as we were leavin'—"

"The rifle slug scored a clean hit on my belt buckle," Johnny informed them. "Knocked the air right out of my innards." He added further details.

Quinn Taylor said, "Gawd, you were lucky."

"Ranger luck, cowboy." Johnny grinned.

The two punchers scowled when Johnny told of finding the sheriff's badge and plug of tobacco. Neither could remember what sort of teeth Norton had. Johnny asked, "What happened in Rawhide City, if anything?"

"Not a thing," Taylor replied. "Of course that skunk could have turned off the road someplace and hid along the way, but I've got a hunch he kept straight on into town. Jehovah only knows where he went then; I don't. He could have slipped into a number of different buildings."

"We gave the hitch racks a good looking over,"

Slim put in, "but we couldn't find nary a hawss that looked like it had been run hard recent. Looked in the livery stable too, but the proprietor said nobody'd come in for the past three hours. We didn't state why we was looking."

"Everything was pretty well closed up." Quinn Taylor took up the story. "One restaurant and the Blue Gem Saloon were the only places left open. The restaurant's an all-night joint, and the Blue Gem was about to shut its doors."

Johnny asked, "Did you see Norton in the Blue Gem?"

Quinn shook his head. "Nope, the barkeep said he'd left some time before to go to bed. Exactly how long before, the barkeep couldn't remember—or wouldn't state, I don't know which. He was just plumb vague about the time, and accordin' to him it could have been anywhere from one to three hours. I was all for going to Norton's place and rousing him out, but Slim figured that mebbe wouldn't suit your plans. Cripes! I wish now we had gone to his place. We might have learned something."

Johnny shrugged muscular shoulders and ran his fingers through his thatch of unruly red hair. "Damned if I know. It might have been a good idea; maybe it wouldn't have. Howsomever, what we know and the sheriff doesn't know won't hurt us a bit. What say we turn in? It's been a long day. I'm obliged to you two for making that ride."

Quinn and Pickens told him not to mention it.

Ten minutes later the lights in the bunkhouse had been extinguished and the men were snoring in their blankets. Only Johnny remained awake, staring up into darkness, his active mind milling with speculation. Could Norton have been mistaken in identifying the Falcon? It could have been possible. If he wasn't mistaken, the sheriff could have lied. There was something queer at that angle that would have to be cleared up. Exactly how honest was Banker Caldwell? Oh, there were problems to be settled. Regarding the disappearance of the money, suspicion, in Johnny's mind, turned toward the sheriff, though that was largely a hunch and something Johnny couldn't explain. If Norton had secured the ten thousand dollars, who had helped him in the plot? The sheriff hadn't boldly exchanged the satchels in the street in full view of everybody.

"Well," Johnny mused, "something should break right soon, then I'll learn where Norton stands. . . . And damn his gizzard for wanting to marry 'Rene. Now I have got a real grievance against that hombre. I don't mind being shot at, but when it comes to 'Rene . . ."

A slow smile creased his features as he drifted off to sleep.

# CHAPTER X

## "I'M STAYING!"

IT was still early, the following morning after breakfast, when Johnny and Mike Vallejo saddled up and turned their ponies towards the road that led to Rawhide City. 'Rene was standing in the front door of the ranch house as they rode past. Johnny and the Mexican pulled rein for a few moments and doffed their sombreros.

"I see the gay *caballeros* ride off in the dawn light, on the road to adventure," 'Rene said, laughing.

"As usual, you're wrong," Johnny answered with assumed disgust. "The said dawn light has been gone for some hours now, and that gay *caballeros* and adventure *habla* don't fit into anything as I see it these days. 'Rene, you sound like you'd been reading some of these romantic novels of the golden West. That's the only place I ever hear of poor hardworkin' cowfolks being called gay. Alkali-covered or sweat-streaked, maybe, but no man ever looked gay under those conditions."

"I don't see any sweat or alkali on you, Johnny. And you're no longer cowfolks. Just a plain loafer, as I see it. I should think you'd be ashamed to take the salary the Border Rangers Association pays you."

"I am." Johnny grinned. "Someday I expect

they'll catch up to me and throw me out of the force. I can hear 'em squawking right now when I put a new belt on my expense account."

"That weel look fine—no?" Vallejo grinned. "Expenses—one belt buckle. No cartridges."

'Rene's smile widened. "How is your terrible wound this morning, Johnny?"

"Oh, the poor old belt is doing as well as can be expected. When I consider back, I think it was almost on its last legs last night—or should I say waist? Anyway, I'll have to depend on Matt's belt for a spell. When we get to town I'll drop around to Doc Duncan's and inquire about him."

'Rene sobered. "I'll be in later. I'd like to stay there all the time, but Doc says there's not a thing I can do. Meanwhile, I've been going over Dad's accounts to see what we can save from the wreck when the final blow strikes—"

"I've got a hunch it might not strike," Johnny said. "Remember what I said about keeping a stiff upper lip?"

"I'll remember." 'Rene nodded. "Did you men find any sign last night, after I went in?"

"Plenty," Johnny replied. "I'll tell you about it later—probably to-night."

'Rene wrinkled her nose. "That sounds like a hint for an invitation to call."

"It wasn't," Johnny answered promptly. "It was a demand. . . . Maybe I'll see you in town this afternoon."

126

"Not if I see you first." The girl laughed.

"That," Johnny observed seriously, "was extremely unkind. Well, if your womanly curiosity won't give you any rest, ask Tex Houston what we found last night. I'm betting your eyes will pop out—and, by the way, said eyes are looking a heap brighter this morning."

"My eyes?" 'Rene looked puzzled. "Why should they?"

"That's simple. They've been resting on me," he replied complacently.

"Who's simple now?" the girl scoffed. "Johnny Barlow, you're a conceited wretch."

"That's your fault. Always boasting about me the way you do."

"I do no such thing. You'd better start riding. I can't waste more time listening to such empty talk. Take him on his way, Mike. He's light in the head. It's my guess he's been smoking marijuana."

Vallejo showed his white teeth in a wide smile. "Ah, *senorita,* with you to look at, the marijuana ees not necessary."

"Very nicely put, Señor Mike. And flattering! I think both of you had better hurry on your way. You're turning a pore innercent gal's head."

"You're a-whoopin'. I'll be taking him on his way." Johnny grinned. "I can't compete against that sort of *habla.*"

The two men rode off laughing. 'Rene gazed after them until they were far down the road, then turned back and re-entered the house.

Occasionally, as they rode toward town, Johnny and Vallejo sighted small bunches of white-faced cows branded on the left flank with the Lazy-Double-M iron. Halfway to town they paused beneath the cottonwoods and let their ponies drink at the shallow-flowing Creaking River. They took a few moments for rest and the rolling of brown-paper cigarettes, then the horses were reined back to the hoof-worn trail and the riders loped on.

It was around nine o'clock when they first sighted the buildings of Rawhide City. Johnny pulled to a slower pace and Vallejo followed suit. Johnny announced, "I've been thinking."

The Mexican smiled. "Don't strain what you call the ol' bean, Johnee."

"I reckon there isn't much to strain," Johnny said disgustedly. "I've been thinking and thinking, but I can't seem to get any of my thoughts to dovetail. Now I think it is pretty clear in your mind and mine that Sheriff Norton didn't kill the Falcon. The question is, does Norton know it, or has he just made a mistake somewhere along the line? By tomorrow I figure we should have a chance to settle that question—though it might take longer. Meanwhile, it seems like we're just wasting our time."

"Always Johnee, you are in the hurry. But you are correc'. How can I help?"

"That hombre, Mex Louie—who some folks

seem to think was killed instead of the Falcon—interests me a heap," Johnny went on thoughtfully. "Mike, I wish you'd sort of circulate around the Mexican Quarter in town and see if you can learn anything about him. You know how it is. The Mexican folks will likely talk to you, where they might not feel like taking me into their confidence for fear I might tie 'em up to trouble somehow. Find out if anybody in town knew Mex Louie well enough to state whether or not he has been in town within the past few months."

"I weel do eet, Johnee." Vallejo nodded his approbation of the idea. "And you—what do you plan to do?"

"I figure to talk to Kirk Norton just as soon as possible. You'd better stay with me until I've seen Norton, otherwise he might catch us apart, see you first, and start some of his roughshod methods with you. I'm not sure exactly where we'll find him; maybe in his office, maybe at the Blue Gem, or he may just be around town someplace. We want to be straightened out with him after that warning he gave us to leave town. I'm afraid he's the type hombre who might shoot first and then make explanations later. After I've talked to him I plan to just sort of loaf around town and see if I can pick up anything worth while. There'll always be men to give you their ideas; the job is to sort out the really important ideas from those based on thin air or speculation."

"I'm theenk eet is the good plan."

The two men pushed on into town, alighted in front of the Blue Gem Saloon, and entered. Except for the barkeep, Jiggs, the place was deserted. He paused midway in polishing a liquor glass, and his eyes widened. "You two got a nerve coming back—" he commenced.

"I haven't asked you for your opinion," Johnny said sharply.

"All right, you haven't," Jiggs said sullenly. "Just the same, you should know I can't serve a Mex—"

"We didn't come here for service," Johnny snapped. "I'm looking for Norton. Now let's have less talk and some information. Where is he?"

"He was in here about an hour ago," Jiggs replied, much of the belligerence gone from his tones. "Maybe you'll find him down at his office. You won't have no trouble locatin' it. Got a sheriff's sign hangin' in front. But I don't think you'll get far with Kirk. He runs this town with a hard hand, and just because you're a Ranger—"

Johnny's soft laugh interrupted the barkeep's words. "Good news travels fast, doesn't it? So I'm a Ranger and Norton doesn't like Rangers maybe?"

That laugh was infectious. The barkeep chuckled. "It ain't my place to say what the boss likes, and I wouldn't want to go on record, but I'll sure admit it wasn't good news to Norton, Barlow.

He's sort of put out, after he had that—that little misunderstandin' with you last night. Take my advice and don't rub him the wrong way, or you'll find his spurs rakin' your flanks."

"Not my flanks, he won't," Johnny said easily. "And I like to rub some folks the wrong way. Sometimes I find out things that way."

"Don't get over confident," Jiggs advised, "just because you're a Ranger. Kirk don't care no more for Rangers than he does anybody else. Your authority won't scare him none."

"And his don't scare me," Johnny replied, "so that makes us even. Who told him I was a Ranger? Vink Deever, maybe?"

"Maybe," the barkeeper said noncommittally. "I couldn't say for sure. And it ain't my business. It could be I've already talked too much. Kirk might not take it kindly if he thought—"

"Don't worry, mister," Johnny said. "Just because you thawed out enough to give me a warning against your boss is no sign I'm going to run to him with tales."

"I ain't said nothin'," Jiggs protested.

"Nope. You ain't." Johnny smiled. "And thanks for your kind consideration—which same I don't figure I'll need."

At that moment Vink Deever entered the Blue Gem. He stopped short and glanced nervously at Johnny. Johnny said, "Where's Norton, Deever?"

Deever shrugged his shoulders. He looked as

though he couldn't decide to run, or beat a retreat. There was a sort of puzzled look in his eyes. "How do I know where he is?" Deever replied in an uncertain voice. "He might be at his office, but I couldn't say. I ain't his keeper."

"That's plain. But he's yours, isn't he?"

"Damned if I know what you're talkin' about," Deever answered sullenly. "But just to show there ain't no hard feelin's, I'll go see if I can locate him. I'll tell him you're looking for him—"

"That's not necessary, Deever," Johnny commenced, but Deever had turned and departed hurriedly through the swinging doors.

Johnny glanced at the bartender and saw the scornful look in Jiggs's eyes. The bartender swabbed at the long counter with a soiled towel. "Maybe," Jiggs said quietly, "there is something to this Ranger authority, where some folks is concerned."

"Maybe there is." Johnny smiled.

"That Vink sure looked scared," Jiggs continued, "and I don't remember that you even said 'Boo!' at him. Oh well, it's none of my business. I'm just paid to follow Kirk Norton's orders."

Johnny nodded. "Well, we'll see you again."

"Sorry I can't buy a drink," Jiggs said half apologetically, "but you know how it is. A man does what his boss has ordered."

"I know how it is, feller," Johnny replied.

He and Vallejo left the saloon. They hadn't pro-

132

gressed far along the plank sidewalk when they caught sight of Meticulous Jones approaching a few yards away. Johnny said, "How are you, Deputy?"

Jones returned the salutation gloomily. "Mornin', Ranger man." He paused and looked cautiously both ways along the street. There were a number of pedestrians in view, walking on the shady side of the main thoroughfare, mostly. A few horses and vehicles were tethered at hitch racks on either side. The deputy's eyes came back to meet Johnny's. He glanced momentarily at Vallejo. "How you doing, Mike?" Again he paused, then the words came in a rush: "Dammit to hell, Johnny! Why didn't you tell us you were a Ranger? It might have saved a heap of trouble."

"I haven't had any trouble. What's wrong?"

"Kirk's pretty damn riled this mornin'. Got a temper like a bobcat that's been chawin' a buzz saw. He jumped all over me like it was my fault you come to Rawhide City. Says I'd best learn who's comin' to town, or turn in my badge."

Johnny chuckled. "Well, why don't you?"

Meticulous looked indignant. "Cripes A'mighty! I got to live, ain't I?"

Johnny asked, "Why?" in a surprised tone.

"Why?" Meticulous blurted. "Why does anybody have to live?" A sort of sickly smile passed over his morose features. "Aw, you're just joshin' me. But don't think I wouldn't be glad to give up

133

this deputy job. It don't bring me no pleasure. I've already looked for other jobs, a coupla times, but there's always some sort of work connected with 'em. My heart just won't stand hard work."

Johnny laughed. "In that case, it's a good thing Norton didn't give you the job of making us leave town."

"Gawd forbid!" Meticulous said fervently. "It looks like you got your mind made up to stay, Norton or no Norton."

"I'm staying."

"Just when did Norton spread the news I was a Ranger?" Johnny asked.

"Last night," Meticulous answered sourly, "sometime after supper hour was over. I'd seen you and Mike when you were riding out of town. Then, a coupla minutes later, I ran across a hombre what says he'd been in the Blue Gem and saw you throw a gun on Kirk Norton. I figured him as havin' had too much redeye to be sensible, but decides I'd better drift down to the Blue Gem to learn the truth of the statement. When I got there, Kirk and Vink Deever was sittin' on the porch, out front. I spoke to 'em, but neither answered me, so I went on inside. The boys was still talkin' about a run-in you two had with Kirk and Vink. Me, I was plumb surprised to hear how it come out—"

"So were Vink and Norton." Johnny grinned.

"I betcha." Meticulous nodded agreement. "The fellers said that Norton had even appealed to some of his customers to take a hand and help him—" He broke off, shaking his head. "That's the first time I ever knowed Kirk to yelp for help. Anyway, a few minutes later, Kirk and Deever come inside. It was then that Kirk announced that you was a Ranger. He didn't say how he learned that, but I've got a hunch that Deever knowed you someplace before."

"You're a good guesser, Meticulous. Who was in here when Norton was talking about me?"

The deputy considered. "Lemme see—Banker Caldwell and Jay Summerton dropped in, right after Kirk started talking—"

"I mean, who else?"

"Cain't say I just recollect, at present. Just the usual run of barflies, some cowhands and so on. Caldwell and Kirk got to chewin' the rag and the conversation got sort of short-tempered."

"Is that so?" Johnny said casually. "What did those two have words about?"

"Oh, it didn't amount to much. Kirk acted mighty sore, though. He accused Banker Caldwell of asking an investigation by the Border Rangers regardin' that missin' money of Matt Melville's. Kirk allowed as how he could run his own territory without no help from Rangers or anybody else. Caldwell denied sendin' for you, but then he got snappish too, and stated plumb definite that maybe it was a good thing if the Rangers did come in to do somethin'. He was so mad he got sort of pale in the gills and the sweat commenced to bead on his forehead. Jay Summerton, he sided with Caldwell. Caldwell's voice had got so shaky that he let Summerton carry on the argument for a few minutes. Course, Kirk quick beat Jay into silence, like he does everybody else. Finally, Kirk allows as there ain't no use arguin', and he bought a drink all around. Me, I took bourbon as usual. Then Summerton and Caldwell left."

"Uh-huh." Johnny nodded. "Well, Caldwell would be a fool to get in wrong with Norton on my account. I hope they patched up their difficulties." Meticulous said it looked like they had; anyway, they'd both cooled down. Johnny said next, "Meticulous, have you got any chewing tobacco on you?"

"Sure enough, Johnny." The deputy reached to a hip pocket, then stopped. "Cripes! I plumb forgot I'd run out. I was just on my way to buy me a plug when I run into you two. If you want to wait until I drop into—"

"Forget it, Meticulous. I'll buy some myself, or borrow a chew from Norton when I see him. He chews, doesn't he?"

"Plenty," Meticulous said. "Nigh on to a plug a day, anyhow. I suggested to him once that it might be cheaper for him to chew scrap, but he told me to mind my own business. And I did, from then on henceforth. Say, you figurin' to see Kirk now?"

"If I can find him. Want to come along?"

"Not me, brother—not me," the deputy exclaimed fervently. "I'd just as soon you didn't mention we'd been talkin'. He'd prob'ly accuse me of fraternisin' with the enemy. Kirk's humour ain't what you'd call pleasant this mornin'. I'm aimin' to walk wide and scary around him, until he gets over this mad. If you had good sense, you'd stay away from him too."

Johnny laughed. "Oh, I reckon he won't bite me. Well, we'll see you again, Meticulous."

"I hope so," the deputy said gloomily, "but I ain't so sure. When Kirk's mad, he's like as not to eat a man for breakfast."

"He'll get a bad case of indigestion if he tries to eat me."

"Betwixt you and me," Meticulous said cautiously. "that wouldn't cause me no great grief neither."

He passed on and turned into the Blue Gem. Johnny and Vallejo continued on to the sheriff's office. On the way Johnny stepped into a store and purchased a plug of Indian Head chewing tobacco, which he shoved into one hip pocket.

# CHAPTER XI

## REWARD NOT WANTED

THE combination sheriff's office and county jail was situated the distance of a city block farther on. It proved to be a solidly built structure of rock and adobe. At the rear of the sheriff's office was an iron-barred door which led to a row of prisoner's cells. At the front of the building was a wide porch; jutting above it was a wooden awning that reached to supporting posts placed at the edge of the plank sidewalk. Followed by Vallejo, Johnny stepped quietly to the porch and glanced through the open doorway. In one corner of the office stood a cot upon which rested a neatly folded pile of blankets. A topographical map of the county and a meat-packer's calendar decorated the rear wall. At a side wall stood a rack holding guns, and a number of pairs of handcuffs were suspended on pegs. One corner of a desk showed through the open door of the office. Johnny was about to knock on the doorjamb when he heard Norton's harsh voice:

"Well, don't stand there spying around. If you've got business with me, come in, Barlow."

Johnny and Vallejo entered. Johnny said quietly, "I thought we'd better make sure we were not interrupting important business, Sheriff, before we came barging in on you. I'd like time for a bit of talk—"

"You'll get it," Norton snapped. "I got eyes." He gestured toward the wide window of his office, facing on the street. "I saw you when you first arrived. I want to talk to you too."

The sheriff was seated, smoking a long cigar, behind his desk. His pale blue eyes gleamed balefully as his visitors came farther into the room. Johnny said, "First, let's get it settled that we had no intention of spying on you. I think I have information that might be to your interest. If you don't want to listen, all you have to do is say so, and we'll get out."

For a moment, Norton didn't answer. His temper was already close to the snapping point, but he managed to hold it in check. Finally he spoke, ignoring Vallejo, and saying to Johnny, "Have a seat."

There were a couple of straight-backed wooden chairs in the office. Johnny shoved one toward Mike and dropped into the other. Johnny commenced, "You and I, Sheriff, seem to have gotten off on the wrong foot last evening—"

"You put one over on me last night." Norton half snarled the interruption.

"That trouble wasn't of my making," Johnny pointed out. "I seem to remember you saying something about burning powder if I cut your trail again. Well, I've cut it, Norton. The next move is up to you."

Norton's features tightened angrily and for a brief instant Johnny expected trouble, but the man relaxed after a moment. "All right," he conceded, "up to a point I'll admit I talked too soon. But that wasn't solely my fault. You should have made yourself known as a Border Ranger the instant you struck town. Taken all around, that's made an awkward situation for me. You threw a gun on me—and got away with it. That's something that just doesn't happen here—"

"But it did happen," Johnny interrupted. "If you'll be honest with yourself, you'll see I couldn't have done anything else, the way you were acting."

"I'll be honest with myself. I always am." Norton clipped the words short. He exposed his large, even white teeth momentarily in what was intended for a smile, but which more closely resembled a snarl. "Because I'm honest with myself, we'll overlook your gun work. You probably saved bloodshed." He said again, "We'll overlook it."

"I suppose it was Deever told you I was a Ranger," Johnny said.

Norton nodded, his face flushing slightly. "And that's made it awkward for me too. I'd never have hired Deever if I'd known he was an ex-convict."

"A good many ex-convicts have gone straight and made good citizens," Johnny said slowly. "Are you firing Deever now?"

Norton gnawed at his long yellow moustaches and gave the question consideration. "I'm damned if I know what to say," he muttered angrily. "I'm supposed to be running an efficient law-enforcing office in this county. Folks trust me. They know I save the taxpayers' money; since I've held office it hasn't been necessary to pay the expenses of a town marshal or city jail. As county officer I take care of both—"

"I'm asking what you intend about Deever."

"I'm making my position clear, I hope," Norton interrupted half savagely. "You and Deever have put me in a spot, Barlow. If people around town knew of Deever's reputation, I'd have to let him go. It just wouldn't do for me to have a known ex-con. in my employ. I have his story. What can you tell me about him?"

"It was a matter of stolen cows," Johnny said. "He was mixed in with the wild bunch. I arrested him and saw he was brought to trial. Deever and I traded some lead on the way, and I happened to be a mite faster than he was. That's all there is to it."

"Just about as he told it to me," Norton said, "except he claims he wasn't guilty and it was all a mistake."

Johnny smiled. "Pleading not guilty isn't uncommon among cow thieves."

"I'll concede that too." Norton almost smiled. "For that matter, some of the biggest cow outfits in this country are based on stolen cattle originally. If a man got caught he went to jail; if not, in some cases he became a cattle baron. . . . But I'm damned if I can decide what to do about Deever. He's been a good man to have on my pay roll. He knows cattle and rods my spread with ability. Not a particularly congenial man, but I pay for work, not smiles. I suppose I should fire him, though."

"If Deever wants to go straight and has been living on the level," Johnny said quietly, "I'll not spread any story of his past life. I haven't any grudge against him, even after last night. It's a matter for you to settle with him."

Norton frowned. "I'll have to think it over." He changed the subject. "I suppose you'll be leaving Rawhide City shortly."

Johnny smiled and shook his head. "I hadn't planned it that way. You see, the Melvilles are old friends of mine. I'm aiming to stay here until that missing money is found, or at least until we can learn what became of it." Norton started to speak, but Johnny cut him short. "I'll be vouching for Mike Vallejo here, so you won't need to run him out of town, either. In fact"—and a trace of steel entered Johnny's quiet tones—"I'd take it rather hardly if you tried to order Mike out. He's my *amigo*." He turned to Vallejo and said, "Mike, there's no use of you staying if you feel like ambling around or dropping into the Clinic Saloon.

Sheriff Norton and I can get along all right. We've things to talk over."

"*Si,* Johnee." The Mexican rose. "*Adios,* Sheriff Norton."

Norton scowled but refused to answer. Vallejo laughed softly and stepped into the street. His footsteps died away on the plank walk. Norton spoke then, sarcastically: "Your bodyguard, Barlow?"

"Who, Mike?" Johnny laughed genially. "Sheriff, you know better than to ask a fool question of that sort. Do you really think I need a bodyguard?"

"To tell the truth, I don't," Norton said grudgingly.

Johnny rolled a cigarette and lighted it. Norton touched fresh flame to his cigar, which had gone out. "See here, Barlow"—Norton spoke suddenly—"it's none of my business if you want to visit with the Melvilles, but it's not at all necessary that you stay in town. I'm capable of handling my county and uncovering the disappearance of that money."

"I've already made up my mind to stay," Johnny said lazily through a cloud of tobacco smoke. "I don't like to change it. I'm mighty curious to learn exactly what became of that money."

"I'll take care of that matter." Norton's voice was cold, his mouth, beneath the yellow moustaches, hard. "I'm following up clues now. I expect to make an arrest shortly. Maybe two."

"Who are you arresting? What are your clues?"

Norton spaced his words evenly. "They are solely my business, Barlow, and I don't intend to tell you. Border Rangers aren't needed—nor wanted—in Rawhide City. Dammit! Hasn't it occurred to you that I could force you to leave, charging interference with my duties? I could have you recalled mighty *pronto.* With my good record, I could manage that easily."

Johnny shook his head, laughing softly. "That doesn't go down, Sheriff. I don't bluff easy. Sure, I don't doubt you have connections that are powerful. Any sheriff does. But hasn't it ever struck your mind that I could be in a similar situation? The influence isn't all on your side. I'd like to remind you that the governor is a mighty close friend of mine."

Norton's clenched fist crashed down on the desk. "I don't give a damn for any seat-warming politician in this country, Barlow. I'm running this county—not the governor. I'd just as soon run him out of town as I would—"

"Me?" Johnny supplied the word with a grin.

"Yes, you!" Norton thundered. "I will not allow the Rangers to come meddling in my county. I'm warning you, Barlow—keep your hands off my job!" He was on his feet now, eyes glaring down into Johnny's.

Johnny rose slowly. He was smiling, but in his gaze burned cold flames of righteous anger. "Any man who throws a warning at a Border Ranger,

Norton, had better be sure of his ground, or he's a heap likely to encounter a mess of trouble. You can't intimidate me—not any. And I'm telling you something in just two words: I'm staying."

"You'll regret it," Norton snarled.

"That sounds like a threat, Norton. All right, I'll keep my eyes peeled. If you aim to stir up something, that's all right with me. I've been threatened before, but you'd better soon damn get it through your head that I'm not leaving this country until I learn what happened to Matt Melville's money—"

"We'll see about that—" Norton commenced wrathfully.

"I'm doing the talking, Norton, and I'm going to tell you a few things. First, you're acting like a blasted fool." He motioned to the star of office pinned to Norton's vest. "You're disgracing that badge. You were elected to enforce the laws of this county, but the folks who elected you *didn't* figure on putting a dictator in office. After all, you're nothing but a public servant—"

"I was elected—"

"Keep still until I finish," Johnny snapped. "From all I've heard, Norton, you've been one hell of a good sheriff, but that's no sign you can ride roughshod over this whole country. Most sheriffs are glad to have help from the Rangers. You are entitled to that help, and you're going to get it whether you want it or not. Get that, straight! Whether you want it or not. Maybe you're jealous of your reputation here. I can understand that. But right now we're facing something that's bigger than your rep., bigger than the rep. of any single man. You need help, but you won't admit it. Right now you're facing a problem that has you stopped cold. That's where I come in. I may not finish what I'm starting, as you've intimated, but I'm aiming to keep trying until hell freezes over—"

"By God, Barlow! You can't talk like this to me—"

"I can and I will and I am! Hold up! I'm not through yet. An attempt was made on my life last night. Somebody doesn't want me here. I'm figuring to learn who that somebody is. Last evening you ordered me out of town. Do your orders also include ambushing?"

"What in the devil are you talking about?"

Johnny explained in terse tones. "Last night when I was leaving by the rear door of the Lazy-Double-M ranch house, somebody threw a chunk of Winchester lead my way. I was lucky. He—he missed. We heard the lousy bustard riding off, hell-bent for leather. Afterward, we read 'sign' on him—"

"What did you find?" Norton's voice was eager. His tones showed less anger now.

"Do you expect me to tell you? You mentioned clues you had, awhile back, but you claimed they were solely your business and you refused to tell me of them."

"This is a different matter. I'm entitled to any evidence you can give regarding an attempted crime in my county. I insist that—"

Johnny said in a weary voice, "Oh hell, I'll show you co-operation." He asked a question. "That silver star you're wearing, Norton. When did you pin it on?"

"What?" The single word cracked angrily. Johnny repeated the question. Norton looked puzzled, then, "I don't know why you've changed the subject, but—hell! I don't remember when I pinned it on. Maybe three or four days ago. I might have changed it from my coat then. It depends on the weather. Sometimes I wear it on my vest, sometimes on the coat."

Johnny was looking closely at the sheriff's vest, but could see no evidence of a recent tear, where the pin might have pulled loose. He said, "Where's your coat?" Norton indicated the long black coat hanging on a hook against one wall. Johnny crossed the floor and examined both lapels. The cloth here was also intact, though faint pin holes could be observed. He came back to the desk, then dropped into his chair. "Sit down, Sheriff," he suggested. "We still got a lot of talking to do."

With a savage grunt Norton dropped into his seat and took up his cigar, which had once more gone out. "Barlow, what in hell are you driving at?"

"You asked me if we'd found any 'sign',"

Johnny explained patiently. He took from one pocket the badge he'd found the previous night and tossed it on the sheriff's desk. "We picked that up not far from where the ambushing bustard mounted his pony. There's one answer, Norton, as to why I'm intending to stay around here a spell."

Norton looked sharply at Johnny, then down at the badge again. He picked up the badge from the desk and examined closely the tarnished silver star. An almost imperceptible emotion hardened the lines of his features. When he finally spoke, his words sounded strained:

"I don't suppose it would do any good to tell you I had nothing to do with any dry-gulching that went on at Melville's place last night."

"*Attempted* dry-gulching," Johnny corrected coldly. "That's your badge, isn't it? Now if you've still got it in mind to try to have me recalled from Rawhide City, you just play that hand to your limit, Norton. I'll have a story of my own to tell."

For a full minute Norton didn't speak. He drew out one of the drawers of his desk, glanced within it, rustled some papers about, then slammed the drawer closed again. He puffed furiously on his cigar while Johnny waited in silence. Finally, Norton said coldly, "It's my badge, all right. It would be useless for me to deny that, I suppose, though I might be able to convince you. But that I refuse to try. My office isn't built on lies. . . . Yes, it's my badge, but it's an old one." He gestured

148

toward the bright badge pinned to his vest. "If you care to take a close look, you'll see this badge has the name of the county stamped on it. It was issued to me nearly two years back. This old badge doesn't bear the county name. You can check on all this if you care to, learn when the new badges were issued, and so on."

"Maybe I'll take your word for that."

Norton nodded grimly; his eyes narrowed. "This old badge has been lying in my desk for months. Since we rarely have prisoners in the jail, I often leave the door of my office open. Anybody could have slipped in here and stolen this old badge from my desk."

"But who could have known just where you kept it?"

"God knows; I don't. Someone may have seen me place that badge there. Perhaps he took it, or told someone else where it was."

"It might be a prime idea," Johnny suggested dryly, "to keep your office door, or your desk, locked from now on."

The sheriff didn't appear to have heard him. When he finally spoke the words came with reluctance. "I'm willing to grant, Barlow, that you may be right. Maybe it would be a good idea for you to stick around for a spell. I don't suppose you'd believe me if I swore it wasn't me that shot at you last night."

Johnny laughed softly. "The Sheriff Norton I've

been hearing about wouldn't have worked it so clumsily. I've got a hunch that somebody who knows you and I aren't exactly friendly is trying to frame you, or create trouble between us, providing the bustard failed to kill me last night. No, I never did figure it was you lost that badge, Norton. Somebody guessed we'd look for 'sign', and dropped that badge on purpose for us to find. Then probably it was expected that I—or one of the Lazy-Double-M hands—would come tearing into town with accusations that would knock you plumb out of your job. Maybe those clues you mentioned are hotter than you think, Sheriff. Somebody's feeling plenty uncomfortable."

Norton sent a quick look toward Johnny. "Exactly how did you come to the conclusion it wasn't me lost this badge?"

Johnny said, "If it had worn through the cloth on your vest and dropped off, the pin would still be fastened in its clasp. The pin on this is wide open."

A thin smile touched the sheriff's lips. "Y'know, there's a lot of men wouldn't think of that."

"Border Rangers are trained to look for things most men wouldn't think of."

Norton looked more relieved than he had a few moments before. He drew a big bandanna from his pocket and mopped perspiration from his forehead. "I'm sure glad you got reasoning powers, Barlow."

Johnny shrugged. "Sometimes I wonder about

that too. Sheriff, you left the Blue Gem fairly early last night, didn't you? Where'd you go?"

"I was right here in my office for a couple hours, making out my monthly expense account. After that I went to bed."

"Where was Vink Deever last night?"

Norton frowned and settled back in his chair. "By God, if it was Deever done this—" He broke off, then continued, "No, Deever left the Blue Gem at the same time I did. He said he was going out to the Quarter-Circle-N—that's my spread y'know. I haven't seen him since. I told Deever to keep out of your way, so as to avoid any trouble—"

"Deever's in town now," Johnny said. "I saw him shortly before I came here. He didn't come here, eh?"

Norton appeared not to have heard the question. He was turning the old badge over and over between his fingers. "Some bustard is trying to get me," he muttered angrily, half to himself. He glanced uneasily at Johnny, then back to the badge. He drew on his cigar, which had again gone out, then reached for a match.

"You seem to have trouble keeping that weed lit," Johnny commented. "Here, you'd better join me in some eating tobacco." He drew out the plug he had purchased a short time before, bit off a generous chew, and proffered the remainder of the plug to the sheriff.

Norton said, "Thanks," in an absent-minded sort

of voice and accepted the plug. Reaching into a pocket for a clasp knife, he opened the blade and sliced off a chunk of the plug. Popping the tobacco into his mouth, he returned the plug to Johnny. Johnny replaced what was left in his pocket and watched Norton. Norton chewed meditatively, spat a long stream of brown juice into a sawdust-filled box near his feet; a scowl deepened on his face. "Yes, dammit," he stated, chewing with angry vigour, "there's no doubt of it. Some son-of-a-buzzard is trying to frame that dry-gulching job on me."

"It could be—probably is," Johnny conceded carelessly. Then, in the same easy tones, "I note you cut your chew, instead of biting it off like most hombres."

"What?" Norton glanced up suddenly as the words interrupted his abstractions. "Oh, yeah sure. I don't like strange teeth biting into my plugs, and I sort of figured you might feel the same way." He again dropped his eyes to the tarnished badge.

"Yes. I never thought of it that way before, though," Johnny said. He shoved his Stetson to one side of his red hair and climbed lazily to his feet. "Well, I reckon I'll be drifting along. Then it's set-tled, Norton, that you've no further objections to me staying here?"

Norton looked up suddenly and spoke in cold tones. "My mind on that score hasn't changed, Barlow. I'd sooner you weren't here. I can run my job without outside help. However, under the circumstances, and until this badge matter is cleared up, it might be a good thing for you to stay. I might want to ask you some questions, later—"

"What sort of questions?"

"I haven't decided yet." He concluded bitterly. "You stay as long as you like."

"In that case, why wouldn't it be a good thing for us to work on the Melville case together?" Johnny suggested. "You said something about having some clues—"

"My clues are my own," Norton said frigidly. "You work your way, and I'll work mine. I'll be frank; I'm out to beat you in solving the disappearance of that money. I want to teach you Border Rangers once and for all time, that I don't need any help."

"Stubborn cuss, aren't you?" Johnny smiled. "Plumb unreasonable, as I see it. Still holding a grudge, I imagine. Well, that's all right with me. We'll get together yet." He started toward the doorway, then turned back. "There was one more thing I wanted to ask. What made you so sure in identifying the Falcon after you killed him?"

Norton's eyes narrowed. "I don't have to tell you, but I will; I'd seen a reward bill with the Falcon's picture and description on it. That suit you?"

"No, it doesn't. Have you still got that reward bill? It seems that would give you very little information to go on so fast. As I get it, you stated it was the Falcon robbing the bank the instant you laid eyes on him—and him with a bandanna across his face."

Norton stated in cold tones that he no longer had the reward bill, that he didn't know what had become of it. "In the first place," he went on, "I'd heard—somewhere—that the Falcon was headed this way. I recognised his build from the description on the reward bill. Later, when he was dead, I was able to state definitely he was the Falcon."

"I don't quite get that 'definite' part," Johnny persisted.

"I expected you to say that." Norton appeared to be trying to keep patient. "I'll explain. Some time back I was down in Mexico. The Falcon was pointed out to me at a *cantina* down there. I never forget a face. Now are you satisfied?"

Johnny laughed softly. "I should be, shouldn't I, Norton? But I still think there's a chance you could be mistaken. . . . By the way, Norton, Elson Trigg will be in town to-morrow. You know Trigg, don't you? Sheriff of the next county to the east. Got his office at Capitol City."

Norton frowned. "What in hell does Trigg want here?" he snapped.

"I sent him a letter by stage last night. It's not much of a ride, so I'm expecting him in to-morrow morning."

"I'm asking what he's coming here for."

"He's one of the nearest men I know of who can

identify the Falcon for sure," Johnny explained quietly. "I heard you hadn't notified the reward authorities, and I figured you could use the money."

Norton's face had gone crimson, then white with rage. "God damn it!" he roared. "More of your damn meddling! Why can't you Rangers learn to mind your own business? I identified the Falcon when I killed him. There's no sense—"

"I'm plumb sorry," Johnny said contritely, "if I've put my hoof in a corral where it's not welcome, but somebody else who knows the Falcon will have to identify the body before you can collect the reward offered—"

"Hell's-bells!" Norton flamed. "I'm asking no reward for doing my duty. I figured to let that part go, but now you've come, butting into something that is none of your affair."

"I'm mighty sorry you're taking it this way, Norton," Johnny said meekly. "I just aimed to do you a good turn and show you I didn't hold a grudge for that little fuss we had in the Blue Gem last night. Well, if you don't want that reward money, you can donate it to charity; either that, or maybe give it to the Melvilles to sort of make up to Matt for what happened—"

"Dammit! Don't tell me what to do," Norton snarled. "All I ask is that you mind your own business. And I'll be thanking you to get out of this office—right now—before I have to throw you out—"

"Don't try it, Norton," Johnny said sharply. "I'm going. Maybe after you've calmed down a mite you'll realise I've acted entirely legal. You should know a body has to be identified by two people in a case like that—two, at least. If you get cooled down, after a spell, let me know, and maybe we can get together."

The only answer was a muttered curse from the sheriff, still seated at the desk. Johnny nodded and stepped out to the street. As he sauntered slowly away from the sheriff's office, he thought: "He sliced that plug with a knife. That might, or might not, prove something eventually. On the other hand, I'm pretty nigh sure it was not Norton who dropped that badge. Hell! This is sure one mixed-up tangle."

Drawing abreast of the Blue Gem, Johnny crossed over and glanced above the swinging doors, but among the customers there, there was no one in whom he was interested. He wondered what had become of Vink Deever, and if Vallejo, going through the Mexican Quarter, was having any success in turning up news of Mex Louie. A few moments later Johnny disposed of his cud of tobacco and continued on down the street, heading in the direction of the Clinic Saloon.

# CHAPTER XII

## A POOR RISK

ERNIE BRAUGHN was presiding at the bar of the Clinic Saloon when Johnny entered. There was no sign of Doc Duncan or any other customers in the bar. Johnny said that he'd like a bottle of beer. Ernie had only nodded when Johnny came in. Ernie set the beer and a glass on the bar, then exploded: "Sufferin' tomcats, Johnny! Why didn't you announce yourself as a Border Ranger when you were in here yesterday?"

Johnny laughed. "I didn't see any particular reason for advertising that fact. Does it make any difference?"

"You're dang right it does. You've raised merry hell in town. Sheriff Norton dropped down on me like a ton of bricks last night, bawled me to the king's taste, and was about ready to throw me in the clink—"

"How come he jumped on you?"

"Norton had figured I knew you was a Ranger, and he felt I should have let him know. I had a hard time convincin' him I didn't know it. He cooled down after a spell, but I ain't likely to forget—If I ever forget anything—that cold look in his blue eyes. I'd sure hate to have him holdin' a grudge against me."

157

"I can't see why Norton figured you should know anything about me."

"We-ell, it's just sort of unusual for a Ranger to drop into a town and not announce himself. Norton learned you came here first and he tooken it for granted you had said who you were."

Johnny drank some of his beer. "Sure, when a Ranger comes to a town on a job, he states who he is, generally. But, Ernie, I didn't come here on a job. I was on a furlough. I didn't even want to think about working."

"Well, you sure got under Norton's skin. He jumped all over Meticulous too. He's been giving that deputy a rough time the past few hours."

"I know. I saw Meticulous a spell back. He's keeping out of Norton's way. I saw Norton, too, this morning."

"T'hell you did! What happened?"

"Nothing much. We came to a sort of agreement."

Ernie looked curious, but he didn't ask what the agreement was. He whistled softly, poured himself a small drink of liquor, and downed it. "That drink," he announced, "was drunk to the man who threw a gun on Kirk Norton and got away with it—"

"Got away with it so far," Johnny amended with a grin. "May you enjoy many more drinks like that one, Ernie. After what happened last night. I've got a notion your sheriff doesn't like me too well."

"I just got the outstandin' details. Tell me about it."

Johnny related what had happened at the Blue Gem the previous evening. When he had finished Ernie said, "That's as I heard it all right. The news is spread through town, and Kirk Norton's prestige has fallen a heap. . . . And so you come here to clear up that matter of the stolen money."

"I didn't say that. Didn't you hear me say I'd come here on my furlough."

"Just to enjoy the climate, I suppose," Ernie said sceptically. "All right, don't tell me if you don't want to. But I'd sure like to know exactly—"

Johnny chuckled. "Ask me no questions and I'll tell you no lies. Ernie, I'm not sure enough of any of my facts to talk about 'em yet."

The two conversed desultorily for a few minutes Johnny finished his beer and lighted a cigarette. He asked where Doc Duncan was, and inquired after Matt Melville's condition.

"Doc says he's getting along fine and should be able to have visitors pretty soon. Doc was in a spell ago, but he said he was going home to stretch out awhile. He stays up nights a lot, with Matt."

Two cowmen entered the saloon. Ernie introduced them to Johnny as Guy Gerard, owner of the Rafter-G Ranch, and one of his hands, Fargo Delroy. Gerard was grey-haired, smooth-shaven. Delroy was tall, nearly middle-aged, with stooped shoulders and faded overalls. The two looked curiously at Johnny and shook hands.

Gerard laughed and said, "So you're the Ranger

159

we heard about almost as soon as we struck Rawhide City. I understand you sort of tipped over Sheriff Norton's apple cart last evenin'."

"We just had a little misunderstanding, that's all," Johnny said quietly. "I'm afraid folks have been exaggerating a mite. There's no real bad trouble between Norton and me right now. People just like to make mountains out of molehills. I just left Norton's office about half an hour ago."

Ernie saw that Johnny wasn't inclined to talk about the Blue Gem argument, so he inserted a question: "Johnny, where's Mike this morning?"

"He's around town someplace," Johnny replied. "Be turning up eventually."

Gerard inquired after Matt Melville's health. Ernie gave him the same report he'd given Johnny. Gerard said that sounded fine. The conversation, after a time, turned to the holdup and the shooting of the Falcon. Certain questions were directed at Johnny, but Johnny shook his head and said that he'd not yet found any clues relative to the affair. He asked, "Did either of you gents witness that holdup?"

Fargo Delroy was studying the glass of whisky Ernie had placed before him. He said, without looking up, "I was in town that day. Ernie, you saw it, didn't you?"

Ernie Braughn shook his head. "Saw only what I could see from the entrance here. I couldn't leave the bar. I didn't get a close look at the Falcon, neither."

Johnny said to Delroy, "Tell me everything you saw, as near as you can remember it."

Delroy marshalled his thoughts, choosing his words carefully. "Well, lemme see . . . I was standing on the Blue Gem porch right after that first shot was heard. Fact is, I wa'n't exactly on the porch, just at the edge. There was quite a bunch of us massed at the swinging doors, lookin' out. We'd been at the bar when we heard the shot. I saw the Falcon come out of the bank with the satchel in his hand. Then he commenced throwin' lead reckless-like, both directions along Main Street."

"You didn't make any start to try and stop him, eh?" Johnny asked.

Delroy flushed. "Me, I'm just an ordinary everyday cowprod. I don't make any pretensions to bein' a gun slinger. And I didn't like the way the Falcon was shakin' lead outten his barrels in all directions. A stray slug might have come up on the Blue Gem porch. 'Bout the time that thought struck me I turned tail and got back inside the Blue Gem as fast as I could."

Johnny smiled. "I don't blame you. I reckon you didn't have any option on that idea either, did you?"

"From all I hear," Guy Gerard put in, "nigh everybody scuttled for safety and shelter, plumb simultaneous and immediate."

Delroy nodded. "That's the plain truth. I ain't yet met anybody who admitted to seeing the Falcon from the time he got on his bronc until Kirk Norton downed him. Kirk showed plenty nerve that day." He paused, considering. "Kirk started out, then found he didn't have his hawg laig on. He come back into the bar and got a Winchester. That spelled the Falcon's finish."

Johnny frowned thoughtfully. "For a few moments, then—possibly the space of half a minute or maybe less—nobody was watching the Falcon."

"That's the way it looks to me," Delroy replied. " 'Course, I don't know who was watching from other buildin's, and maybe there was those in the Blue Gem who risked one eye to peek, but I wa'n't one of 'em. Next thing I knew, somebody yelled that Norton had downed the Falcon, and then the whole street was fair swarmin' with folks. I ran up the road to take a look at the body, but there was quite a crowd around it before I got there."

A fleshily built man with a round pleasant face came pushing through the swinging doors of the Clinic bar. He was middle-aged and dressed in citizen's clothing, though he wore a stiff-brimmed black Stetson atop his thin, greying hair.

"H'yuh, Mr. Caldwell?" Ernie greeted.

"Howdy, Ernie. Hello there, Gerard. Fargo, how's the world treating you these days? And speaking of treating, let's all have a drink at my expense." He paused and looked inquiringly at Johnny.

162

Ernie performed the introduction. "Mr. Caldwell, shake the hand of the man who thrun down on Kirk Norton and lived to tell it. Johnny, this is Frank Caldwell, Rawhide City's premier banker."

The two shook hands. Frank Caldwell possessed an ingratiating laugh and a white-toothed smile. He said, "I've already been hearing things about Johnny Barlow. Young man, I don't think you'd be a good risk for my bank to lend money to, unless you had mighty good security. You're just too damn careless about your health."

Johnny grinned. "I heard you done some bearding of the lion in his den last night, so maybe neither of us are good risks. I understand Norton got riled with you for a spell."

Caldwell sobered. "I'm sorry about that argument. Kirk and I have always gotten on well—not close friends, you know. Nobody could be real friendly with Kirk. He's too stiff. But, as I say, we get along. He's a good sheriff; been good for Rawhide City. But in this particular instance I think him wrong in objecting to you being here. He could use some Ranger help in locating Matt Melville's money. So far as the argument goes, I guess the fault was mine as much as his. I lost my temper and said things I shouldn't have. My cashier, Jay Summerton, got into the argument then. I suppose we're both in the bad graces of Norton now, but I think he's too big a man to hold a grudge. I'm going to try and have another talk with him to-day sometime, and see if we can't bury the hatchet. For that matter, things had pretty much simmered down by the time Jay and I left the Blue Gem last night."

"How much do you know about Summerton, Mr. Caldwell?" Johnny asked.

"Quite a little—" Caldwell commenced, then broke off, "Here's Ernie with our drinks. Let me have a minute to wet down my throat." He tilted a neat two fingers of whisky into his mouth, coughed, shuddered, and wiped his lips with a handkerchief. The others occupied themselves with their drinks. Johnny poured some more beer into a glass.

Caldwell continued, "We were talking about Jay. He's a good man—been with me quite a spell now. Jay Summerton arrived out here, broken in health, and when he asked for a position in the bank I was somewhat dubious about taking him on. I didn't expect he'd live three months. But I hired him and it's the best move I ever made. He knows banking, and he's had plenty of experience. He acts as cashier and takes care of all the books as well—we both work on the books, of course. Jay has got it into his head that he owes me something for hiring him, and he's unusually loyal. Matter of fact, he doesn't owe me one damn thing. I needed a cashier and Jay filled the bill. That's all there is to it. Jay Summerton is square all through, and I'd trust him with my last dollar."

Johnny nodded. "You certainly give him a high recommendation. We were just talking about the bank holdup—or the holdup of Matt Melville's money, whichever you like—before you came in. That day the holdup occurred, before the Falcon entered the bank, did you count out that ten thousand dollars yourself and place it in the satchel?"

Caldwell shook his head. "No, I didn't even see the money until later. Jay counted it out, put the money in the bag, and then brought it into my office, where Matt was waiting. Matt counted it, though, and I watched him, checking to see that he didn't make a mistake. Then, just as he was leaving, the Falcon stepped in—"

"Excuse me for interrupting," Johnny said, "but I know about that part. There's something I'd like to know though. Did Matt lock that satchel after he closed it?"

Caldwell's brow furrowed with thought. "Er—no—no—I don't think he did. Just closed the snaps, as I remember. I don't recollect having a key there. Anyway, knowing Matt as I do, I don't think he would have bothered to lock it, key or no key."

"Uh-huh," Johnny said absent-mindedly. "Do you happen to have any idea who the thief might be—whoever it was got the money away from the Falcon, or how it was gotten?"

Caldwell shook his head helplessly. "I've not an idea in the world. It's the worst puzzle I've ever encountered. As a matter of fact, I was too excited that day to think of anything but Matt and the money. If it hadn't of been for Kirk Norton—"

"I'll say you was excited," Fargo Delroy interrupted, laughing. "Excited is no word for it, Frank. You were just plain stampeded. I'll never forget how you looked. Hair mussed. Ink spilt all over your pants. Your collar had come unfastened and was stabbin' you in the off ear, while your necktie was trying to build a loop on your other ear."

Caldwell laughed sheepishly. "I did get pretty well mussed up, I guess. You see, Johnny, in my effort to get out of the Falcon's gun range I'd sprawled on the floor, knocking over my ink as I went down. Kirk Norton took me to task right severely for not having my gun handy, but, great Caesar! I'm no gun fighter. I wouldn't have stood a hound-dog's chance against a shot like the Falcon."

There was some laughter at this, then the men talked awhile longer. Little of import to Johnny came out of the conversation. Finally, Caldwell said it was time for him to be leaving. He shook hands with Johnny again and wished him luck, then took his departure. A few minutes later Gerard and Delroy also headed for the street. Johnny remained lounging at the bar, frowning at the nearly empty beer bottle before him. Ernie started to speak, then paused and turned instead to polishing glasses. Ten minutes passed in silence. No other customers entered.

# CHAPTER XIII

## HIRED KILLER?

JOHNNY finally roused from his abstractions. "Ernie," he asked abruptly, "how long have you known Fargo Delroy?"

Ernie gave the question but an instant's consideration. "Twenty years, three months and two days," he replied.

A grin crossed Johnny's face. "Regular old memory wizard, aren't you? What do you know about Delroy?"

"Nothing bad. I know him as well as any of the cowhands who come and go around Rawhide City. Fargo has worked for various outfits part of the time, and part of the time he hasn't worked. I figure him as an honest cowpoke without too much ambition."

Johnny nodded. "Is Guy Gerard on the square?"

"I don't know positively of anything against him. He pays his bar bill prompt. There was some talk a long while back that he had started his herd with other men's cows, but I'm probably the only one who remembers that, nowadays. Shucks! What if he did? I figure there's plenty stockmen in this country got their start the same way."

"Norton said something similar to that when I was talking to him. He said in the old days when a man got caught rustling he was jailed. If he didn't get caught, he became a cattle baron."

"That's sure the truth in a lot of cases. I wonder what brought cow stealing to Norton's mind?" Ernie looked expectantly at Johnny.

"That's something I can't go into right now," Johnny said. Before Ernie had a chance to ask why, Johnny went on, "Have you known Caldwell long?"

"All my life, I reckon. We're about of an age, though he was away from Rawhide City for quite a spell. But we started out here. I was a kid, scrapin' at jobs here and there, when Caldwell went to work as a button on the old Circle-Y— known as Jim Cross's Circle-Cross now."

Johnny said, "I kind of thought Caldwell had cow sticking to him, in spite of his clothes and ways. How come he started a bank?"

Ernie shrugged. "I don't know all the details— never heard 'em. While he was working at the Circle-Y an uncle of his up in Utah decided to adopt him. That's when Frank went away. I guess the uncle had money. Anyway, when the uncle died, Caldwell got the pile. That's as I heard it. Frank had got an education while he was away too, and studied banking. Then he come back here and bought stock in the Rawhide City bank. I reckon by this time he holds a controllin' interest."

"I had a hunch he was well fixed with cash."

"He ain't wantin' for food," Ernie agreed. "Still,

at that, I wouldn't trade places with him, for all his money. His health isn't so good as he'd like it to be. I never yet saw him take a drink that he didn't give a shudder when the liquor went down. Maybe he's got a bad stomach, I don't know. He gets lumbago bad, at times, and suffers to beat the devil. Then he don't hardly dare to bend over or move sudden. I noted he was walkin' stiff-like this mornin', so I reckon he's been having some twinges."

"What he likely needs is some good exercise," Johnny said. "No man can keep fit working at a desk. He's got to have exercise. If Frank Caldwell would just sit a saddle for an hour or so every day, instead of a cushioned seat at a desk chair, it would do him a world of good."

Ernie's loud laughter sounded sceptical. "What! Frank Caldwell sit a hawss? Cripes! Johnny, his riding days are over. I don't think Caldwell has been on a pony in fifteen years—and don't ask the exact time, 'cause I never heard how long it is. But I heard him say once as how he was all through riding since he took to branding mortgages instead of cows."

"I suppose that's how it is. Well, every man to his own job, Ernie. . . ." He glanced at the heavy gold watch he carried in a pocket. "It's getting along toward noontime. 'Rene Melville said she'd likely be in to-day, and it's about time I found Mike. I'd best be getting along. I'll see you again, Ernie."

"Make it soon, Johnny."

Johnny pushed through the entrance and stood a few minutes beneath the wooden awning that jutted from the front of the Clinic Saloon. Four or five passers-by, men he didn't know, spoke to him. Johnny replied with a smile. Apparently he was becoming known in Rawhide City. What was it the man had said? Fame and bad fortune travel on wings of lightning swiftness? Something like that. Anyway, folks in town were learning about him. Trouble was, Johnny mused, such notoriety as he had gained came from having thrown a gun on Kirk Norton and lived to tell of it, rather than from the fact of his being a law-enforcing Border Ranger. When folks, Johnny mused, learn to put more stock in the law and less in gun throwing, the world will be a better place to live in. He rolled and lighted a brown paper cigarette, and leaned against one upright of the porch roof, inhaling thoughtfully.

Miguel Vallejo passed on the opposite side of the thoroughfare. Johnny hailed him: "Anything new, Mike?"

The Mexican shook his head disgustedly, called back something to the effect that he'd see Johnny later, and proceeded on without stopping.

Johnny frowned. "I reckon," he told himself, "Mike must be finding it hard going to trace that Mex Louie hombre." He heaved a long sigh. "Time sure hangs heavy on a man's hands when he's waiting to learn things. I suppose I might as well drift down to the Blue Gem, get my pony—and Mike's—from the hitch rack, and see that they get a feed and water."

He left the Clinic Saloon porch and moved leisurely along the sidewalk until he had rounded the slight curve in the road that brought the Blue Gem into view, the distance of half a city block farther on. At that moment he saw Kirk Norton and Vink Deever standing on the sidewalk before the Blue Gem, talking earnestly. Both appeared to be angry. They were too far off for Johnny to hear their words but he judged from certain irate gestures that all was not well between the two. Finally both turned and entered the Blue Gem.

"Now I wonder what those two were scrappin' about," Johnny mused. He paused in the deep shadow beneath a wooden awning stretching from the front wall of a feed store and pondered the matter. "I wonder if Norton was accusing Deever of stealing that badge and leaving it for us to find. Deever certainly had the appearance of making a vigorous denial of—something. He and Norton are doing a heap of wondering, or lying, about now, I'll bet." He chuckled softly. "Life may be hellish, but it's never dull when the Border Rangers hit a town."

His gaze wandered idly across the street toward the brick structure that housed Caldwell's bank. A slimly built, bareheaded man had just come out of

171

the wide doorway. An instant later Frank Caldwell hurriedly emerged from the bank and joined the bareheaded man. Caldwell had caught at the other's arm and started talking earnestly. They, too, appeared to be arguing with Caldwell doing most of the talking. This continued for several minutes and Johnny wished he could hear what was being said. Finally, the bareheaded man reluctantly turned back into the bank, and, with Caldwell close behind, disappeared within the building.

Johnny's brow furrowed. "I wonder if that was Jay Summerton, the cashier? He fitted the description. And what in the devil were he and Caldwell chewing the rag about? Summerton looked sort of put out."

While Johnny stood lounging in the shade of the feed store, Caldwell once more emerged from the bank, crossed the roadway diagonally and entered the Blue Gem Saloon. Johnny's frown deepened. "Folks are certainly busy hereabouts today," he mused. "Caldwell said he planned to have a talk with Norton to-day, to sort of bury the hatchet after last night's fuss. Maybe Summerton was wanting to talk to the sheriff too, and bury the hatchet—in Norton's skull. It could be, though, that Summerton isn't interested in hatchets, either way, but felt called on to take up Caldwell's argument. Or maybe he's thought up some argument all on his own. Jeepers! I'm probably clear off the trail. Summerton could have been headed someplace else—maybe to see about some bank business with somebody. That's the trouble with my mind. It clicks, but I can never tell what way it's clicking, or how. All I know is, I got a hunch things are moving."

He dropped his cigarette butt on the sidewalk and ground out the ember with the toe of one boot, then sauntered on toward the Blue Gem Saloon. As he came abreast of the place, Vink Deever came reeling out. Deever had taken on a load; that he had a skinful, there was no doubt. His breath smelled like a distillery. He stopped short on seeing Johnny, then braced himself against an upright of the Blue Gem porch roof, where he surveyed Johnny with bloodshot, malice-filled eyes.

"I was jush—just headin' to find you, Barlow," he growled.

Johnny came to a full stop. "I reckon I've saved you some trouble then. Why don't you try to avoid making more for yourself?"

"Don't you tell me what to do," Deever said hotly.

"All right. You've found me. What's on your mind, Deever?"

"I wancha—want—to—know what in hell you mean by tellin' Kirksh—Kirk—I took a shot at you last night."

"I might mean a hell of a lot," Johnny said sharply, "if I'd told Norton that. As a matter of fact, I didn't. I merely asked Norton where you were last night. Norton must have jumped to conclusions."

"I'll tell you where I wash—I was ridin' to the Quarter-Circle-N—no plash else. Anyway, I think you're a liar, Barlow."

"Take it easy, Deever!" Johnny's tones were crisp. "You've been drinking or you'd have more sense than to talk that way."

"You ain't got nothin, on me—"

"At the rate you're travelling, I will have, unless you slow down. You'd best go someplace and sleep off that jag you've taken aboard."

Deever swore violently. "You ain't tellin' me my business, Barlow. You bested me once, but that ain't shayin you can do it 'gain. One of these days, you'n me will meet on even terms, Ranger man— and the shooner the besher." He was fast working himself to a killer rage.

Disgustedly, Johnny started to turn away and enter the Blue Gem. Deever took a quick lurching step and barred the way. "Where in hell do you think you're goin'?"

Johnny snapped, "I warned you, Deever. Go slow! I'm going to tell Norton to put you where you can cool off. Either he does it, or I will."

There were voices from within the saloon now. Steps were approaching the entrance, drawn by Deever's angry tones. Deever snarled, "Like hell you'll tell Norton." He tried to seize Johnny's arm.

Johnny whirled away to avoid the clutching

hand. Momentarily he was facing away from Deever. Deever cursed him again, and Johnny caught the meaning inflection in the tones. Spinning completely around, Johnny drew his six-shooter as he moved. His hand abruptly mushroomed with smoke and flame. A haze of burned black powder filled the air.

Deever reeled back, a yell of fright parting his loose mouth. A bullet from Johnny's Colt gun had struck Deever's holster just as the man started to draw. He was uninjured, but his eyes were wide with fear and he was suddenly sobered. Backing away, hands flung high in the air, he half screamed, "Don't shoot me, Barlow. Don't shoot! I'll—"

"Cripes A'mighty! What goes on here?" Kirk Norton's harsh voice.

The sheriff had come pushing out, followed by Caldwell and several other customers. Johnny had just started to turn and face Norton, when he felt something round and hard boring into the small of his back. "What in hell do you think you're doing, Barlow?" The sheriff's tones were cold, vicious.

Johnny stiffened, then relaxed. Suddenly he laughed softly, and slid his own gun into holster. "You'd best take your hardware away from my spine, Norton. You're heading for trouble."

"Nobody can shoot up one of my men and get away with with it, Border Ranger or not. Nobody! You hear, Barlow? I'm running this town."

Again Johnny laughed. "Nobody's shot up your

man, Norton. I've ruined his holster and maybe damaged the gun some too, but if you had good sense you'd be glad of it. Deever's not harmed any. He picked this fight, but he sure lacked what it took to see it through. I'd like to suggest that you use your brains, if you have any."

"Look here, Kirk"—Caldwell's tones trembled slightly—"this is no way to treat a Ranger. You're just making trouble for yourself. Why don't you put that gun away? Barlow's holstered his."

"I didn't ask for your advice, Caldwell," Norton growled savagely. "You keep out of this. I run this town as I see fit and I don't want any interference." Already his finger was quivering on the trigger of his six-shooter.

Drawn by the sound of the shot and the loud voices, a crowd of men had gathered before the Blue Gem. Exclamations of excitement came from farther down the street and there was the sound of running feet on the sidewalks.

Abruptly, Johnny threw discretion to the wind and whirled suddenly to face Norton. "All right, shoot and be damned, Norton!" he snapped. "And remember that when you do, you'll have the whole Ranger force on your back. Now go ahead! Pull that trigger and see where it gets you."

Norton hesitated. The crimson rage slowly faded from his taut features. He opened his mouth to speak, closed it again without uttering a sound. Slowly he lowered the gun bearing on Johnny, his hard blue eyes still glaring into the Ranger man's.

Johnny was first to break the silence. He said coldly, "You showed good sense, Norton. Now put that gun away and have better sense than to draw it on a Ranger again. I could break you for this little stunt—have you removed from office—but I won't. Maybe you're just over zealous, too anxious to enforce the law. Anyway, we'll lay it to that—and forget the matter. I was on my way to tell you to put Deever where he won't make further trouble. If you refuse to do it I will, but seeing you're sheriff here, I prefer to let you do it."

Norton turned his angry countenance on Vink Deever. "Deever, you and I are through. Come on inside. I'll pay you off."

Without another word Norton turned and pushed through the swinging doors into the Blue Gem. Deever followed reluctantly, a hangdog look on his face. The batwing doors slowly swung to a stop. Johnny drew his gun, plugged out the empty shell and inserted a fresh load in the cylinder. Then he stepped out to the sidewalk. The crowd commenced to disperse. One or two men spoke to Johnny, trying to draw him into conversation, but he shoved on past without replying and started along the street.

He had gone but a short distance when he heard his name called, and turned to see Frank Caldwell hurrying after him. Caldwell's face was streaming with perspiration and he still looked rather shaken.

"I'm sorry that had to happen, Johnny," Caldwell panted, mopping at his features with a bandanna. "It's as you said, Kirk is over zealous. It hurts his pride to have anyone else show authority here. Besides that, I don't think he likes you."

Johnny's sudden laughter filled the air. "That," he exclaimed, "is an understatement if I ever heard one. First Norton orders me to leave town. To-day he throws a gun on me when my back is turned. And now you say he doesn't like me." Johnny chuckled. "Y'know something, Caldwell? I'm commencing to suspect that you may be correct."

Caldwell's face crimsoned and he looked sheepish. "That did sound foolish as hell, didn't it?" he said. "But what I meant was—well, I think you get what I meant, anyway. Sorry the whole damn mess had to break now. I'd just finished having a long talk with Kirk. I thought I had things fixed up and that I'd convinced him it would be best to work with you. Norton has a frightful temper, but I know after he has time to think things over he'll regret his actions—"

"I've reached the point," Johnny said tartly, "where I don't much care what Norton thinks. And Vink Deever had better keep clear of my trail too. If Norton has sense he'll throw Deever into the hoosegow for a few days, or order him to get out of Rawhide City—which would be cheaper for the taxpayers."

"It likely would," Caldwell agreed. "Deever

always has been a rather hard drinker. And quarrelsome. I never could understand why Kirk kept him on his pay roll."

"For a few moments," Johnny stated deliberately, "when Deever started to draw on me, I thought I knew."

Caldwell's jaw sagged. He stared at Johnny, then said weakly, "You—you don't think Norton hired Deever to kill you?"

"Why not?" Johnny asked. "It would solve one problem for Norton. He doesn't want me here. And Deever wasn't quite as drunk as he pretended to be, either. Oh, sure, he'd been drinking, but he'd had just about enough to give him fighting courage. Go on back to the Blue Gem, Caldwell, and ask Norton who's been paying for the drinks Deever has slopped up the past hour or so. I'll lay you a bet they were on Norton. The sheriff just had to stoke the furnace to get it blazing hot—"

"I—I can't believe it," Caldwell protested. There was a look almost of horror in his eyes. "Kirk's reputation has always been of the best here. No, it can't be as you say, Johnny. Norton isn't that kind. If he wanted to kill you, he'd do it himself—or try to—not hire such work to be done."

"As sheriff," Johnny pointed out, "Kirk Norton couldn't afford to kill a Border Ranger; an act of that sort would finish him."

Caldwell shook his head; his hands made futile protesting motions. "I still can't believe you're right, Johnny," he said, helplessly, "but I must admit that Kirk has been acting queerly since you arrived here."

"Too queerly to suit my fancy," Johnny said dryly. "Right now he's done enough to warrant his removal from office. I could have him thrown out of his sheriffing job—only I don't do business that way. Give a man enough rope, you know . . ." He left the sentence unfinished. "Oh yes, there is something else, Caldwell. Is your cashier in the bank now?"

"He's always there during banking hours unless I am," Caldwell replied. "Why? Do you want to see him?"

Johnny nodded his head. "No hurry, though. I'd just like to hear what he has to say about the Falcon holdup and so on—you know, get his slant on the business."

"That's a good idea, though I doubt Jay can tell you much. I wonder if you'd mind waiting until closing time, this afternoon. This is the end of the month, you know, and Jay is head over heels busy, balancing his accounts. He'll likely think clearer when he doesn't have his mind occupied with both ledgers and clients. So if you don't mind waiting until we close—"

"Sure, sure," Johnny interrupted carelessly. "I'm in no particular hurry. Any time will do."

They walked on. After a few minutes Caldwell crossed the street and turned back towards his bank. Johnny glanced at his watch. It was one o'clock, and nearly time for 'Rene to be arriving. At that moment he spied the girl loping into town on her little sorrel gelding. She looked attractive in her mannish flannel shirt, divided riding skirt of deerskin, and high-heeled riding boots. Her wealth of dark hair was tucked beneath a worn fawn-coloured sombrero. Johnny stepped out to the middle of the road and raised one hand to stop her.

## CHAPTER XIV

### "DAD COUNTED THE MONEY"

'RENE and Johnny went first to Doc Duncan's house. The doctor's combination residence and office was an attractive looking frame house, with a huge live oak in the front yard, and a white picket fence surrounding the building. The house was situated at the eastern end of town, some short distance north of Main Street. Duncan himself met 'Rene and Johnny at the door. "Saw you two walking up the path toward the house," he greeted them. "Have you been set afoot?"

"Johnny was about to take his and Mike's ponies to the livery, and I thought mine might as well get a feed and rub down at the same time," 'Rene said. "How's Dad to-day?"

"Getting along famously, 'Rene," Duncan said as he closed the door behind Johnny and the girl.

181

"I allowed him to talk for a few minutes this morning. I told him Johnny Barlow was here. It seemed to brighten him up considerably." Duncan glanced at Johnny. "Matt thinks a lot of you."

"I'm glad to hear it, Doc. That feeling isn't all on one side, either. Is there anything I can do to help the cure along?"

Duncan shook his head. "There's very little anyone can do now, except my wife. She's a mighty capable nurse, and that's about all Matt needs now. I often think that nursing is more important in bringing about recoveries than a doctor's ministrations. Good air, the right food, plenty of rest will do more for a convalescent than anything I know of. An efficient nurse will take care of anything else that's needed. And Mrs. Duncan has had plenty of experience with bullet wounds since we've been married. For a time here, my practice consisted almost entirely of taking care of the unhappy results of gun fights. Then Rawhide City sort of calmed down. Later, Sheriff Norton took a hand in keeping things quiet—Ah, here's my wife now."

A pleasant-faced, middle-aged woman in a stiffly starched nurse's uniform had entered the room. She said, "Hello, 'Rene," and 'Rene returned the greeting.

"Sophie," Doc Duncan said to his wife, "this is Johnny Barlow. Shake hands with a Ranger man. I think there's a chance that Johnny may clear up this stolen money business."

Johnny grinned. "I can't make any promises, but I'm certainly aiming to try and recover that money." He liked the firm hand Mrs. Duncan gave him.

Duncan winked at Johnny, then said, "Sophie, I've just been telling 'Rene and Johnny that I thought Matt would recover in spite of your nursing. It's too bad we haven't a *good* nurse in Rawhide City. I think I'll have to import one from the capital—preferably a young one—"

Sophie Duncan's scornful chuckle interrupted the words. "Doc Duncan," she stated firmly, "you know very well your bungling would lose nine tenths of your patients if I wasn't on hand to save them. You just try bringing any pretty young nurses in here and see what happens to your practice." She turned, smiling, to Johnny and 'Rene. "The doctor doesn't realise it, but if it wasn't for me, he wouldn't get any business. He just has a lot of luck with his cases."

"Now, Sophie—" Duncan started a protest.

Mrs. Duncan laughed. "I'll never forget the first case he had in Rawhide City. Doc was young then, and nervous. The proprietor of our general store came to be treated for a stomach disorder. He was in pain, of course, and he told Doc that he felt sure he was standing in the very doorway of hell—"

Doc Duncan groaned. "Aren't you ever going to let me forget that, Sophie?"

"And Doc said to him, in what was meant to be an encouraging manner, 'Don't worry, Charlie, I'll pull you through.' And to top it off, the town undertaker dropped in at that time to pay a visit. Charlie took one look at Doc and another at the undertaker, and said, 'My Gawd, you fellers sure do work together,' and decided not to remain for Doc's treatment."

Doc said stubbornly, "Anyway, he never had any more stomach trouble, did he?"

"No, you scared it out of him," Sophie Duncan retorted.

'Rene and Johnny laughed with her, and Doc finally joined in. When the group had sobered down again, 'Rene asked, "Are you going to let me talk to Dad to-day, Doc?"

Duncan nodded. "For only a few minutes, though. You'll have to keep that in mind. You don't want to risk weakening Matt."

Johnny asked, "Is it all right for me to see him too?"

Duncan looked dubious, then shook his head. "I'd rather you didn't, Johnny. Too much excitement might bring on a relapse. I just can't risk that. He hasn't seen you for a long time, remember, and seeing you and 'Rene at the same time might tire him, set him back. I'm sorry, but—"

"Sure, Doc, I understand how it is," Johnny said. "You know best. I wonder if it would be all right for 'Rene to ask him a question for me?"

184

"What's the question?"

"I'd like to know," Johnny explained, "if Matt took time to count that money before he started out of the bank with the satchel—you know, just before the Falcon came in and shot him. What I'm getting at, I'd like to know for sure if the money was in that satchel when Matt started to leave."

Duncan frowned, started at first to refuse to allow the question to be asked, then relented. "Maybe a question of that sort wouldn't do any particular harm," he said slowly. "Matt's got a strong heart. He already knows the money is gone. It might encourage him to know you're working on the case, Johnny. With a start like that, he might even remember other details, things that would help you. 'Rene, do you understand what Johnny wants?"

The girl quickly nodded. "All right," Duncan continued. "You can have just five minutes with your dad. Go on in."

'Rene and Mrs. Duncan left the room. Doc offered Johnny a chair and the two men sat down in the doctor's office. A glass-doored cabinet of instruments stood in one corner. There was a leather couch, and a white-enamelled metal table in the centre of the room. Duncan's desk was placed near a side window, and to the right of that were shelves which held medicine jars and bottles, some of them bearing on their labels a red skull and crossbones. A framed diploma from a medical school hung on one wall. The floor was covered with linoleum. For that day and age it was quite a modern-looking office.

Duncan stuffed some tobacco in a briar pipe and struck a match. "Have you run across any clues yet, Johnny?"

Johnny shrugged his muscular shoulders. "Nothing that I could call real important. One or two ideas are clicking in my mind, but I can't seem to make things dovetail to suit me. . . . I dang near stopped a slug of lead last night, though." He told Duncan of the night rider who had shot at him, but neglected to mention the finding of the shaved plug of chewing tobacco and sheriff's badge.

Duncan scowled and drew steadily on his pipe. "That sort of thing seems to indicate that somebody doesn't like the idea of a Border Ranger being here."

Johnny said dryly, "That idea has occurred to me too. By the way, do you know Sheriff Trigg, from the next county? He'll be in town to-morrow, I expect."

"Yes, I know Elson Trigg well. What's he coming here for?"

"I sent for him to identify the Falcon's corpse."

"You mean you're going to open the grave?" Johnny nodded, and Duncan went on in a puzzled tone, "But I thought Norton had already identified the Falcon's body."

Johnny said, "It will have to be identified by a

second person as well, before Norton can collect the reward offered."

Duncan's face cleared. "Oh, I see. It's a wonder Kirk didn't take care of that sort of thing. But then I suppose no one else in town knew the Falcon."

"Probably not. Anyway, Norton told me he didn't want a reward for doing his duty—said he wasn't interested in the money."

"That could be so," Duncan said. "Kirk is like that. A cold, hard individual, but just as upright as they come. A mite quick on the trigger—and temper too—at times. But we all have faults."

Johnny smiled. "Norton has his, I reckon. Say, Doc, were you in the bank the day they opened the satchel and found the money had been replaced with chunks of rock?"

"Yes, I was there."

"Was there any chance that the satchel of money might have been exchanged for a satchel of rock after it came into the bank?"

"Not a chance," Duncan said promptly, "as I see it. I was working over Matt, of course, but just the same I don't think any switch of the satchels could have been made at that time. Also in the bank, besides myself and Matt—though Matt was in no condition to be alert right then—were Norton, Caldwell, Jay Summerton, and Meticulous Jones. Even if one of those men was guilty, he couldn't have exchanged satchels without the others seeing the transaction."

At that moment 'Rene and Mrs. Duncan re-entered the doctor's office. The girl was smiling cheerfully. "Doc, Dad seems ever so much better than I expected. You've worked wonders." Duncan said something about all credit being due to the nurse. 'Rene turned to Johnny: "I asked Dad about counting that money."

"Well, did he?" Johnny asked eagerly.

'Rene nodded her head. "Jay Summerton brought the satchel of money into Mr. Caldwell's office. Dad signed the note for it, then opened the satchel and counted the ten thousand. The amount was correct. He replaced the money, closed the satchel, and started to leave. At that instant, the Falcon appeared. Father remembers being shot, and he has a sort of vague recollection of seeing the Falcon leaving the door with the satchel, but that is all. He says everything was pretty blurred about that time. . . . Does this help you any, Johnny?"

"Maybe it does," was the noncommittal reply, "but then again maybe it just tangles things worse. Danged if I'm sure which."

The four talked a few minutes longer, then 'Rene and Johnny took their departure, walking slowly, and closely together, in the direction of Main Street. Once back on the principal thoroughfare, Johnny said, "Now we'll go to the Kansas City Chop House and stow away a bait."

"Johnny, that would be lovely, but I can't. I've

got to get back home. I've been going over Dad's papers. Things are in a terrible mess, financially. We're going to be cleaned out—"

"If I die," Johnny said solemnly, "it will be all your fault."

"Die?" 'Rene looked startled. "Die of what?"

"Starvation, undernourishment, anemia. I've waited all this time for you to arrive and help me choose the proper food. Now if you won't help me, you'll just have to be responsible for the consequences. Right now, I'm so weak I could sag in the gutter—"

"But, Johnny—" 'Rene commenced.

"But me no buts. This is no time to debate, woman. Look at me. This is a critical period in our lives. I'm so feeble from lack of chow I can scarce walk straight, and it's all your fault—"

'Rene laughed. "Johnny Barlow, with those legs you never did walk straight."

"That's right," Johnny said aggrievedly, "poke fun at a feller because his saddle pins are slightly warped. Well, you're wrong, if you think they got this way from riding. It come about by accident. I'd been swimming and I sat too close to the fire when I was drying out. Really, 'Rene, I ain't bow-legged. It's just that my pins are sagging from weakness. Blame it on the lack of beans and pie and beef." Johnny's tones were plaintive. "I was so desperate for food a spell back that I even took to eatin' tobacco, to tide me over until you arrived."

"Johnny Barlow!" The girl wrinkled her nose distastefully.

"It's a fact. Come on with me and I'll tell you all about it while we're eating."

"Johnny, I can't. Honestly. Come out to the house to-night and tell me about it."

Johnny grinned suddenly. "I knew I'd get an invite to come calling. Just can't resist me, can you?" His face fell suddenly. "Jeepers! I should stay in town to-night."

"We-ell, in that case," 'Rene consented, "I suppose I could come with you. I do have to eat dinner sometime—"

Johnny grinned. "Suppose nothing. You know you're really anxious to eat with me. It isn't every girl I'd give that chance to. I'll bet a lot of folks will get to wondering why I honour you in this way."

"Of all the conceited, no-account, fresh—"

"I deny the last two accusations. I admit to being conceited, though. Cripes! Who wouldn't be conceited with a pretty girl like you to take to dinner?"

"Well, that's a little better." The girl's eyes sparkled. "Aren't you exaggerating a little bit, though."

"Not a mite. I'm understating, and talking fast to make up for all the years I haven't seen you."

"Why should you?"

"That's something I'll tell you while we're eating. C'mon."

190

Arm in arm, they walked, laughing, along the street, until they'd reached the Kansas City Chop House. At the restaurant they lingered long over their cups of coffee, and ordered additional cups while 'Rene rolled cigarettes for Johnny. At this hour the restaurant was deserted; only a cook and waitress were in the kitchen washing dishes.

". . . and after I leave here," Johnny was saying, "I'll slope back to headquarters and resign. When they ask why, I'll tell 'em how you promised to marry me—"

"But I didn't—"

"You're going to, aren't you?" anxiously.

"Johnny, you work too fast—"

"I told you I had to make up for lost time. You are, aren't you?"

A mischievous light sparkled in 'Rene's dark eyes. "You tell me you're going to resign," she said in dubious tones. "And I'm going to be flat broke. And you forget, the upstanding sheriff of Creaking River County has asked me to marry him."

Johnny swore under his breath. "You said 'no' to him once," he reminded.

"Did you ever see a woman who couldn't change her mind? It's a woman's prerogative."

"That's a good word. Let's not overwork it though. As for Kirk Norton, I'd like to wring his neck, or get something on him," Johnny finished savagely.

"Could that neck wringing be arranged before I married him, Johnny? I'd hate to be a widow."

He gazed at her in sudden admiration. "You'd look beautiful in black, 'Rene—if you were in mourning for Kirk Norton—"

"And a girl does have to consider her appearance," 'Rene said thoughtfully. "Maybe I will marry him first."

Johnny assumed a look of horror. " 'Rene! You couldn't! Norton's got a vice—he chews tobacco."

"You were going to wring his neck right after I married him, anyway, weren't you? So what difference—" The girl broke off and became serious. "Johnny, Tex Houston told me about you and Mike finding his sheriff's star and the plug of tobacco."

Johnny nodded. "That was something I intended speaking to you about—and how come I took to chewing this morning."

"Was it Kirk Norton's badge?"

"It actually was. But I'm not so sure the tobacco was his. Here's what happened since I saw you last. . . ." From that point Johnny continued and related the various incidents that had taken place since he and Vallejo had left the Lazy-Double-M that morning.

When he had concluded 'Rene looked serious. Something of fright had touched her dark eyes. "Johnny, Johnny," she said, shaking her head, "I don't like it—not at all. And that Deever! I'm sure he intended to kill you. And even the sheriff! With his temper—" She paused. "Isn't there some way all this trouble can be settled without you risking your life—?"

"You know better than to ask that, 'Rene. And I'm not running much risk. I aim to keep about a mile ahead of whoever is stirring up all this skulduggery. I'm behind in the running now, but I'll catch up—you'll see!"

'Rene still looked worried, despite his assurances. "But you will be careful, won't you, Johnny?"

"Any special reason?" Johnny asked carelessly, trying to keep his tones steady.

"Something more?" A new voice broke in. It was the waitress standing at their table; the girl had been eyeing Johnny and 'Rene from a discreet distance for some time.

Johnny glanced up. "Yeah," he said with a smile, "there was a lot more to come, but I guess you wouldn't understand. . . . Oh no, there was nothing wrong with the dinner. It was *muy elegante*—fine!"

'Rene broke in. "Johnny, it's way after three o'clock now. I've got to get home. Besides, Mike is probably looking for you."

They rose and left the table. Johnny paid the bill. Outside, he accompanied the girl to the livery stable to get her horse, though she spurned his help in getting into the saddle. The sorrel gelding moved out to the street, Johnny walking by the horse's head. He said, "I'll be seeing you to-night, then."

"Why, you said you had to stay in town to-night."

"I used your woman's prerogative to change my mind." He grinned.

"That is a pretty good word, Johnny."

"It's a pretty good woman, if you ask me," he said with a laugh. "And I plan to see her again to-night."

"You're not letting me interfere with your duties?" 'Rene asked.

"Certainly I am. Love always interferes with duty, work, thought, or anything else. On the other hand, I've got to get certain ideas into your head, or I won't be able to 'tend my duties. Anyway, Mike wants to win his *pesos* back from Soup-Kettle—"

"That has nothing to do with you. Had you intended to stay in town for anything important?"

"Just to see if I could pick up a clue around some-place," he said dryly, "but shucks, to-morrow will do. There're always plenty of clues lying around waiting to be picked up—according to what I read in books, anyway. Trouble is "—he was serious momentarily—" I just don't always see 'em waiting. I can blame my thick head, I suppose. Or maybe sometimes I just go plain blind—"

"But what did you mean, to-morrow will do?"

"We-ell," he said hesitantly, "if something happens, I'll know that—well, that something has happened."

'Rene looked exasperated. "You're just exuding information, aren't you?"

"Not information—perspiration. I'm really working, girl, even if I don't look it. To tell the truth, 'Rene, I just can't explain yet what will happen. It has to do with identifying the holdup man's body. And I can't tell you the details about that either—not until I have more time."

"Right, cowboy, you're the boss." She sat her saddle easily, looking down at him.

Johnny glanced up, met her eyes. "Will you admit that one year from now?"

"I'd be lost," she said in a steady voice, "if I ever admitted anything to you."

"And then you'd need me around to help you find yourself."

The girl didn't answer that. She touched spurs to the sorrel, called good-bye, and loped the pony out of town, in a cloud of dust.

Johnny stood grinning happily after her, until, suddenly becoming conscious of the curious looks directed his way by passing pedestrians, he reddened sheepishly, mumbled replies to two or three people who had spoken to him, and then set out in the direction of the Clinic Saloon.

# CHAPTER XV

## WORD OF MEX LOUIE

H E was halfway to the Clinic Saloon when Johnny saw Vallejo advancing along the sidewalk. The Mexican's eyes lighted up when they fell on Johnny, and an expression of relief passed across his features.

"Johnee!" Vallejo said when they'd come abreast. "You are all right? Ees good."

"Why shouldn't I be all right, Mike?"

"I was not sure. Firs', where have you been? I'm look from one end of theese town to the othair, but of Johnee Barlow there ees no sign. I was growing worry."

"Jeepers! I'm sorry. 'Rene came to town. We went to Doc Duncan's to see about Matt, then 'Rene and I had dinner at the Kansas City Chop House. Somehow we got to talking and drinking Java and time just passed on. I should have left word with Ernie where we were."

Vallejo smiled and shrugged his shoulders. *"No importa."*

"T'hell it's not important!" Johnny contradicted. "It always matters when a pard is worried about a friend. I'm sorry as the devil. But you were just wasting your time bothering over my welfare."

196

Mike's smile broadened. "And you—deed you waste also of the time, Johnee?"

Johnny reddened. "I sure talked, *amigo,* but I don't think I've got her convinced yet. I told her we'd be out to the ranch to-night."

"Yes?" Vallejo looked surprised. "I theenk you plan to stay in Rawhide Ceety to-night. Ees that not what you say?"

"I was thinking of you, Mike," Johnny said hypocritically. "I remembered you liked to shuffle the pasteboards, and figured you'd want to make a try for getting back the money you lost to Soup-Kettle Simpson. That poker game will likely be going again to-night—"

"But I'm theenk we plan to stay and keep the eye on Sheriff Norton to-night—see what he do."

"All right." Johnny's flush deepened. "I give up. To tell the truth, Mike, I'm going to the Lazy-Double-M to-night because I'm in love, head over heels in love with—"

"—weeth the sweetes', deares', girl in the world," Vallejo finished with considerable irony in his soft laughter. "Johnee! I have listen to hondreds of hombres say those very word. Men are all the same when they are een love. Love, eet is a disease of the heart that affect the brain and then burst in the purse, I'm theenk. No?"

"Maybe you've hit it, Mike." Johnny grinned foolishly.

"Of course I'm heet eet. *Bueno!* Good, Johnny,

*amigo.* I cannot blame you. 'Rene is lovely, and I'm theenk will provide for you the ideal *compañera. Si,* you make the ride to the ranch. I shall stay and watch the sheriff."

"Nothing doing," Johnny refused abruptly. "If I'm going to loaf on the job, you can have your pleasure too. After all, it doesn't matter too much. If something happens to-morrow, when the time comes to identify that corpse, we'll know that Norton didn't make a mistake when he called the dead man the Falcon. He knew what he was doing." Johnny paused. "Have you learned anything?"

Mike nodded, and the two started in the direction of the Clinic Saloon. "I'm tell you what I have learn in a minute, Johnee. But first, I'm hear you have the run-in with Vink Deever and Sheriff Norton."

"It didn't amount to much." Johnny shrugged. He told Vallejo what had taken place.

The Mexican looked soberly at Johnny. "You take too many of the chances, *amigo.* Eet is bes' that you be more careful."

"I don't think this is the time to be careful, Mike. We've got certain people in Rawhide City asking themselves questions they can't answer. Now's the time for us to keep the pressure on, show 'em we can't be buffaloed. No, I'm not worrying about anything Norton might do. As for Vink Deever—"

"I have also hear that Deever was seen leaving town."

Johnny nodded. "Norton said he was going to fire the bustard. You sure Deever has left?"

"He was seen rideeng away. I hear he has told all of hees friends good-bye."

"Maybe it's true, then. It could be that Deever and Norton have parted company for good—certainly it couldn't be for bad. I somehow wonder, though. Maybe they're both staging an act to fool me. And then, maybe it's all on the level. Anyway, we'll learn eventually. . . . Have you found out anything regarding Mex Louie?"

"A little. Pairhaps to you eet will mean a lot. After much searching I found the *padre*—the father—of Mex Louie. He is a vairy old man— more than one hondred year. What you call feeble in the mind. And een the body. Hees teeth are but few—how you say it?—snags? *Sí,* that ees eet. Hees teeth are a few snags. Ah, that padre of Mex Louie, he have not many more days on theese earth. He lives alone. At firs', he could not remembair if Mex Louie had come to Rawhide Ceety recently. Then it comes to him and he recollects that Mex Louie was een town at the time of the holdup."

"Now we're getting some place," Johnny commented grimly. "This begins to sound like pay dirt, Mike. But I'm interrupting. Get on with the story."

"Mex Louie has been away from Rawhide Ceety for many year," the Mexican continued. "Then, of a sudden, he appear at hees home to visit hees padre, and to beg for food. *También*—also—he demand of hees padre a few coins the old one have save. Mex Louie, I theenk, have nevair been the good son. Hees padre call heem the *ladron*—a thief—if not worse. With the coins he goes to buy liquor. Within time he returns. He has had the liquor and talks much, telling he has met the Señor Sheriff, and of how Norton has work for heem the next morning, work that will bring in many of *pesos*. Mex Louie does not tell what sort of work. Then once more he goes away. Hees padre has not see heem since. That is all. Does theese mean anytheeng to you, Johnee?"

"It sounds mighty important." Johnny sounded enthusiastic. "So Norton was going to give Mex Louie work, eh? Work that would bring in many dollars. Mike, we'll yet put a rope around Norton's neck. Now we know that Norton was definitely acquainted with Mex Louie at the very time he denied the holdup man was Mex Louie. Unless"— Johnny's face fell—"unless the father was mistaken, or lying."

"Can you theenk of a reason why he should lie?"

"I'm damned if I can, Mike—unless his feeble mind was dreaming up things. Good work! Have you learned anything else?"

"About Mex Louie, no," Vallejo replied. "Regarding the cashier of the bank, yes."

"Jay Summerton?"

"That ees the hombre. I visited the livery stable.

200

Last evening theese Jay Summerton hire a saddle horse. The horse was not return ontil theese morneeng."

Johnny whistled softly in surprise. "Jay Summerton! Good lord, could it be Summerton who rode out to the Lazy-Double-M last night and took that pot shot at me? . . . Hmmm . . . I've got to see that hombre, question him a mite, and learn how he shapes up. It must be nearly closing time at the bank."

He glanced at the sun. It was swinging far to the west, toward the peaks of the Sangre de Santos Range. "Close to four o'clock," Johnny commented. "Well, I told Caldwell I'd not bother Summerton until the bank had closed. I'll keep my word. Mike, here's the Clinic just ahead. What say we drop in and wash some of the alky dust out of our gullets? That's a good excuse, anyway."

The Mexican smiled. "For a drink I do not need the excuse, Johnee."

The old wall clock hanging above the Clinic bar showed the time as eight minutes to four when Vallejo and Johnny entered the saloon. Guy Gerard and Fargo Delroy were standing at the bar, conversing with three or four other customers, all in citizens' clothing. Two punchers from the HB-Connected were playing a desultory game of seven-up at a round wooden table in one corner of the bar-room. Johnny and Mike spoke to the men at the bar, then gave orders to Ernie Braughn.

Ernie set out a bottle of beer and Mike's usual tequila set-up.

"Back again, eh?" Gerard smiled. "You sure make to ambulate around, Ranger man. I hear you had a little ruckus with the sheriff and Vink Deever this morning. I got there too late. Sorry I missed it."

Johnny nodded casually. "You didn't miss much. Norton lost control of his temper for a minute, but things turned out all right. He run Deever out of town, and that's what I was after."

"You make it sound simple," Fargo Delroy put in. "That's not the way I heard it. I heard Norton had a gun on you and was about to pull trigger until you bluffed him into backing down."

"Jeepers," Johnny said wearily, "you can hear a lot of things in this town." He poured some beer into his glass and sipped it appreciatively.

One of the HB-Connected punchers playing cards glanced around and spoke to Johnny. "Did you say Deever had left town?" He looked surprised.

"Yes, so I understand," Johnny replied. "Friend of yours, or did he owe you some money, cowboy?"

The puncher swore softly at the hand of cards he had drawn, then glanced back at Johnny. "Neither," he answered. "Only Curly, here"—he motioned toward the other card player—"and me spoke to Deever at the edge of town when we were riding in."

Johnny cocked one inquiring eyebrow. "That right? What was he doing? How long ago did you boys ride in?"

"An hour or so back," came the reply. "Deever was sitting in the shade of that big cottonwood tree, at the east end of town. His hawss was staked out, croppin' grass. It didn't look to me like Deever was takin' out. I figured him as just sittin' there, killin' time, while he waited for somebody—or somethin'. It don't seem likely if he was goin' away he'd stop to rest that soon."

"No, it don't, does it?" Johnny agreed idly. He appeared to have lost interest in the subject.

"Maybe," Guy Gerard put in, "Deever figures to head across those alkali flats south of town, and ride for the border, when it gets cooler."

"That's possible," Johnny shrugged carelessly.

The card players continued with their game. Johnny and Vallejo lounged over their drinks at the bar. They rolled cigarettes and lighted them. Vallejo spoke to Johnny a couple of times, but Johnny appeared to be but half listening. He was lost in thought: where did Jay Summerton fit into the puzzle of the missing money? More and more Johnny was beginning to feel that Summerton might prove to be the key to the solution. But why? Johnny shook his head hopelessly. It was, he admitted readily, pure instinct—call it hunch, perhaps—which persistently continued to intrude Summerton's form into the picture. Actually, there was nothing to go on. Just pure hunch, Johnny thought gloomily. And how often could a man depend on a hunch to give him the right lead?

Johnny spoke to Vallejo. "I'm going to drift up to the bank within a few minutes and see if I can talk to Summerton. Do you want to come along?"

The Mexican considered, then shook his head. He kept his voice low as Johnny had done. "Pairhaps eet is bes' eef you go alone, Johnee. If theese Summerton knows anytheeng of the robbery, he might talk frankly to one man, where he would-what you call heem?—clam up weeth two. I have hear that Summerton is a very quiet hombre. Often these quiet hombre are the mos' suspicious, and weel not talk at all if they get scar'."

Johnny shoved his sombrero to one side of his head, and ran long fingers through his red hair. "I know," he admitted; "that's what I'm afraid of. If I go bargin' into the bank and tell Summerton I want to talk to him, he's likely to get plumb wary—if he does know something about the holdup. But how am I going to get to talk to him, otherwise? I can't wait too long for chance to throw us together. But if I appear too eager, he might shy off. Clam up, as you call it."

"You theenk he knows sometheeng of importance?"

Johnny nodded. "But don't ask why I think so," he said irritably, "because I'm not sure. Call it hunch, if you like. Maybe it was seeing Caldwell

204

and him arguing on the street to-day—at least the man fitted the description I've had of Summerton. Though I'm damned if I know what they were arguing about. Likely I'm crazy as hell. If the truth was known, the argument was probably whether Zeke Cowraiser's beef stock was worth lending money on and if so, should Zeke be charged five or six per cent. Mike, I've thought and thought on this blasted business, until my head's in a whirl—and the faster it whirls, the less I know."

Before Vallejo could reply, a narrow-shouldered, pale-featured individual close to thirty years of age entered the saloon. He wore a narrow-brimmed soft hat and his clothing was of some greyish-black material. His pale eyes peered nervously about the saloon as he paused uncertainly just within the entrance.

Ernie Braughn spoke to him. "Hello, Jay. Lost your dawg?"

A wan smile crossed the man's face. "You should know, Ernie, I never owned a dog." He nodded to Gerard and Delroy, then continued, "I'm looking for that Ranger fellow who came to town."

Johnny stiffened slightly. Ernie had called the man Jay. This was likely Jay Summerton. It was the same man he'd witnessed arguing with Caldwell. A certain elation ran through Johnny. Maybe this was the break he'd been hoping for. This could be it! He turned lazily, unconcernedly, toward Summerton. "Would you be meaning me, mister?"

Summerton studied Johnny a moment, then came to a decision. "If your name is Barlow—Johnny Barlow—that's who I mean."

Johnny suppressed a yawn. "I'm Johnny Barlow. And I'm a Border Ranger. What can I do for you?" He was sizing up the man as he spoke. Undoubtedly, Summerton was nervous. He was a rather weak-looking individual, his eyes vacillating, his chin none too pronounced.

Ernie Braughn broke in, "Johnny, this is Jay Summerton, Banker Caldwell's cashier. Jay, shake hands with our Ranger man."

Summerton crossed to the bar. Johnny took his hand and noted the limp, soft-fingered grasp. Well, he thought, he shouldn't hold that against Summerton. After all, the man wasn't too well.

Summerton said in an uncertain voice, "I wonder if I could see you for a few minutes, Mr. Barlow."

"Sure," Johnny replied casually, "longer than that, if necessary. I was sort of figuring on walking down to the bank to see you, after a spell. Nothing important. I just wanted to get your ideas regarding that Falcon business."

"Yes, Mr. Caldwell said he asked you to wait until the bank was closed. It was his idea that maybe we could both answer your questions—but I don't know. I thought maybe you'd like to hear what I had to tell you—"

"Sure enough, Summerton. What's on your mind?"

The cashier hesitated, then, "I'd like to see you privately if possible."

Johnny nodded. "I reckon that can be arranged."

Ernie Braughn broke in. "Say, Johnny, why don't you and Jay go in my back room there?" He jerked one thumb over his shoulder, toward the door of a back room at the rear of the saloon, "You can close the door and be as private as you like. Or, if it's too stuffy there—gets pretty close some afternoons— you can continue on out the back way. There's nothing back there but a pile of rubbish—tin cans, old bottles, and so on. The nearest buildings are some distance off. You can be as private as you like."

"Thanks, Ernie," Johnny said. "That back room will just fill the bill."

He led the way to the back room, followed by Summerton. Once within the small back room, he closed the door at their backs. Only a murmur of voices from the bar reached through the pine partition. In the back wall of the room was a low window, somewhat scratched by the sandy blasts of desert winds, and a closed door. A cot with folded blankets was placed against one wall. At its head stood a small stand holding a washbowl and pitcher. A couple of towels hung on a rack. The floor was of bare pine boards.

Johnny motioned to the two chairs and table in the centre of the room. "Guess we can talk here without being interrupted, Summerton. There's no need for us to go outside."

He dropped into one of the chairs, making certain that Summerton took the remaining one facing the window. He wanted to study the cashier's face in the light that penetrated the scratched surface of the glass. Somewhat timorously, Summerton sat down; his nervousness had increased and he seemed at a loss how to begin.

To place the man at his ease, Johnny said genially, "Shucks! I forgot. Can I have a drink brought in for you?"

Summerton shook his head. "No, thank you. I never drink. The state of my health—well, I'm just better off without it." He paused. "Mr. Caldwell— er—that is—well—" Again he fell silent, as though trying to marshal his thoughts.

Johnny said quietly, "You've worked for Caldwell a number of years, haven't you?"

"Yes, I have. He's a very good man to work for. I feel that he just about saved my life when I first came out here. When nobody else would give me work, he gave me my position in the bank. I owe him almost more than I can say." He paused, as though doubtful what to say next. Johnny began to get an impression that Summerton wished he'd never taken this step.

Abruptly, Summerton changed the subject. "Mr. Caldwell tells me you had some trouble with Vink Deever to-day."

Johnny shrugged his shoulders. "It was Deever who had the most trouble. It didn't bother me to any extent. I got what I wanted when Sheriff Norton ordered Deever to leave town."

Summerton looked surprised. "Is that right? Are you sure? Why, I saw Deever on Main Street just a few minutes before I came here."

"That's possible, I suppose," Johnny said easily. "Maybe he changed his mind about leaving. More likely Sheriff Norton gave him twenty-four hours to get out, and he's taking full advantage of his time."

"No doubt that's it," Summerton said nervously.

"Oh well," Johnny went on, "we don't have to waste time talking about Deever—or did you come to see me concerning Deever?"

"Oh no—not at all." Again Summerton halted.

"In that case," Johnny prompted, "there was something special you wanted to talk about, I suppose."

Summerton nodded reluctantly. "Yes. Or so it seems to me. I understand you're here looking into that robbery the Falcon perpetrated. Maybe I can give you a clue. On the other hand, you may not think it means anything."

"There's no telling until I hear what you have to say. I want to hear about it anyhow."

Again Summerton hesitated. "I spoke to Mr. Caldwell about it," he continued slowly, "but he said it wasn't worth while to bother you with. I started out to look for you this noon, but Mr.

Caldwell persuaded me there was no hurry and I might just as well wait until the bank had closed. I suppose he was right—it wouldn't do to keep clients waiting."

Johnny said, "I saw you standing on the sidewalk talking to Frank Caldwell around noontime. Then you went into the bank together. Were you discussing this clue you mention then?"

"That's right," Summerton answered, and fell silent.

Johnny smiled. "Your clue may be important or it may not, Jay," he said in friendly tones, "but I want to hear about it. You've got my curiosity aroused. Are you going to keep me in suspense all afternoon? After all, if you know something worth while—and I'll decide if it is or not—it's your civic duty to tell me about it. So go right ahead. Speak up. If it's anything that's likely to harm some innocent person, you have my word that I'll act with discretion."

Thus reassured, Summerton began. "Now I wouldn't want to get anybody in the wrong with the law," he said earnestly, "and what I'm going to tell you, I'd like you to keep secret. I wouldn't want to harm an innocent man, even if appearances did seem to be against him—" He broke off, swallowed hard; his eyes roamed nervously around the room.

Johnny suppressed a wave of impatience. "I'm waiting, Jay. I've already told you no one who is blameless will be harmed if I can help it. Now let's have your information."

Summerton's tongue licked at dry lips. "This may not amount to a thing," he continued. "Mr. Caldwell has already spoken to Sheriff Norton and—" Again came that exasperating halt in Summerton's speech.

Mentally, Johnny gave vent to a certain profanity. Good lord! Was this Summerton hombre going to have to have his story dragged out of him a few words at a time? Johnny decided to shock the man into a greater volubility. He said casually, "Jay, I've been wondering if your story has anything to do with that pony you hired at the livery last evening?"

The question brought results. Summerton's jaw dropped. He slumped in his chair. "How—how did you know—about that?" he stammered.

With an effort he pushed up out of the chair, his eyes darting here and there like those of some trapped animal. His usually pale features were now the colour of dirty ashes. His frightened gaze went to the rear door, then shifted to the window, as though seeking a way out. The look of fright on his face abruptly changed to one of extreme horror. He staggered back, one arm upflung before his head, as though to ward off some unexpected attack.

"What the hell's wrong?" Johnny exclaimed, but even before the words were out of his mouth there came the shattering roar of a Colt six-shooter.

# CHAPTER XVI

## POWDER SMOKE!

EVEN as the broken glass was jangling to the floor and the vibrations of the shot were blurring his hearing, Johnny was up, kicking from behind him the chair on which he'd been seated. His movement came not an instant too soon. The gun at the broken window roared a second time, and Johnny sensed, rather than heard, the whine of the bullet as it passed dangerously close to his body. The drawing of his own weapon had been a miracle of swift reflex action, and Johnny felt the butt of the weapon jump into his hand almost before he realized it, his gaze and the muzzle of the six-shooter turning toward the window at the same instant.

Even as he fired at the disappearing face of Vink Deever, Johnny knew his shot had missed. Powder smoke swirled in the room. As he leaped for the door, Johnny saw from the corner of an eye the struggling form of Jay Summerton trying to rise from the floor. But there was no time to attend to Summerton now. The men in the saloon could do that.

Ernie Braughn's voice and the startled sounds of the customers reached Johnny through the partition. He was at the back door now, one hand fumbling at the knob. As luck would have it, the door was locked. The key wasn't in the lock. Johnny looked quickly about, hoping to find it on a nail somewhere, but it wasn't in sight.

From the bar-room came the sound of running feet. The next moment Miguel burst into the small room, other men following closely behind.

"Johnee! What is wrong? Are you hurt?" Then, as the Mexican discovered Jay Summerton on the floor: "*Poder de Dios!* What is happen?"

Crash! Johnny had hurled the full force of his muscular body against the locked door. It yielded a trifle, but the lock held. "Not hurt," he panted. "Vink Deever—shoved his gun—through the window—"

There came a sharp splintering sound as Johnny again flung his weight against the door. He drew back for a third try, still talking: "See to Summerton, Mike. He took one of Deever's slugs. See if he'll talk—"

A third time Johnny charged the stubborn door. This time the hinges ripped loose from the frame. The door fell outward. Johnny fought to save his momentum, but it was too late. He went sprawling after the door, and fell in a heap in the dust beyond the doorway.

Fortunately the fall saved his life: a leaden slug ripped into the doorjamb at a point covered by his body but an instant before. A few yards away, Vink Deever defiantly sat his horse, six-shooter raised for another shot.

Catlike, Johnny rolled over and over, until he had gained the partial shelter of a pile of rubbish. A bullet from Deever's gun raised dust from the pile. Johnny was still moving. He came to his feet, his right hand spurting lances of white flame. He steadied himself, then unleashed two more shots, close together.

Abruptly Vink Deever's body stiffened in his saddle. Frightened at the explosions of the heavy-calibre weapons, Deever's horse shied to one side. Deever had dropped his gun by this time and both hands clutched frantically at the saddle horn. An expression of dismay, combined with pain and hatred, contorted the man's features.

Quite suddenly he relaxed his grip and slid to the earth. A spasmodic shudder ran through his body, and then he was still. Black powder smoke drifted lazily in the clean air.

Johnny didn't stop to examine Deever's body. It wasn't necessary. He'd seen small puffs of dust rise from Deever's vest, and knew his shots were fatal ones. Plugging out his empty shells, Johnny reloaded and started back for the rear door of the Clinic. Already men were emerging from that door. Pushing through them, he gained the small back room once more, then passed on into the bar where Ernie and Vallejo already had Summerton laid on a table. The cashier's eyes were closed and for a moment Johnny thought he was already dead.

Men were crowding in at the front entrance of the saloon. Ernie sent a man running to Doc Duncan, then dashed around the corner of his bar for whisky and water. Johnny and Vallejo loosened the wounded man's clothing. A great crimson blot welled out of the cashier's breast.

Johnny shook his head. "You can't argue with that kind of a wound. Summerton's a goner. I'd sure like to know what he was going to tell me though. Blast such luck and damn Vink Deever!"

Vallejo looked up suddenly. "You got Deever?"

Johnny said grimly, "There isn't any Deever—not any more." He called to the barkeeper. "Speed up with that liquor, Ernie."

Ernie came hurrying back. Johnny forced a few drops of liquor between Summerton's pallid lips, then bathed his face with water. He spoke to the ring of curious bystanders: "Keep back, will you, men? Summerton needs all the air he can get." The men moved back. Some of them went out the rear way to learn what had happened to Vink Deever. There was a good deal of yelling and the sounds of running feet, both on the street and at the rear of the Clinic Saloon.

Sheriff Norton came shoving through the crowd. "What's wrong here?" he demanded harshly. His eyes were cold on the unconscious form of the cashier, then his gaze went to Johnny.

Johnny didn't speak, or even look up. Ernie Braughn explained briefly, "I didn't see it, Kirk, but I guess Deever tried to kill Johnny. Summerton got hit in the mix-up."

"Deever!" Norton's tones expressed surprise. "You sure? I gave Deever orders to leave town."

Johnny spoke coldly over one shoulder: "I reckon your orders don't mean much, Sheriff. Deever came back." He again bent to the wounded cashier.

"Where's Deever now?" Norton demanded with an oath. "I'll tend to that bustard plenty fast—"

"You're too late to do that, Norton," Johnny cut in without looking up. "I've already sent him out of town. You'll find his carcass out back."

Cursing angrily, Norton again pushed through the ring of spectators and headed toward the rear doorway. Johnny let a few more drops of whisky trickle down Summerton's throat. Summerton's breath was becoming more shallow every minute that passed. Finally his eyelids fluttered, then opened. He gazed vacantly about, then tried to speak.

"Listen, Jay," Johnny said, "don't waste words. Just try to tell me what you started to."

Summerton's lips parted, then he caught his breath sharply. He tried to speak. Blood welled up in his throat, choking him. A groan of pain worked through the crimson-stained lips. With a clean bandanna, Johnny wiped away the blood, held the glass of water to the man's mouth and followed it with more whisky.

"Try to tell me, Jay," Johnny begged. "I know it's important. You've simply got to give me a hint—"

He broke off. Summerton was trying to say something. The words were thick, faint, unintelligible. Johnny placed one ear close to Summerton's mouth. His brow was creased with concentration, but it did little good. He straightened up and swore in exasperation.

"Damn! I can't get it—can't make out what he's trying to say." He looked appealingly at Mike, then once more bent close to the dying cashier. "Try again, Jay, please."

Once more came the faintly spoken words, the accents blurred with approaching death. Johnny shook his head, glanced at Vallejo. "It sounded like Summerton said 'to . . . coat closet.'" He turned back to Summerton. "Is that it? To coat closet? The Falcon made you get into the coat closet? We know that, Jay"—as Summerton's eyes brightened a trifle—"but what happened next?"

Caldwell's voice was heard at the entrance. Summerton gasped, more clearly this time, "Caldwell." The final syllable trailed away into silence. Already Summerton's eyes had begun to assume a glassy look, then they slowly closed. Johnny straightened up, defeat written plainly on his features. "It's all over," he said hopelessly.

Then Caldwell's voice again: "God Almighty! It's Jay!"

"He called your name a minute back," Johnny said slowly.

"Is that all?" Caldwell produced his handerchief and loudly blew his nose.

"He was trying to say something else," Johnny went on, "but all I could make out was something about the Falcon shoving him into a clothes closet."

Doc Duncan came hurrying in, carrying his black bag. He took one look at the lifeless clay and asked Johnny, "Am I too late?"

Johnny said, "Too late, Doc. I doubt you could have done much anyway. He was hit bad, and didn't have too much strength to begin with."

Caldwell bowed his head and turned away. A minute later he asked, "Will some of you men help me carry poor Jay to the undertaker?"

Norton came bristling back. He glared at Johnny. "I suppose you know you killed Deever."

Johnny said, "*I* told you that before you went out back. You're a mite late with your news, Norton."

Norton's eyes hardened, then he relaxed. "You don't need to be so proddy, Barlow. Maybe we don't always agree, but in Deever's case I call it good riddance to bad rubbish."

Johnny smiled frigidly. "You're certain'y fiddling a different tune, Sheriff. I expected you'd be trying to arrest me."

Norton glared at Johnny, then ignored the words. His gaze went to the dead cashier. "Summerton's finished too, eh? Did he make any sort of statement before he passed out?"

"Didn't live long enough," Johnny replied, "for which I'm mighty regretful."

"We agree on that," Norton rasped. "I think he might have been mixed up in that Falcon business—him and Deever—"

"That's a hell of a thing to say, Kirk," Caldwell interrupted, "about a dead man who can't defend himself. They didn't come any squarer than Jay Summerton. Just because you and he had a little argument last night is no sign you can blacken his character now that he's gone."

"Oh, to hell with it, and you too, Caldwell," Norton growled. He turned to Johnny. "I want a line on how all this business happened, Barlow. How come you and Summerton were together when Deever started his lead slinging?"

Johnny told him briefly what had taken place. Norton scowled. "What in hell sort of clue could Summerton have to give you? Didn't you get anything from him before Deever fired?"

"If I did," Johnny evaded, "I'm not talking about it now."

Norton relaxed somewhat. "Personally, I don't think you got a damn thing that's worth while. If you did, you wouldn't be hanging around here. You'd be taking action."

"Think what you like," Johnny said shortly. He turned to Caldwell. "Frank, Jay did say he'd men-

219

tioned something to you regarding the clue he thought he had."

Caldwell nodded. "He did. It didn't amount to anything, and I told him so. To satisfy him I passed the information on to the sheriff—"

"Oh, that," Norton said disparagingly. "Cripes, no! That stuff was worthless—no use even giving it any thought."

"I'm still wondering what Jay thought he had," Johnny said. "Frank, you say you know. Let's have it."

"It's not worth your bothering with, Johnny, but here it is. After the holdup Jay said he remembered the Falcon had talked with a sort of stutter—"

"And you don't think that's important?" Johnny said.

"No, I don't. I think Jay was mistaken. Remember, I heard the Falcon talk too, and I didn't hear any evidence of a stutter. If he stuttered when Jay heard him, it was probably from nervousness—something like that."

"And do you think," Johnny asked, "that that is what Jay wanted to see me about?"

"I don't know of anything else," Caldwell replied. He turned away and spoke to the others. "I think we should get poor Jay's body down to the undertaker's. It seems indecent to leave it lying here."

"Anyway," Norton put in, "Summerton being hit instead of Barlow is very lucky—for Barlow. And for our town. Thanks to our visiting Ranger man who has rigidly upheld the traditions of his organisation, the community is rid of one no-good hombre—namely, Vink Deever. Had I known what a bustard Vink was, I'd gotten rid of him long ago. But it has remained for our gallant Ranger to accomplish the deed—"

"Cripes!" Johnny protested. "Cut out the sarcasm, Norton. I can do without it."

"Anyway, you must admit," Norton sneered, "that Jay's getting in the way of Deever's slug saved your life, Barlow."

"I wonder," Johnny said, eyes narrowing on the sheriff, and then again, "I wonder. I'm not sure but that Deever intended to shoot Summerton first."

"What!" Norton exclaimed. "Now why in hell should Deever want to kill Summerton?"

"I'll let you figure that one out," Johnny said quietly. "You pretend to know all the answers."

Norton bent a sharp look on Johnny. "What exactly do you mean by such talk?" he demanded.

"There's no certainty Deever would have killed me," Johnny said promptly. "He certainly didn't have any luck when he tried."

"No, you had all the luck," Norton growled. "I knew Vink. He was a fast man with a gun."

"Sheriff," Johnny said, "you sound as though you almost admired that speed."

"And you sound crazy as hell," Norton blustered. "That Deever bustard didn't mean anything to me, as you should know. The instant I learned what he was really like, I got rid of him. He came back. You did a good job snuffing him out."

Without waiting for Johnny's reply, Norton turned and stalked indignantly out of the saloon. A slight smile curved Johnny's lips as he gazed after the departing sheriff.

Meticulous Jones arrived, heard the story of what had happened from a half-dozen men, then passed on through the bar-room to take care of Vink Deever's corpse. Various friends helped Caldwell carry away the dead body of the cashier. Most of the crowd drifted out of the Clinic, after first giving it a vigorous run of business for a short time.

It was almost dark when Johnny and Vallejo left the saloon. They went to the T-Bone Restaurant for supper, but Johnny ate only a little. He sat scowling into his coffee cup and muttered something that had to do with his hating killing.

"But, Johnee, eet was hees life or yours." The Mexican shrugged. *"Por Dios!* But for the grace of the good fortune, you would not now be here at suppair weeth me."

"Meaning?" Johnny smiled thinly.

"The poor aim of Deever's firs' shot."

Johnny looked thoughtful. "I still think, Mike, that it was Summerton who Deever was after, first—"

"No!" Surprise tinged the Mexican's tones.

Johnny nodded. "When I went in that room with Summerton, I half suspected there might be some sort of skulduggery arranged to get me, so I didn't take chances. I seated Summerton where the light from the window would fall on his face. I was watchful for a trap. If anything was due to happen to me, I figured Summerton's eyes would give him away. But as it turned out, I feel sure now the poor hombre was on the level when he came to me to give information. I was watching him close, and by the look on his face I'm certain he was just as surprised as I was—maybe more so—when Deever appeared at the window." Johnny paused to roll a cigarette and light it.

"And then?" Vallejo prompted.

"I'd been sitting with my side to the window—matter of fact, I almost had my back to it. It would have been almost as easy for Deever to shoot at me first. But it was Summerton he threw his lead at, probably figuring to get me later, if possible—"

"But, Johnee," Vallejo protested, "there is somebody here that wants you killed. Are you sayeeng eet is more important that Summerton be killed first?"

"Exactly what I'm saying. I feel certain Summerton had important information to give. Deever had orders to stop that information getting out. If he'd killed me first, Summerton might have escaped to tell his story to somebody else."

"Pairhaps you are correc', Johnee," the Mexican said thoughtfully. "But who would peeve theese order to Vink Deever and tell heem to kill Summerton?"

"Who do you think, Mike? After all, Deever was Norton's man."

Vallejo frowned in perplexity. "*Was* Norton's man. But Norton fired heem, told heem to get out of town—"

"Norton *claimed* he fired Deever," Johnny contradicted. "Of course I may be mistaken, but that's how the setup looks to me. Think it over."

"*Socorro!* Now you have told me, I do not have to theenk," Mike exclaimed excitedly. "Eet ees all clear like the bell. Summerton had words to say wheech Norton did not weesh you or anyone to hear. And so Norton geeves the order to Deever to kill Summerton."

"You've got it. And with Summerton dead, we're set back on our heels again. I have a feeling that Summerton could have given me the key to the whole tangled mess. And now he's gone."

"You think Summerton had something additional to tell, beside theese talk of a bandit who spoke with the stuttair?"

"I feel certain of it, Mike. That story about the Falcon talking with a stutter didn't ring true to me."

"Pairhaps," Vallejo suggested, "Summerton only made up that part to tell Caldwell—"

"Why should he?" Johnny asked quickly.

Mike shrugged his shoulders. "*Quién sabe?*—who knows? Eet ees all beyond my poor mind."

Johnny frowned. "Summerton did give the effect

of protecting someone who was innocently mixed up in the holdup. Could it be Caldwell—?" He broke off suddenly. "Let's get off the subject for a spell. It's driving me cuckoo."

They left the restaurant and sauntered about Rawhide City for a time, talking to anyone who might have witnessed the holdup, but witnesses were difficult to find and they could learn nothing new.

"Come on," Johnny proposed at last, "we'll get our ponies from the livery and ride out to the Lazy-Double-M. I've got a hunch I might feel more cheerful out there."

Getting their horses from the stable, they mounted and loped swiftly out of Rawhide City.

## CHAPTER XVII

### NO IDENTIFICATION

JOHNNY'S face was wreathed with smiles the following morning as he and Vallejo pushed their ponies toward Rawhide City. "Jeepers!" Johnny exclaimed, "I can't say I feel very mad at anybody this morning. There's a nice breeze lifting across the range, and look at that blue sky, Mike. Have you ever seen anything so blue? And just a couple of little wispy clouds chasing each other around. What a day!"

"Ees eet the day, or something else?" The

Mexican chuckled. "Nine times out of ten eet ees a girl who produce such enthusiasm."

"Could be a girl has something to do with it," Johnny admitted, grinning.

Mike laughed. "Always, the gay *caballéro* rides weeth love in the saddle. It mus' be the Señorita 'Rene lent no inattentive ear to your talk of last night, Johnee." He added ironically, "Can it be that she, *tambien,* at long las', has fallen in love?"

"Maybe she hasn't fallen yet," Johnny said, "but I've got a hunch she's slipping."

Mike's face assumed a saddened expression, and he spoke as though to himself: "Poor blind hombre. My *amigo* cannot see that already the light of hees eyes gazes on heem weeth the look of one who worship."

"Huh?" Johnny blurted. "What's that?"

"*Es verdad,*" the Mexican nodded, smiling. "I speak truth. I, Miguel Vallejo *y* Cordano, could see so much, personal weeth my own eye, the firs' evening the Señorita 'Rene sees you. Always, I know at once, Johnee, she have always love you. But you are so blind, you mees eet, complete."

"Well I'll be damned!" Johnny exclaimed, his jaw dropping. His pony slowed to a walk, and Mike reined in at his side. "Say," Johnny demanded, "are you running a whizzer on me, or should I have talked just a mite longer last night?"

The Mexican's dark eyes brimmed with laughter.

"I know not what you say to her las' evening, but I feel in my heart that you have—how you say eet?—made the bull's-eye weeth your lady."

"You really think I've scored a hit, then? I don't know, Mike. Maybe I'm dumber than I've always figured—if you know so much before I do."

Mike nodded. "Een matters of the heart, I'm theenk you are very stupid, Johnee. Eef you could read a killer's intentions no bettair than you interpret a woman's mind, I'm theenk you would have been one dead hombre many year ago—no?"

"Maybe you're right—" Johnny commenced dubiously.

"There ees no doubt," Vallejo cut in.

"There'll be no doubt about us missing the arrival of that morning stage, either," Johnny said suddenly, "if we don't fan our tails a mite faster. I want to be on hand when Sheriff Trigg arrives."

He kicked his pony in the ribs. The two horses jumped into a swift, ground-devouring pace, sending up drifting clouds of dust at their rear. Before long, Johnny and Mike were moving along the main street of Rawhide City at a fast running walk.

Leaving their mounts at the hitch rack in front of the Clinic Saloon, the two men crossed the street to the post office, where the stage was scheduled to stop. Sheriff Kirk Norton was already on hand, accompanied by two men carrying spades and picks. A number of other citizens lounged in the shade of the wooden awning that extended out over the sidewalk.

Johnny and Miguel nodded to the sheriff. Johnny said pleasantly, "I see Elson Trigg hasn't arrived yet."

"A man don't need much eyesight to tell him that," Norton replied harshly. He angrily shifted his cud from one cheek to the other, then spat a long brown stream. "This is the damnedest piece of foolishness I ever heard of," he commented bitterly. "Digging up a man that's been dead a week or more."

"If you killed the Falcon," Johnny maintained stubbornly, "you're entitled to the reward. To get the reward, the body's got to be identified by someone other than the killer. And to be identified, it has to be dug up. If you know of a better way, let me know. Is that clear?"

"It's clear that you don't know enough to mind your own business," Kirk Norton growled. "I'm not asking a reward for doing my duty. The county pays me and pays me well—"

"In that case," Johnny suggested, "why not turn the reward over to the county? It might ease the taxpayers' burden some."

"You know damned well it wouldn't be a drop in the bucket," Norton said harshly. "Besides, how are you going to be sure about identification at this late date? After a man's been dead so long, his features change sometimes—"

"Not in ten days," Johnny stated. "I reckon we won't have trouble identifying the Falcon—providing the body proves to be the Falcon's—"

"God damn it!" Norton exploded. "I said once it was the Falcon. That should be enough identification. I'm not used to having my word doubted—"

"Hey, Kirk," a bystander interrupted, "is that right? Are you aiming to dig up the Falcon's body this morning?"

Norton gave the curious one a baleful look. "What business is it of yours?" he said coldly.

"Aw-w, you don't need to get riled, Sheriff," the man said. "As a taxpayer I got a right to know what's going on in the county—"

"As a taxpayer," Norton snapped, "you talk too much. And if you feel like remembering that when election time comes up again, I won't be bothered any. I'd sooner not be elected than be put in office by a pack of jackasses."

The man fell silent and moved uneasily away.

"After all," Johnny said with a laugh, "the jackasses have to elect a leader, Norton. Aren't they the same ones elected you before, and aren't you still kicking up dust in the same corral?"

"Are you inferring that I'm a jackass, Barlow?" Norton thundered.

Johnny's grin widened. "Don't pin me down, Sheriff. I'll leave it to Rawhide City to decide. A few more days should tell the story."

Someone in the crowd before the post office

snickered. Norton's face went crimson. A week previous no one would have dared laugh at him. The look he directed at Johnny was full of hate, but he held his temper in check:

"Damn the luck," he growled. "Now the news will get all over town that we're digging up the Falcon. There'll be a regular stampede out to Boot Hill. This is all damn foolishness."

Johnny laughed. "Well, it won't hurt to give Rawhide City a mite of entertainment."

As the news spread, more and more people collected before the post office, curiously eyeing the sheriff and the men with the digging tools. Questions commenced to shower on the sheriff, all of which he ignored. The spade bearers, however, weren't so reticent. Norton was on the point of telling them to shut up when someone announced the impending arrival of the stagecoach.

A cry went up: "Here she comes!"

The Concord stage was just entering the eastern end of Main Street. The heavy vehicle swayed and rattled as it rumbled along the dusty street. Hoofs pounded; there was a jangling and squeaking from harness and other equipment. A rising cloud of dust at its rear nearly enveloped a group of small boys who were giving chase in the hope of jumping on for a ride, or just for the fun of helping to announce the stage's arrival. In front of the post office the driver pulled the horses to an abrupt halt and footed the brake amid a cloud of flying dirt and scattered gravel.

"There's Elson Trigg now," Johnny said. He and Mike pushed through the crowd. A stout man with curly, sand-coloured hair was just descending from the coach. He wore corduroy pants, a battered grey Stetson, a Colt six-shooter, and a size seventeen collar, which was by now wilted and bedraggled.

"Blasted hot ride," he wheezed to everyone in general, then, catching sight of Johnny, "Hi there, Johnny Barlow, you young hellion!" His round red face beamed genially on Johnny as they shook hands. Johnny introduced Vallejo. Trigg said to the Mexican, "You're in bad company, young feller, when you run around with this Barlow limb of Satan."

Johnny chuckled. "Elson, I reckon Mike knows where I got my bad habits. My dad might have known it wouldn't be good when I was a youngster to let me go hunting with you. That's when I learned all the cussedness you mention."

Trigg guffawed and waddled up to the sidewalk. Norton came forward to greet him. "Hi-yuh, Kirk," Trigg bellowed, sticking out his hand.

"Glad to see you, Sheriff Trigg," Norton said stiffly.

"I'll be damned if you look glad," Trigg puffed. "Come down off'n your high horse, Kirk. Don't act so dignified. You're just human like the rest of us, only mebbe you got ice water in your arteries."

Trigg's perspiring face was wreathed in smiles of genial good nature.

"This grave-exhuming business is all damn nonsense," Norton stated abruptly. "If I'd known Barlow intended to write you, I'd have tried to save you a trip. There's no need for this business. However, as I didn't know in time to prevent your coming, I considered it my duty to co-operate in any possible way. I've hired diggers, but don't for one minute get an idea I condone this foolishness—"

"Foolishness, my eye!" Trigg snorted. "If you killed the Falcon, you're entitled to reward money. Anyway, I was glad to make a trip over here, at county expense. I figure to ride out later and visit my old friend Jim Cross, at the Circle-Cross. Ain't seen him for months. . . . Well, let's get started. Got a hawss ready for me?"

"I thought we might walk out to Boot Hill—" Norton began.

*"Walk!"* Trigg's body shook with uproarious laughter. "My Gawd, Kirk, you ain't expectin' me to walk? Why, hell's-bells on a tomcat! I ain't walked more'n the distance from one saloon to another since Hector was a pup. Me, I just ain't built for that sort of ambulation."

"All right," Norton said disgustedly, "I'll get horses."

Not many minutes were lost while horses were procured from the livery stable. Johnny and Mike got their ponies from in front of the Clinic Saloon, led them up the street and waited for Norton to appear with mounts. Meanwhile, the crowd had scattered, some to get horses and others to start the short walk to the local cemetery. There was some further delay while Elson Trigg entered the nearest saloon to down a few bottles of beer. Finally he announced he was ready.

As they were mounting, Norton said, "Look here, Sheriff Trigg. Are you sure you can identify the Falcon's body?"

"Me?" Trigg exploded with laughter. "Reckon I should be able to, if anybody can. It was me he was holdin' a gun on in that El Paso del Norte saloon holdup, four months back, and I couldn't do one solitary damn thing about it, except get a good look at his face. He got plumb away, slick as a whistle, too, with a posse on his tail—What? No, I wa'n't with the posse. I got no authority down there. Me, I just happened to be visitin' in El Paso at the time."

With considerable heaving and grunting, Trigg managed to get himself settled on his horse's back. "I tell you, Kirk," he went on, deftly rolling a cigarette with the fingers of one stubby hand, while his other hand searched for a match, "you deserve a heap of credit for downin' the Falcon. He created plenty hell among the desert towns, and other spots as well. But he liked to hole up in the desert, and then come out for his raids. Only you should have reported the killing yourself, 'stead of leaving Johnny Barlow to start the wheels of reward moving."

"I was trying to avoid all this fuss," Norton said sullenly.

Sheriff Trigg eyed him with some awe. "Damned if I can understand you, Kirk Norton—callin' it 'fuss', when you'll be collecting fifteen hundred dollars reward. Brother, that kind of money ain't buffalo chips, y'know."

"Let's get started," Norton said coldly.

A cavalcade of riders moved off, with a number of lately arrived pedestrians strung out at the rear. The Boot Hill Cemetery was situated just a short distance south of Rawhide City. It wasn't located on a hill at all, but was simply a cleared space, fenced with wire and dotted by occasional head-boards; here and there a stone marker showed above a grave. A series of rough paths from which broken bits of rock had been cleared meandered in and out among the low mounds of earth.

Arriving at the cemetery, the men dismounted and made their way on foot through a wide gateway. Here they paused and stood talking for a few minutes. Eventually those who were coming on foot arrived, panting and covered with perspiration. Finally Norton, with his two spade men, led the way between graves, with Johnny, Trigg and Vallejo at their heels. Other men came trailing behind them.

Trigg mopped perspiration from his florid countenance and complained of the walking, but managed to keep pace with the others. "I see it," he panted suddenly, as Norton came to a halt between two mounds of earth. "It's that one that looks fresh dug."

"Why shouldn't it look fresh dug?" Norton demanded in surly tones. "It's only a mite over a week since we buried the Falcon. And there's been no rain to settle the earth."

"Well, I didn't say anythin' to make you riled, Kirk." Trigg mildly protested the other man's tones.

"This whole damn business riles me," Norton snapped. "Putting this extra expense on the county is sheer waste."

"You can make it up to the county with your reward money, Kirk," Trigg said with a throaty chuckle.

Norton said, "God damn that reward. I don't want to hear any more about it." He turned angrily away and ordered his men to start digging. The onlookers, full of morbid curiosity, gathered closer to the spot. "They do say," one of them remarked to a companion, "that a dead man's whiskers keep on growing after he's dead. Now we'll see if it's true."

"I don't believe it myself," another man said sceptically.

"Suppose it is true, though," a third fellow put in.

"They'd have to shave the Falcon to make sure it was him, did the whiskers grow very long."

Someone burst into loud laughter. "I can just see the look on Barber Jake's face should the Falcon be carried in to be shaved. Can't you just see Jake bending down solicitous to ask, 'Does the razor pull, sir?' "

The laughter grew in volume. Norton turned irritably and told the men to shut up. They shut up. One of the diggers commented that the earth was soft enough so the picks wouldn't be needed. "You should make better time, then," Norton growled. "Go on, put your muscles into it. I'll pay for any tools you break. Only hurry up!"

Johnny and Mike talked to Trigg and smoked cigarettes. The sun beat hotly on their bodies. Far overhead a lone buzzard soared and floated on sluggish wings against the expanse of blue sky. A few flies began to gather. Norton stood near the grave, in an aggrieved silence. The shoulders of the two spade men dropped lower as they shovelled out loose earth. Finally there came the sound of steel striking against wood.

"We've struck it," one of the diggers announced.

"You made good time, boys," Trigg complimented the men.

The other digger paused momentarily in his labours. "It wa'n't as bad a job as I expected. Earth hadn't packed down yet. . . . Where's them ropes, Tim?" to his companion.

The last earth was cleared from the top of the box, the ropes were looped around the ends, then the crude wooden coffin was lifted out and placed on firm ground. The crowd, open-mouthed, gathered nearer.

Trigg said, "I'm surprised your local undertaker didn't come out to see how his work was standin' up."

Norton laughed harshly. "He wanted to, but I told him it was none of his business. I know that scavenger. He'd try to do some additional work at county expense before we buried the stiff again. I told him to keep away."

Johnny cast a quick look at Vallejo. The Mexican looked slightly pale and Johnny saw him cross himself. Johnny turned back to Norton. "What are you waiting for, Sheriff?"

Norton said curtly to the two diggers, "Open it up."

One of the men inserted the blade of his spade under the lid of the coffin and pried. A board creaked, splintered, then broke off at one corner. "Hell of a job of coffin building," he commented disgustedly. "Nails all twisted and bent; boards cracked—"

"No siree! That was a good job," protested a stout voice in the crowd. "I help build the coffins for the under taker—"

"Maybe I'd better suggest that the undertaker get a new carpenter, then," Norton said sharply. The man's voice drifted to silence.

"It sure looks like a hurried job of carpentry to me," the man opening the box went on. He tried again and another board splintered off. Inserting his blade under a third board, he quickly removed that too, muttering something meanwhile about bent nails causing cracks in the wood. The crowd pressed closer. The removal of the third board allowed more daylight to enter the box. The man with the spade was about to remove the next board when he stopped short, his face paling.

"Now what in the devil—" he commenced.

"What's wrong?" Trigg asked quickly.

"Lookit"—the man pointed a shaking finger toward the interior of the coffin—"we got grave robbers around here."

The others closed in, Sheriff Norton first of all. An expression of surprise was allowed to flit across his features before he resumed his usual cold mask.

"Grave robbers is correct," Johnny exclaimed after a single look.

"Well, may I be skinned for my aunt Minnie's tomcat!" Sheriff Trigg exploded. "Nothing but three sizable chunks of sandstone in this box. Kirk, what do you make of this?"

The others, crowding in to look at the box, now dropped back and waited for Norton to speak.

Kirk Norton forced a rueful smile. "It appears," he commented sourly, "that someone isn't in favour of me getting that reward, and has removed the body to prevent my getting it. I've known for long that I had enemies, but I didn't suspect anyone of going to this length to make things disagreeable for me. Well, I've maintained right along I didn't want that reward. Perhaps this will settle the matter."

"But where's the Falcon's corpse, then?" Trigg puffed.

Norton shrugged his shoulders. "I've no idea. It's got me stopped. Strangest thing I've ever encountered. This is the very spot where he was buried. You can ask anybody."

Two or three others spoke up:

"This is the right grave, all right."

"It's the right spot."

"I ought to know, I helped bury the Falcon."

"Damned if I understand this." Trigg frowned.

"Well, you know as much as I do," Norton said tersely. "However, there's no use hanging around here, looking at a box of rock." He cursed long and fervently. "And now I got grave robbers to contend with. If this sort of thing keeps on, Creaking River County can get itself a new sheriff."

"Somebody's sure good at exchanging rocks for other things," a man commented. " 'Member how Melville's money was exchanged for rocks? I'll bet if you can find the hombre that stole the Falcon's body, you'll find the missing money too."

Norton sneered. "That shows how dumb you are.

Like's not, some of the Falcon's relatives heard about him being buried here and they come out and took the body away."

One of the diggers said, "You want we should bury this box again, Sheriff?"

Norton stared at the man in disgust. "What in hell for? Sure, go on and bury it, but put your own dumb carcass in the box first."

He strode angrily out of the cemetery, climbed on his horse and loped off without waiting for the others. The crowd began to disperse, though Trigg, Johnny, and Vallejo stood talking for a time beside the empty box and mound of heaped earth. Finally they went out to their waiting ponies.

Trigg said, climbing to his saddle, "Well, looks like I had this trip for nothin'."

"I'm plumb sorry," Johnny said, "that you had to come all this way to look at an empty box. But you did have your trip for nothing—the county pays your expenses."

Trigg guffawed. "For nothin' is right. It doesn't cost me a cent."

Johnny and Vallejo were mounted now and the three set out toward town, walking their ponies. "Nope," Trigg went on, "I don't mind this trip a bit. It'll be something to tell Jim Cross when I reach his place. Jim will sure be surprised. . . . Well, if you're in town to-morrow, Johnny, I'll be seeing you some more. I aim to stay the night at the Circle-Cross with Jim. *Adios*."

Johnny said good-bye and Vallejo added, *"Vaya con Dios, amigo."*

Trigg turned east to strike the trail that led to the Cross Ranch. Norton had long since reached Main Street in town. Johnny and Vallejo rolled cigarettes. Johnny struck a match and held it to Mike's smoke. They exchanged knowing glances across the flame as their eyes met, but neither man said anything as they settled once more to saddles.

## CHAPTER XVIII

### JOHNNY GETS AN IDEA

As Johnny and Mike were dismounting in front of the Clinic Saloon, Tex Houston, Murphy Swartz, Slim Pickens, and Quinn Taylor rode up.

Johnny grinned. "Well, it looks like an invasion by the Lazy-Double-M. All we need now to make it unanimous is 'Rene, Jovita, and Soup-Kettle—"

"And 'Rene will be in later," Houston said.

"But what are you hombres doing in town, Tex?" Johnny asked as the men started to pile off their horses.

"I just ain't certain," Houston replied. "Boss's orders, though. After that fracas you had with Deever yesterday, 'Rene gets to worryin' about your narrow escape. Somehow she got it into her head that somebody else might be primed to put a slug into your carcass. I told her and told her you was capable of lookin' after your own skin, but nothin' would do but we should come in to help you out if anythin' happened."

The girl's thoughts for his safety sent a pleasurable glow through Johnny, and his mind was only half on what Houston was talking about when he replied, "Well, nothing's happened yet, but I'm hopeful—" He stopped short, reddening.

"Ain't it?" Houston grinned meaningly. "I thought from the way 'Rene was acting that maybe everything had been decided."

"I mean," Johnny said sheepishly, "that nothing much has happened in town that spells trouble for me, but you never know when it might, of course."

The others laughed. Tex said, "I knew you'd be all right, but 'Rene wouldn't listen to me. You know how a woman is."

"I don't know if I do," Johnny said uncertainly.

"Leastwise," Houston said, "she gives the orders and we carry 'em out. She's the boss, y'know."

Johnny chuckled. "That's the truth if I ever heard it—"

"So don't blame us," Tex went on, "if you don't want us around. It ain't our fault. I said to her, I said, 'Now Johnny can take care of himself. He's already proved that—' "

"Forget it," Johnny interupted, "and let's go get a drink."

"That's the smartest suggestion I've heard today." Houston chuckled an acceptance.

They all trooped into the Clinic. Already an excited group of men were gathered at the bar talking of the empty coffin that had been dug up and speculating as to what could have become of the Falcon's missing body. Johnny took up the tale at the beginning and brought the Lazy-Double-M cow-punchers up to date on what had taken place. That brought forth more ejaculations of astonishment.

Somebody wondered if perhaps the missing money might not have been buried with the Falcon. While there was no basis for such an idea, the thought took hold and conversation increased. An excess of talking results in dry throats, and another round of drinks went along the bar. Pipes and cigarettes were lighted, and for a few minutes Ernie Braughn found himself caught in a rush of work.

"Anyway," a cowhand from the HB-Connected commented, "you can count on one thing—greed for gold generally brings on killin'. Look at the score to date: Matt Melville just pulls through by the skin of his teeth. He nearly gets killed. The Falcon does get killed and then his corpse is snatched. Then, yesterday, there's two more gets bumped off. Mind you, in one day, two! Summerton and Deever."

Another man nodded. "That's right. A desire for gold makes folks do crazy things."

Johnny had been idly listening to the conversation. Now something clicked suddenly in his mind. He called Ernie Braughn to his end of the bar.

"Ready for another drink, Johnny?"—eyeing Johnny's only partly empty bottle of beer.

"It's another kind of service I'm wanting now," Johnny said. "I want to check myself on something, Ernie; make sure that I heard correctly. This is a job for that memory of yours."

"Shoot," Ernie said. "If I heard it, I'll remember it."

"Yesterday," Johnny explained, while those near him listened interestedly, "when Jay Summerton was dying, he tried to tell me something. Do you remember his exact words?"

"But I didn't hear 'em," Ernie reminded. "All I heard was what you told me Summerton said."

"That's good enough," Johnny replied. "I just want to make sure that I haven't got the words twisted since I first heard 'em. What did I tell you Summerton said?"

"Give me a few moments to think, and I'll repeat your exact words, Johnny," Ernie replied, screwing up his forehead. Then he relaxed, smiling. "Here it is. You said, 'It sounded like Summerton said to . . . coat closet.' Then, Johnny, you said to Summerton, 'Is that it? To coat closet? The Falcon made you get into the coat closet? We know that, Jay, but what happened next?'"

"That's it, Ernie." Johnny looked pleased. "That's as I remembered Summerton's words, but I wanted you to check me."

"Cripes," Ernie said proudly, "that was an easy

one to remember. Then, just before Summerton died, he sort of gasped out one word, 'Caldwell'. I heard that myself."

"You're a marvel, Ernie," Johnny said.

Tex Houston asked, "What's that all about, Johnny?"

Johnny said evasively, "I'm not sure yet, Tex. I've got to think something over first."

Conversation along the bar picked up again. Johnny gave Mike a short nod and started for the door. Houston looked at him inquiringly. Johnny smiled and said, "No, Tex, there's no need for you and the boys to come with me. I'm just going to catch a breath of air and see can I learn something. I'll be back after a spell."

"That's all right with me," Houston said, "only if the boss gives me Hail Columbia for not bird-dawgin' you, you'll have to square me with her."

"I'll square you," Johnny promised.

Houston and the others turned back to the bar. Johnny went through the doorway to the street, followed by Mike.

On the sidewalk Johnny said to the Mexican, and a certain excitement tinged his tones, "Mike, I just had an idea."

Vallejo smiled lazily. "Eet ees not the first time, Johnee."

"Listen. Be serious a few mintues. What that HB-Connected cowhand said in there a few minutes back started me thinking. You remember he said something about greed for gold leading to killing. Then he added that yesterday two were killed in one day. Two. Summerton and Deever."

"I remembair, Johnee. I am as good as Ernie—no?"

But Johnny ignored that. "When that hombre said 'Two' and 'Summerton' almost in the same breath, an idea clicked. Yesterday Summerton tried to tell me something."

"That also I remembair: 'To . . . coat closet'."

"No, that wasn't it at all, Mike. We understood him wrong. He was really trying to say ' two'— t-w-o. Not 't-o'. See? And then he pronounced Caldwell's name."

"Yes?" The Mexican looked blank. "Johnee, eet does not make good sense—'two—coat closet— Caldwell—' "

"But it *does* make sense, Mike. It gives us what we're looking for."

Mike's eyes widened. There was dawning understanding in his face. "Of course, Johnee—you have hit eet—"

"I've hit it!" Johnny exclaimed. "What are we looking for? A satchel, isn't it? A missing satchel that was exchanged for—"

"*Sí, sí,* Johnee!" Mike exclaimed excitedly. "When Summerton said ' two . . . coat closet,' he meant there were two satchels in Caldwell's coat closet. He was not talking about the closet in which he had been placed by the Falcon—"

"Come on!" Johnny grabbed the Mexican by the

arm. "Let's go to the bank and see what Caldwell can tell us. I've got a hunch we're getting warm."

"I theenk we get hot—no?" Vallejo amended.

They hurried along the sidewalk until they'd reached the bank. Just outside, Johnny started to laugh and pulled Mike to a slower pace. "Take it easy, *amigo.* We're rushing in like we already had everything settled."

Casually, the two men entered the bank, just as a customer was taking his departure. The front two thirds of the large room was bare except for a table and chairs placed against one wall for the convenience of clients. On the table were arranged printed withdrawal and deposit forms, blotters, pens, and two bottles of ink. Hanging above the table was a calendar advertising a hay-and-feed company.

A third of the distance from the rear of the building a high partition divided off the back of the room, and placed in this partition was a closed door and a grilled window, several feet apart. Behind the grill, Johnny could see Caldwell. Caldwell was so engrossed with some papers before him that at first he didn't see Johnny and Vallejo. Glancing above the partition, Johnny sighted the top of a heavy steel door, which he guessed stood open at the vault. A short distance from this was a second door, which probably led to Caldwell's private office.

Johnny said, "Mike, I guess, we'll have to jolt him to life. C'mon."

# CHAPTER XIX

## GUILTY!

SUDDENLY Caldwell glanced up, peering at Johnny and Vallejo through his grilled window. "Why, hello, boys," he said genially. "I didn't see you there. Did you come to borrow money or open an account?"

"No, we came to close one," Johnny said quietly.

"Close one?" Caldwell's forehead furrowed. "I don't understand."

"You will," Johnny assured him. "We want to look around."

Caldwell asked if he was looking for clues. Johnny nodded. "Clues have been raining down all around me, but I'm just beginning to understand 'em. Now I want a few more to dovetail with what I've got."

Caldwell chuckled. "I like your way of putting it. I'm pleased to hear you're making progress. But could you come back later, when I'm not so busy? Summerton and I have always managed things by ourselves, but with Jay gone I have to do the work of two men—"

"We won't take long," Johnny insisted. "I'd sure appreciate it if we could look around now."

Caldwell beamed. "Well, if you put it that way, I can't refuse to accommodate you. I don't want to give you an impression I'm another Sheriff Norton with no consideration for other people's wishes."

"I'm sure you're not another Sheriff Norton," Johnny said bluntly.

A momentary frown appeared on Caldwell's forehead, then he said, "One moment and I'll let you in." His face vanished from the grilled window and an instant later they heard a key turn in the door placed in the partition. The door swung open and Caldwell said, "Come right in, gentlemen," in a voice indicating he had assumed the pomposity befitting his character as town banker.

Johnny and Mike passed through the doorway. Caldwell closed the door and turned the key in the lock. Johnny said, "Do you always keep this door locked?"

"Certainly. Otherwise anyone would have easy access to my office and the vault, if it were open. There's generally currency near that grilled window too."

"Was this door locked the morning the bandit entered?" Johnny asked.

"No—worse luck. Or there'd have been no robbery. Jay must have left it unlocked by accident. He was a trifle careless at times."

Johnny laughed softly. "I'm surprised to hear you say that, Caldwell. Think how it sounds—a banker employing a careless cashier. That doesn't impress me as being good banking practice. You're sure it wasn't *you* who left this door unlocked that morning?"

"Good lord, no! And I didn't mean that Jay was careless in his financial matters. Quite the contrary. A very careful boy, Jay, and the very soul of loyalty."

"I can believe that," Johnny said. He didn't at once pursue the matter of the unlocked door again, but stood gazing around. Directly ahead of him was the closed door leading to Caldwell's private office. Caldwell led the way a little farther along the space enclosed by the partition. Now Johnny and Mike could see through the grilled window to the outer part of the bank. There was a short counter below the grill, and at one side was a partitioned box holding coins and paper money.

Caldwell said, "Jay was standing right there at his window when the Falcon entered that morning while Matt and I were fixing up that loan in my office. There was no one else in the bank at the time, and Jay said later he didn't see the Falcon enter. It was only a short time before that Jay had brought in Matt Melville's money in that satchel. I suppose he was busy with his ledgers, or something of the sort, at the time, and that is why he didn't see the Falcon come in. Y'know, when you're concentrating on adding a column of figures, you're not likely to see anyone enter until he arrives at the grill. Why, just a few minutes ago, I wasn't conscious that you two had come into the bank until I suddenly looked up and saw you standing there. So you see, it wouldn't have been difficult for the Falcon—"

"Sure, sure," Johnny interrupted. "I can see how the holdup man got in. With that door in the partition left unlocked—" He broke off. "You're sure it wasn't you, and not Summerton, who left that door unlocked?"

Caldwell bridled. "Look here, Johnny, are you inferring that I purposely left the door unlocked so the Falcon could make his entrance?"

"I didn't say that." Johnny smiled easily. "I just asked, that's all. Don't jump to conclusions, Caldwell."

Caldwell forced a smile. "Maybe I am a bit touchy. I don't mean to be, but the events of the past week or so"—he passed one hand across his moist forehead—"well you can see how they'd get on a man's nerves. Anyway, we do know that partition door was unlocked. Jay told us later that the first intimation he had of the Falcon was when the man came through the door, gun in hand, and closed it softly after him."

Caldwell took a deep breath to collect his thoughts, then went on, "Jay was about to yell a warning, but the Falcon motioned him to silence with the gun. Jay put his hands in the air and the Falcon backed him into that closet next to the vault." The banker jerked one thumb over his shoulder in the direction of the closet.

Johnny and Mike crossed the floor to the closet and opened the door. It was an ordinary coat closet. There was nothing within except a hat and a couple of coats hanging on hooks.

Vallejo said, "Eet looks like a tight fit for a man, Johnee."

Johnny replied, "Remember, Summerton was a thin sort of fellow. Besides, when you're looking into a gun you can squeeze yourself into a mighty small space if necessary."

"And that's what happened to Jay," Caldwell continued. "The Falcon forced him into this closet, then closed and locked the door."

Johnny nodded and turned to survey the open vault. There were account books, ledgers, and small metal boxes standing on shelves. There were a couple of closed metal doors. On one shelf was a package of bills and a canvas sack containing coins—at least Johnny judged it contained coins.

"I'm surprised," Johnny said, "that the holdup man didn't clean out your vault while he was here."

"I don't quite understand that myself." Caldwell frowned. "Of course, it would have taken time. Some of those compartments are kept locked except when the necessity to open them arises. Nor did the Falcon touch the ready currency Jay kept near his window. But, with time, he could have got more money from the vault. I was so engrossed with Matt in my office that I'd never have heard him. I wish he had done something like that, and

252

never entered my office. It would have been far better for poor Melville."

"It certainly would've," Johnny agreed.

At that moment a client came to the grilled window. Caldwell excused himself to Johnny and Mike and took care of the man's requirements. When the fellow had departed, Caldwell turned back to Johnny and Mike. "Well, there you are, gentlemen. That's all there is to see, or for me to tell. If you picked up any clues, you're welcome to them."

"We haven't yet had a look at your office, Caldwell," Johnny reminded.

"Shucks! There's nothing to see in my office," Caldwell replied.

"Suppose you let me be the judge on that score," Johnny suggested. "I want to see everything while we're here."

Caldwell sighed. "Well, of course, if you insist. Just a minute while I close this vault door." He closed the vault, turned the handle, then removed from arm's reach the currency box placed near the grilled window. "I don't know what my clients will think if they come in and find no one at the window. It will look highly irregular."

"This seems to be a sort of slow time of day," Johnny said. "Maybe we won't be bothered. If any customers come in, it won't hurt 'em to yell for you."

"We-ell, just as you say." Apparently Caldwell

didn't at at all like the idea of such interruption during business hours, but he led the way to his office door, opened it, and stood aside while Johnny and Vallejo entered. Within, a flat-topped desk and swivel chair were placed near the back of the room, and just beyond was a window equipped with heavy iron bars.

Johnny said, "Don't the bars at that window make you feel like you're in prison, Caldwell?"

"I don't like them there, that's a fact," Caldwell admitted. "But then what can I do? I have to protect the rear of the bank. Otherwise someone might gain entrance at night through that window."

Johnny gestured toward a door in one corner. "Does that lead outside, to the back of your building?"

Caldwell shook his head. "That's just a door to a closet I had built there. There's no back entrance." Caldwell walked around the corner of the desk and dropped into his chair, his back to the barred window. He gestured toward a couple of chairs placed in opposite corners. "Won't you sit down, gentlemen? I don't know as there is a thing more I can tell you about that holdup, but I'll be glad to answer questions if you have any."

"We won't bother sitting down," Johnny said, "but we'll likely think of something more to say. Now, Caldwell, if you'll tell me just where you were at the time of the holdup, we can get started."

"I was sitting here, at my desk, as I am now,"

Caldwell replied. "Matt Melville was just across from me. He had signed the note for the loan, then I insisted that he count the money in the satchel before leaving. He was ready to take Jay's word for the count, you see. Anyway, he was just about to leave with the money when my office door was flung open and the Falcon entered. And the Falcon shot Matt down like a dog and then—"

"What did you do?" Johnny asked quietly.

"I started to reach in my desk for my gun, but the Falcon shot at me—missing, fortunately. Somehow I tripped and fell down—"

"But you just told us you were sitting in your chair," Johnny reminded him casually. "How could you trip and fall out of your chair?"

Caldwell hesitated. "That does sound sort of queer, doesn't it?" he said uncomfortably. "Well, you see I must have got to my feet the minute the Falcon came in—"

"Will you show me where you fell?" Johnny asked, coming around the desk and standing not far from the side of Caldwell's chair.

Caldwell pointed to a spot on the floor in the vicinity of the corner of the desk. He smiled sheepishly. "I really sprawled when I went down. Got some ink spilled all over my trousers in the excitement."

Johnny glanced at a bottle of ink on the desk. It was placed well back from the edge. "I suppose that's where your ink usually stands?"

Caldwell frowned. "It must have been closer to the edge that morning," he said finally. "Come to think of it, I had drawn it toward me to fill the pen for Matt—"

Johnny yawned. "It doesn't matter. So you got ink spilled all over your trousers while you were sprawled on the floor. Is that right?"

"I certainly did." Caldwell was wearing his sheepish smile again. He pointed to an inkstain on his right pants leg. "There's the proof. I had on these same pants that morning. I haven't been able to find one single solitary thing that will take the ink out of the cloth, either. That ink really stains bad."

"It certainly looks it," Johnny agreed. "Don't you think it's sort of queer, though, Caldwell, that when that ink got knocked off the desk and spilled on your pants, it didn't splash on the carpet too?" Johnny was gazing about the floor, scrutinising the faded red carpet. "I can't see one sign of an ink stain on your carpet."

The smile vanished abruptly from Caldwell's face. He swallowed hard. "Come to think of it," he admitted reluctantly, "that *is* funny. I guess the ink bottle must have been nearly empty when it fell off the desk, and just emptied itself on my pants. Just a few drops left in the bottle, maybe—"

"There're other funny things to be explained too," Johnny interrupted. "Just because a man falls down and spills ink on himself is no sign his collar comes unbuttoned and his tie gets looped all haywire. You sort of overacted your part, didn't you, Caldwell? Oh, I know the act was meant to impress folks, but it wouldn't have been necessary to go so far."

"Just what are you hinting at, Barlow?" Caldwell tried to make his tones sound angry, but his face had gone white.

"If you don't know," Johnny said carelessly, "I'll have to make things plainer. Think that would be a good idea, Mike?" The Mexican nodded and Johnny turned back to Caldwell. "Yep, we'll have to just go a little deeper into the subject." He drew from his pocket a partly consumed plug of tobacco. "Have a chew, Caldwell?"

"Thanks, no," Caldwell refused nervously. "I don't use it. Get on with this hocus-pocus you've started, Barlow. I've got—"

"Don't use it?" Johnny looked surprised. He pointed to a small metal tray on the desk. The tray held a penknife and plug of tobacco from which one third had already been cut. "What do you do, keep that there for your customers?"

Caldwell gasped. His jaw dropped open. Frantically, he put up one clutching hand and covered his mouth.

"Good catch," Johnny complimented genially. "That's right, don't let 'em fall out. You'd better take this plug I'm offering you, Caldwell. It's yours. I've been looking for a hombre with broken and loose teeth. I can see now I should have spent my time looking for a man with false choppers."

"Dammit!" Caldwell said hoarsely, "I've no idea what you're talking about. If I have false teeth, that's *my* business. If *your* business is finished, I'll have to ask you to leave. I've neglected the bank and—and—I've got to see Sheriff Norton—"

"I don't doubt that last for a minute, Caldwell. You know you're in a tight now, and you want Norton to save you. Those arguments you've been having with Norton are all bluff too. But it's too late to run to him for help."

Caldwell had started to rise, but now he slumped limply back in his chair. He tried to speak, but his tongue failed to carry the denial he wanted to voice.

Johnny turned abruptly. "Keep your eye on this bustard, Mike."

"I keep the eye on heel." Vallejo nodded grimly.

Johnny strode to the closet in Caldwell's office. The closet door was locked. There was no key in sight. Johnny said, "Caldwell, where's the key to this door?"

"I—I don't know," Caldwell stammered, "I lost it and—and—well—"

Johnny swore, lifted one booted foot and smashed at the lock.

"That closet is empty," Caldwell cried wildly. "There's nothing there to concern you—"

"Shut your mouth, *cabron!*" Vallejo growled. "Or I weel shut heem for you."

Johnny had paid no attention to Caldwell's protests. He raised his foot again; there came the sound of splintering wood, and the door sagged. Johnny flung it back and glanced quickly within the closet. An instant later he uttered an exclamation of triumph and dragged out two satchels, identical in colour, workmanship, and appearance. Both bore Caldwell's initials stamped in the leather. Johnny gave another look at the interior of the closet and found a repeating rifle standing in one corner. He gave Caldwell a short angry look, then laid the two bags and the rifle on the desk.

A flood of explanation rose to Caldwell's lips. "You mustn't connect me with the holdup and robbery on account of those two bags," he protested in trembling tones. "I ordered one from a mail-order house, and by mistake they sent me two. I kept both."

"I can believe that," Johnny said sternly, and, "I haven't accused you of a hand in that holdup yet. You gave yourself away. I'm accusing you now, though. You're guilty, Caldwell. Guilty as hell."

"I'm not, I'm not," Caldwell quavered. "Melville's money was stolen out on the street. There was a third bag—"

"Now you're adding lying to your guilt, and foolish lying at that. We've got you dead to rights, Caldwell, and right now you're going to tell me all about it. It just occurs to me you're a mighty sick man—"

"But I'm not sick—" Caldwell began.

"By God, you're going to be before I get through with you," Johnny said grimly. He turned to Vallejo. "Mike, I don't want any interruptions here for a few minutes. You go stand in the doorway of the bank. If anybody tries to come in, tell 'em the bank's not operating for a short spell. Tell 'em Banker Caldwell has been taken sick, and I'm taking care of him. Just say Caldwell's had a jolt— I mean, a stroke—"

"You—you can't do this," Caldwell broke in.

"I'm doing it," Johnny snapped. "Here, Mike"—putting a hand in one pocket and producing a small gold badge—"should anybody ask questions, show this badge for your authority. I'm deputising you a member of the Border Rangers for the time being. If anybody comes, send him for Doc Duncan. Get Duncan here. I don't want to start a run on the bank, or anything. Folks know Duncan and trust him, where they don't know us. Keep Duncan at the door with you and tell him what's happened. But tell him to keep quiet about it."

"I'm do eet, Johnee." Vallejo started to turn away, then paused. "Suppose eet ees the Sheriff Norton what come to the bank?"

"You've got your gun if he gets tough, Mike. Use it, if necessary. Remember, you're a Border

260

Ranger now, and the Rangers are running things. Sheriff's don't mean any more to us than ordinary folks. Get going, *amigo*—and don't let anybody come back here."

"I am on the way, Johnee." The Mexican turned and left the office.

## CHAPTER XX

### DOUBLE-CROSSER

JOHNNY slammed the office door after Vallejo, and turned back to Caldwell. The banker's face was pasty. He kept licking with his tongue at dry lips, and he was slumped hopelessly down in his chair. Once he tried to rise, but fright had taken all strength from his limbs. Johnny stood looking disgustedly down on him for a few minutes without speaking.

Finally Caldwell raised his eyes to meet Johnny's. "You—you—you're making a horrible mistake," he quavered. "Matt's money was stolen out on the street—"

"In full view of everybody, I suppose?" Johnny said sarcastically. "Damn it, Caldwell. Quit lying to me. That exchange of bags was made right here. I felt from the first it couldn't have been done any place else, but I trusted you at first, seeeing you were a friend of Matt Melville's—or at least Matt thought you were."

261

"I *am* his friend—" Caldwell commenced wildly.

"Don't lie, I told you," Johnny said coldly. "Here's the way I figure it out. You got Matt to sign a note for that money, then left that partition door unlocked so the holdup man could come in and shoot Matt down—"

"No, no," the banker shrieked. "It wasn't me. I didn't do it. It—it was Jay Summerton—"

"Don't try to throw the blame on that dead man, Caldwell. He was loyal to you—loyal as hell. He knew about these two bags, but was afraid to get you in wrong if he told anybody about 'em. Finally, his conscience got the best of him, but you had him shot down before he could tell me—"

"I swear I didn't," Caldwell moaned.

"It was Mex Louie who backed Summerton into that other closet and then came in here. After he shot Melville down, you gave him the prepared satchel, filled with rock, and kept the one containing the money—"

"Mex Louie! You know—" Caldwell broke off. Cold beads of perspiration appeared on his forehead. "I—I—you're wrong—"

"It was Mex Louie who Norton killed that day, not the Falcon. Norton knew it wasn't the Falcon all right, but he figured the Falcon was a good man to blame for such a holdup. Norton claimed to have identified the Falcon from his picture on a reward bill, but the real Falcon never did have his picture printed. We thought, at first, that perhaps

Norton might be mistaken, but when Norton heard that Trigg was coming to make positive identification, that threw a monkey wrench in Norton's plans. He had to plenty quick dig up Mex Louie's body and hide it somewhere else. After being so definite in his identification, Norton didn't dare take chances on being branded a liar. It was the only thing he could do—get that body out of sight. We knew this morning, when that coffin was dug up, that Norton had lied. Norton was the only one who had a reason for stealing that body secretly. And then he loaded rock in the box and nailed it up again—bent hell out of nails and split wood doing it too—just so the coffin would have weight when it was dug up. There was always a chance, you know, that he could think of something to stall off the actual opening of the box—"

"Barlow, I swear before God I know nothing of that—"

"Now, about riding out to the Lazy-Double-M two nights ago and trying to kill me," Johnny went on, ignoring the interruption, "What were you trying to do to the sheriff? It's too bad—for you—that you had to drop your plug of tobacco, but what was your reason for leaving Norton's badge there to be found?" Caldwell was silent, and Johnny went on, "All right, we'll leave it to the court to make you talk. Caldwell, I'm arresting you for robbery, murder, attempted murder—"

"Oh, my God, don't say that," Caldwell groaned.

"You do the talking then," Johnny snapped. "If you'll come clean and give me a confession, you might have a chance to get off without being hung." He chose the correct psychological moment to add, "I've got a hunch that this is mostly Norton's work anyway, all this skulduggery that's been taking place."

"It was! It was!" Caldwell exclaimed frantically. "It's all Norton's doings. He concocted the plan and everything. Damn him for getting me into this. I'll talk, Johnny. Yes, I'll talk. You'll realize I'm not as bad as you think. And if you can help me, say a good word for me, I'll be your friend for ever—"

"Cut out the babbling and talk then," Johnny snapped, the disgust in his tones plain.

Caldwell swallowed hard. After a few stumbling moments he started in. His trembling confession was, at first, a matter of contradictions, accusations against Norton, stammered denials of his own guilt. However, after a few minutes, the words came easier. It seemed to relieve his conscience to share the blame with Kirk Norton. It had been Norton who had instigated the business. Norton had needed additional water for his herds, and had tried to gain possession of Melville's Lazy-Double-M Ranch and the water from Creaking River.

Johnny interrupted the confession. "What was your share to be, Caldwell?"

"Not one red cent."

"I can't believe that," Johnny said sarcastically. "No more lying. I want the truth now."

Caldwell lowered his eyes. "Well, it was like this, Barlow. Before I came to Rawhide City I had some trouble at another bank. I made some investments with the bank's money and lost every cent. My uncle was still alive then, and he made the loss good. I wasn't sent to the penitentiary. Then I came here to make a fresh start and I prospered with the Rawhide City bank. Somehow Kirk Norton heard of the trouble I'd had at the other bank, and he threatened to expose me as a crook unless I consented to help him gain control of the Melville property."

"And you were so damn weak," Johnny said scornfully, "that you lacked the nerve to tell him to go to hell. You could have exposed him for making you such a proposition."

"I didn't dare!" Caldwell cried. "I was afraid my reputation would be ruined here. Norton really forced me into it. I was desperate. Norton didn't tell me he planned to have Matt killed—"

"So you say"—ironically. "Go on, Caldwell."

"The plan was to break Melville financially, then the bank could take over the Lazy-Double-M. When that happened, Norton would buy the ranch from the bank. So I talked Melville into borrowing that money from me. We discussed the matter several times before the loan went through. You see,

Norton wanted me to hold off the loan until he found the proper man for the job. Then Mex Louie came to town. But according to Norton there was to be no shooting to kill when the holdup was staged—"

"You said that before, Caldwell. Can't you talk faster? Now quit stalling and get on with it."

Caldwell nodded weak assent. "After Matt had signed the note and was about to leave with the satchel of money, Mex Louie entered this office and shot Matt, but instead of Mex Louie taking the satchel of money when he left, I gave him the second satchel, loaded with rock. I had it prepared, in that closet."

Johnny's eyes burned hotly. "And you were willing that Matt be robbed and killed to save your own rotten reputation. You bustard!" Johnny's words cracked contemptuously. Caldwell couldn't meet his eyes, nor answer that. Johnny went on, "What was the idea of giving Mex Louie that satchel filled with rocks? He must have seen you take it out of the closet. Surely he knew he didn't have the money."

Caldwell nodded. "Kirk arranged that with Mex Louie. Louie was to have been paid off later, when he'd made an escape. But Kirk was afraid that someone might shoot Louie on the street and recover the money; he also feared Mex Louie might double-cross us and keep going with the ten thousand. It was fixed for Louie to meet Norton secretly that night and receive pay for acting the part of the Falcon. Norton had purposely left off his six-shooter that day so as to to give Louie more time to get started. He had warned Louie that he would shoot at him—but miss. I guess that Mex Louie thought Kirk had hit the horse by mistake when it was downed. You see, at the last moment, Norton decided to play safe and kill Mex Louie. You know"—Caldwell smiled wanly up at Johnny—"dead men tell no tales."

"That sounds like Norton. Treacherous as a rattler. Likely he'd decided from the first to kill Louie. Who else was in on this plot?"

"Only Vink Deever. I swear I didn't know Kirk was going to kill Louie until it happened."

Johnny said dryly, "I'll believe that. I don't think Norton took you into his confidence much."

"Oh, he didn't." Caldwell's voice was eager. "Kirk just did what suited his ideas, and I had to stand for it. I was just helpless. When I learned you were a Ranger, I was more frightened than ever."

"And so you rode out to the Lazy-Double-M and tried to kill me, eh?"

Caldwell gulped and shook his head. "Honest to God, that wasn't my intention. I was just trying to frighten you into leaving, and draw you out near the road where you could find that old badge of Norton's."

Johnny motioned to the repeating rifle on the desk. "Is this the gun you shot at me with?"

"Yes, that's it. I didn't tell Summerton why, but I had him hire a horse at the livery stable for me to ride out there that night. When I returned I kept it out back of my boarding house until Jay could return it for me the next morning. When I rode out to the Lazy-Double-M, I crept close to the house and saw you talking to Miss 'Rene. I felt sure she had called the Rangers in to investigate the holdup and I was nearly crazy with fright. But I never intended to kill you, Barlow, when I shot at you that night. I aimed 'way wide—"

"Either you're a damn poor shot," Johnny snapped, "or that gun was so fouled it wouldn't send a bullet where you aimed it."

"Perhaps that's it," Caldwell said weakly. "After I fired that shot I rode back to town as fast as I could, hoping you would find that badge of Norton's."

"And," Johnny said grimly, "you figured I'd come to town gunning for Norton. If I'd done that, one of us would have been killed, likely. Either way, you stood to win: you either got rid of me, or you got Norton off your shoulders. Very smart, Mr. Caldwell, very smart. But I'm not so dumb as you figured me. The day after I was fired on, I noted that you walked sort of stiff-legged, like a hombre who hasn't been on a horse in a long spell. Ernie Braughn allowed as your lumbago must be bothering you, but I knew better. You'd been hair-pinning a horse."

"But can't you see that Norton drove me to all this?" Caldwell begged.

"He couldn't have if you'd acted like a man from the first. On top of that, you had Summerton killed to shut his mouth. As loyal as he was to you too—"

"Barlow, don't blame me for that. That was Norton's doing. Jay remembered that I had two satchels that looked exactly alike. I told him I'd disposed of one of them, long since, but he figured some one in town must have got hold of it. I've kept those satchels locked in that closet, but yesterday he came in this office, and while the closet door was unlocked for a few minutes, he saw the two satchels."

"And insisted on telling me about them," Johnny put in.

"That's right. He still didn't dream that I had had a hand in the holdup, though. He didn't get a good look at the satchels, and I talked him out of going to you, for the time being. Finally, he must have come to some other decision, because he started out to see you again. I insisted that he wait until the bank had closed. Then I went to the Blue Gem and told Norton that Summerton was about to spoil the whole plan."

Caldwell swallowed hard, then went on, "Norton told me not to worry, that he'd take care of Summerton. I never dreamed what he intended to have done, but I trusted Norton to handle the affair. It was Norton ordered Deever to kill Jay, and then get you too, if possible. But Deever was to get Summerton at all costs. Jay's death came as a great shock to me."

"By God," Johnny said, "I was commencing to think you were beyond being shocked. And then when you learned that Jay had talked to me, on the spur of the moment you fixed up some sort of crazy story about the Falcon talking with a stutter. You and Norton likely thought I'd go chasing off looking for a man with an impediment in his speech. But I didn't fall for that either. The whole story smelled of fake to me. . . . Cripes! What a double-crosser you are, Caldwell. You double-crossed your best friend and had him shot and robbed. You double-crossed Summerton. You double-crossed your pard Norton and dropped his badge, hoping he would get killed—"

"For God's sake, Barlow," Caldwell pleaded, "don't tell Kirk it was me that stole his star and dropped it out there at the Lazy-Double-M. He'd kill me. Kirk thought first it was Deever dropped that star, then when Deever denied it so vigorously, Kirk got to thinking it could be somebody in town who doesn't like him and stole the badge to make it look like he'd shot at you—"

"T'hell with you," Johnny snapped. "You're wrong if you think I'd lift a finger to save your dirty double-crossing hide. . . . That ten thousand you stole from Matt—where is it now?"

"I put it in my vault this morning," the banker quavered. "I didn't dare put it there before, or Jay would have noticed. I've kept it locked in my closet all this time. I'll give it back to Melville. I—I want to do what's right—"

"You're holding two notes on the Lazy-Double-M," Johnny interrupted tersely. "One was signed by 'Rene, the other by Matt, for money he never got. I want those notes."

"They're right here." Caldwell was more than eager to please now. He unlocked a drawer in his desk and gave Johnny two slips of paper. Johnny glanced at them and nodded. "I'll take care of these. One will be paid to the bank in due course. The other won't. I'll turn 'em over to Matt when he gets well."

"But what are you going to do with me?" Caldwell pleaded. "I've been truthful with you. I've told you everything—"

"And tried to throw all the blame on Norton, you double-crossing louse. The *best* I can see for you is a nice long jail sentence—"

"Don't say that, Barlow," Caldwell whined. "Think of my reputation here, my business. I run a good bank for the convenience of my neighbours—"

"And to make money on 'em and rob 'em when you get a chance. It's too late to worry about your neighbours now, Caldwell. Someone else will operate the bank when you're gone."

"God, you're hard, Barlow. Can't you show a little pity—"

"Pity, hell!" Johnny snapped. "Did you show any for Matt or Summerton? You're just damn lucky your punishment isn't left to me. . . . I'm leaving now, Caldwell. Stay right here. If you attempt to escape, it will go harder than ever with you."

He turned, flung open the office door, and, striding through the doorway in the partition, headed for the front of the bank, where he found Mike and Doc Duncan. Mike said, "Johnee, did you get all of hees story? He made the complete confession?"

"I got it all," Johnny said tersely. "It was a pretty dirty setup, all through." He looked at Duncan. "I suppose Mike has told you what we learned, and about finding the two satchels."

Duncan nodded. He looked shocked. "I can scarcely believe it, Johnny. Frank Caldwell, of all men! I trusted him. We all did. He always seemed on the square."

"He was," Johnny replied, "until he could gain something through double-crossing. . . . Have many customers showed up?"

"Only three or four," Duncan answered. "I told 'em Caldwell wasn't feeling well, and for 'em to come back to-morrow. One of 'em needed some ready cash. I give him a note to Ernie, so he could get what was necessary. I assured folks there was nothing wrong with the bank."

"That's fine, Doc. I didn't want people to get scary and start a run on the bank." Johnny looked relieved. "There'll have to be a new banker appointed here. I've an idea everything is in top shape, financially, but the bank examiner will likely have to come and go over the books. Meanwhile, Doc, with the authority reposing in me as a Border Ranger, I designate you to take charge of the bank until things settle down here and we know where we're at—"

"My Gawd," Doc exclaimed, "I don't know anything about banking."

"You're honest—which is more than can be said for the last banker. It'll work out. Meanwhile, you stay here at the door until it's time to close. Tomorrow some sort of arrangement can be worked out. . . . Mike, you go back and keep an eye on Caldwell—and I mean keep an eye on him. He had the drawer of his desk out once, and I saw a gun in it. Take care of yourself."

He gave the two a few more details of the story he'd learned from Caldwell, then handed Doc Duncan a couple of slips of paper. "Hang on to these, Doc. They're Matt's notes—one of 'em sighed by 'Rene."

"But, Johnee, what are you intendeeng?" Mike asked.

"I'm going down to the Blue Gem and look for Norton. If he's not there, I'll look elsewhere, and put him under arrest."

Vallejo looked serious. "You weel nevair take him alive, Johnee. I know that type. Eet is best that Doc keep the eye on Caldwell and I go along with you—"

"This is my job," Johnny said grimly.

Duncan said, "Maybe you'd better take Mike, Johnny. Norton's a dangerous man with a gun."

Johnny laughed shortly. There was no humour in the sound. "What do you think I use my gun for—a plaything?"

"But, Johnee—"

"Don't try to stop me now, *amigo*. I've got my mind made up."

He didn't wait to hear further words, but left the doorway of the bank building and stepped out to the sidewalk.

## CHAPTER XXI

### SHOWDOWN!

HALFWAY to the Blue Gem, Johnny encountered Meticulous Jones.

"You got a look on your face like you was huntin' trouble, Johnny," Meticulous greeted him. "That red hair of yours is fair bristlin' like you was mad about somethin'—and you're walkin' sort of cocky, like a strange dawg on the prod." He fell into step at Johnny's side.

"Maybe I am mad about something," Johnny

said shortly, "but I've got no time to talk about it now, Meticulous."

"You mad about that missin' body of the Falcon's? Tell me about it. I was asleep when you fellers went to Boot Hill—"

"I'll leave that to Norton to explain."

"Norton! *Humpf!*" Meticulous's tones were scornful. "That bustard won't explain nothin'. I already asked him 'bout that business, and he nigh took my head off. A lot of other hombres has asked him, but he just swore at 'em and told 'em to mind their own business. He's as sore as a bitch wolf in fly time. Run all his customers out of the Blue Gem, so he did. Told 'em he didn't want their trade if they couldn't stop asking damn fool questions. And so they got out and left him alone. He's in his bar now, drinkin' with nobody but his barkeep for company," Meticulous finished as they started across the road.

"Good! I'll be seeing him."

"Not if you got good sense, you won't. Better give Kirk a wide berth for the rest of the day. He'll feel better to-morrow—"

"I got my doubts about that too," Johnny said tersely.

Meticulous eyed him strangely. "By Gawd, you *are* lookin' for trouble. You got blood in your eye, if ever I see a man—"

"For your information, Meticulous, I'm putting Norton under arrest."

"Oh, my Gawd!" The deputy's jaw dropped; his eyes widened. "You can't do that. He—why, he's the sheriff—"

"Maybe I can't, but I'm going to try my damnedest. Watch me!"

"Watch nothin'! I aim to keep as far away as possible when lead starts flyin'. You'll never do it, Johnny. He's lightnin' with his hawg-laig." The two men stepped to the opposite sidewalk.

"I've seen lightning before—"

"Well, don't say I didn't warn you. I know Kirk! You don't. Say, what you goin' to arrest him for?"

"You'll hear later."

Meticulous looked dubious. "I'm afraid maybe I won't," he said gloomily. "Norton ain't the type to be arrested."

"That's where we disagree, Deputy. He's the type all right—and mostly tin. You'd better not go too far away; at any minute you might be called on to step into the sheriff's shoes."

For once Meticulous was speechless. They walked on, and within a few minutes drew abreast of the Blue Gem. Johnny said, "Here we are. You coming in with me?"

Meticulous drew back. "Not me!" he refused fervently. "I never did like lightnin'. I'll wait out here." The deputy's face was pale as he lounged back against a tie rail, well to one side of the Blue Gem entrance, and watched Johnny cross the porch and push in through the swinging doors.

It was cool and dark within the Blue Gem after the brilliant glare of the sun-lit street, and Johnny waited a few moments to adjust his vision to the dimmer light of the interior. His spurs clanked along the board floor as he made his way to the bar.

Jiggs, the bartender, was down at the far end of the long scarred counter, just serving a drink to Kirk Norton. There were no customers in the bar-room.

Norton turned slowly and directed a long look at Johnny. An angry flush crept into his cheekbones. He said, "You'll have to go someplace else to do your drinking, Barlow. I prefer to drink alone, and the Blue Gem isn't serving anyone else to-day."

"That so?" Johnny said easily. "Well, that's all right too, as far as I'm concerned. I didn't come here to drink. I came here to see you."

Something in Johnny's manner caused Norton to stiffen. His eyes narrowed, and he nodded quickly. "All right, so you see me. Now you can get out."

"My mistake," Johnny said. "I should have made it plain I want to do more than see you. I want to talk to you."

Norton eyed Johnny warily. "You got some sort of deal you want to talk over?"

"I didn't say that."

"Cripes A'mighty! Come to the point," Norton said irritably. "If you want to talk, get busy. Have a drink on the house and get your talking over with. I'll be frank, Barlow—I don't like you, and I don't like anybody who does."

"I'm going to be mighty frank with you too, Norton—"

Johnny paused as the bartender approached for his order. He looked nervously from Johnny to Norton, then placed a second bottle and glass on the bar.

Johnny was still looking at Norton. He drew a dollar from his pocket and sent it ringing along the bar. "There're some hombres I don't care to drink on," he explained.

Crimson flooded the sheriff's face a second time, but the held his voice steady and answered carelessly, "Every man to his own taste."

"And mine isn't yours," Johnny replied.

Norton occupied himself with his own drink, and for a few moments there was silence in the barroom. Johnny poured a neat two fingers of whisky into his glass, but let it stand untasted. On the wall, over the bar, an old clock ticked the minutes away. The silence, the ticking clock, the presence of this man he so thoroughly hated had begun to work on Norton's nerves—which was exactly as Johnny had planned things, for a nervous man never shoots straight.

"Damn it to hell!" Norton burst out irritably, "if you're going to talk, get started—and then get out. I won't be able to stand the sight of you much longer."

"You won't have to—much longer," Johnny said coldly. He went on, "Did I ever tell you how I come to meet up with Mike Vallejo, Sheriff?"

"You know damn well you didn't. And I'm not interested in your greaser friend."

"You're going to be, Norton. It's all part of what I came to see you about. I ran into Mike down in Mexico. Him and his horse had got bogged down in a quicksand. I pulled 'em out. We got to be right friendly. He told me a heap of things."

"Too bad you don't marry into some family of *pelados,*" Norton said with a sneer. "You seem to like 'em so well."

Johnny smiled coolly. "By the way, Mike happens to be a citizen of the United States. When I met him, he was heading back to his home, up Santa Fe way. He'd been down in Mexico, helping to bury an older brother. The brother's name was Ramón Vallejo. I don't suppose that means anything to you."

"Why in hell should it?" Norton growled testily.

"You'll see, after I've told you some more," Johnny went on. "This Ramón Vallejo was a romantic sort of cuss. He got to feeling sorry for the peons across the border, and he took to holding up banks, just to get money to help poor folks. He was a sort of Mexican Robin Hood. He'd raid a town, then hide out in the desert. A reward was put up for his capture, but he always eluded any posse sent after him. And then, after so many narrow

279

escapes, hard luck stepped in. Ramón Vallejo's pony carried him over a cut-bank in the dark one night. It didn't hurt the pony much, but it landed on top of Ramón and crushed Ramón's body pretty bad. But Ramón was tough—it took quite a spell for him to die."

Norton whirled impatiently to face Johnny. "Damn it! Cut out the palaverin'. Just what are you getting at, Barlow?"

"Don't rush me, Norton," Johnny said imperturbably. "You're going to be a heap interested in Ramón Vallejo. There isn't much more. To cut this story short, Ramón's home address was in his pocket, and the man who found Ramón, barely alive, sent for my pard, Mike. Mike rode hell out of several horses and got there in time to say goodbye to his brother and help bury him. Ramón Vallejo was buried just ten days before Matt Melville was shot and robbed—"

"Barlow, why should I give a hoot in hell about this nonsense? What are you driving at?" Norton's eyes showed red with anger.

"Oh, yes," Johnny added casually. "I should have told you before that Ramón Vallejo was the *real* Falcon. It was a name the peons gave him, and Ramón was right proud of it."

"You're crazy as hell, Barlow!" Norton half shouted. "I killed the real Falcon. This Ramón hombre was likely an impostor—"

"You killed Mex Louie and told folks it was the

280

Falcon. And then dug up the body and carted it off, to cover your lie, when you learned Trigg would arrive to identify it. Mike and I knew the day we came here that something smelled awfully fishy. You see, we knew positively you lied when you claimed you'd killed the Falcon."

The two men had swung away from the bar now and were facing each other, a scant half-dozen yards between them. Norton's features were working with emotion. With difficulty he controlled his temper. His words came hard. "Barlow, you'd better get out of here, or I'll be inviting you to reach for your iron. That's a warning."

Johnny said, "I don't need your warning, Norton. I came here to arrest you. Will you come quiet?"

Norton stiffened. One arm bent slightly at the elbow, then he relaxed. Suddenly he gave a short harsh laugh, turned back to the bar, and reached for his bottle. He poured himself a full glass and glanced quickly at Johnny before downing the drink. Johnny was standing as before, one thumb hooked in his cartridge belt, his eyes alert.

Words exploded suddenly from Norton's lips, hot, angry words. His face was a furious mask of hate. "You can't arrest me, Barlow, even if I did make a mistake in calling that holdup man the Falcon. All right: maybe I was in error. No man can make sure all the time. Now you clear out of here before you find yourself in a mess of trouble."

Again he turned back to the bottle. Johnny didn't

say anything for a few moments. He was waiting for Norton to make the first move. There wasn't a sound to be heard in the bar-room, except the monotonous ticking of the old clock on the wall. Jiggs, the bartender, had moved some yards away, ready to duck for shelter at the first sign of hostility. He was in a half-crouching position, his face white.

Johnny said again, "I came to arrest you, Norton. Will you come quiet?" His tones were cold, even, inexorable. He added, "I've just come from the bank. Caldwell's through. He blames you, Norton. Oh yes, he talked plenty. This is the showdown."

Norton jerked around from the bar, staring wide-eyed at Johnny now. Johnny went on in the same stern voice, "You'll never get a chance to steal the Lazy-Double-M again, Norton. And I know all about you ordering Vink Deever to kill Summerton, too, so he wouldn't tell about those two identical satchels in Caldwell's closet—"

And that was as far as Johnny got. With a wild, animal-like snarl, Norton leaped out from the bar, his right hand flashing to holster. The gun was spurting flame and lead almost before it had cleared holster.

But Johnny had been waiting for that move. The instant Norton started his draw, Johnny threw himself to one side, jerking his gun as he moved. He fired once—thumbed another quick shot—and then a third. By this time he was halfway across the bar-room, moving too swiftly to provide a good target.

Norton stiffened abruptly, spun half around by the impact of Johnny's .44 slugs. The rafters overhead were still vibrating from the heavy detonations of the guns when Norton's weapon slipped from his lifeless fingers. Slowly the man's legs jackknifed, then he pitched forward, face down, on the floor.

Black powder smoke swirled through the barroom, its scent acrid in Johnny's nostrils. He cast a quick glance at the quaking bartender, just rising from behind the bar, then crossed the floor in wide strides to gaze down on the silent form of the crooked sheriff. Methodically, he punched out his empty shells and reloaded his six-shooter before shoving it back into holster.

Behind the bar Jiggs spoke in a husky, strained voice. "Kirk didn't come quiet, did he?"

A grim smile tugged at the corners of Johnny's mouth. "Not very," he replied.

There was a good deal of yelling in the street and the sound of excited voices. A crowd of men swept into the saloon, Meticulous Jones in the lead. "By Gawd, you did beat the lightnin'!" Meticulous exclaimed. He turned to the others. "I allus claimed, didn't I, that Johnny Barlow was faster'n Norton?"

Johnny pushed past the men who tried to detain him with questions and stepped out to the sidewalk. He had gone but a short way when he saw Tex Houston and the other Lazy-Double-M men burst from the Clinic Saloon. He crossed the street toward the bank, and when halfway there, heard the sound of a gunshot. He broke into a run.

Doc Duncan was still at the doorway, and was joined by Mike Vallejo before Johnny arrived. An expression of relief broke across the Mexican's face. He said quietly, "We heard the shooteeng, Johnny. You were fast enough." Doc Duncan was talking too, asking questions.

"I was fast enough," Johnny said tiredly. "What was that shot I heard, Mike?"

Vallejo explained. "Like you say, I keep the watchful eye on Caldwell. Eet was true, he had a gon in hees desk. He opened the drawer and seized eet. Already my gon was out, but Caldwell paid no attention to me. He turned the muzzle toward heemself and pull the trigger."

"Committed suicide, eh?" Johnny exclaimed. "I reckon that's the best way for him, at that. He couldn't stand the shame—"

A quick drumming of hoofs interrupted the words. Johnny turned to see 'Rene storming in on her sorrel gelding. She pulled the little pony to an abrupt sliding halt, and slid out of the saddle.

Johnny was already at her side and felt her arms go around his shoulders. And then he was holding her close. "Oh, Johnny, Johnny," she half sobbed. "You are safe! I heard shots as I entered town, and saw men running. Something told me you were involved. And then—and then—I saw you standing at the bank doorway. Thank God, Johnny . . ." She drew his head down until his eyes were level with her moist ones, and he felt her warm lips on his own. . . .

Some minutes passed before Mike Vallejo's dry tones intruded: "The gay *cabǎllěro* should choose always the night for the speaking of such tender words. The moonlight, I'm theenk, ees bes' for what you two are saying. 'Rene! Johnee! The whole street ees watching you. Have you no shame? *Por Dios!* Johnee! Johnee! Are you deaf een the ears? Ees a spectacle you are makeeng! Take 'Rene out of the street. Go make of the telegraph to your headquarters what have take place. Also, the bank examiner should have the message. *También*—likewise—Matt Melville would welcome theese news. Eet weel make heem get well faster. John-nneee! I insis' you leesten! Take 'Rene away and tell her all about eet. The street, in daylight, ees no place."

Blushing scarlet, Johnny and 'Rene drew apart and glanced around to see a ring of laughing men encircling them. Johnny grinned widely. Taking the girl's hand, he drew her after him through the crowd. Someone started a cheer and the street resounded with the noise. Johnny chuckled. "I've got a hunch that it will be a heap more fun telling her what's going to happen."

'Rene smiled. "That being the case, Ranger man, let's get away from here without further waste of time—not that it was all wasted. But I'm mighty eager to listen."

And with true Ranger expedition, Johnny Barlow wasn't slow to take the girl's advice.

**(Allan) William Colt MacDonald** was born in Detroit, Michigan in 1891. His formal education concluded after his first three months of high school when he went to work as a lathe operator for Dodge Brothers' Motor Company. His first commercial writing consisted of advertising copy and articles for trade publications. While working in the advertising industry, MacDonald began contributing stories of varying lengths to pulp magazines and his first novel, a Western story, was published by Clayton House in *Ace-High Magazine* in 1925. MacDonald later commented that when this first novel appeared in book form as *Restless Guns* in 1929, 'I quit my job cold.' From the time of that decision on, MacDonald's career became a long string of successes in pulp magazines, hardcover books, films, and eventually original and reprint paperback editions. The Three Mesquiteers, MacDonald's most famous characters, were introduced in 1933 in *Law of the Forty-fives*. His other most famous character creation was Gregory Quist, a railroad detective. Some of MacDonald's finest work occurs outside his series, especially the well researched *Stir up the Dust* which was published first in a British edition in 1950 and *The Mad Marshal* in 1958. MacDonald's only son, Wallace, recalled how much fun his father had writing Western fiction. It is an apt observation since countless readers have enjoyed his stories now for nearly three quarters of a century.

**Center Point Publishing**
600 Brooks Road ● PO Box 1
Thorndike ME 04986-0001 USA

**(207) 568-3717**

**US & Canada:**
**1 800 929-9108**
www.centerpointlargeprint.com